Phantom Pain

Also by Arnon Grunberg

Blue Mondays

Silent Extras

Phantom Pain

ARNON GRUNBERG

Translated from the Dutch by Sam Garrett

Other Press • New York

Copyright © 2004 Arnon Grunberg

Translation copyright © 2004 Sam Garrett

Production Editor: Robert D. Hack

Text design: Natalya Balnova

This book was set in 11 pt. Janson by Alpha Graphics of Pittsfield, NH.

10 9 8 7 6 5 4 3 2 1

Library of Congress Cataloging-in-Publication Data

Grunberg, Arnon.
  [Fantoompijn. English]
  Phantom pain / by Arnon Grunberg ; translated by Sam Garrett.
    p. cm.
  ISBN 1-59051-126-3 (alk. paper)
  I. Garrett, Sam. II. Title.
  PT5881.17.R96 F3613 2004

                    2003026913

Contents

1

HARPO

"I'm a natural for the royal family," said Robert G. Mehlman one evening. We were sitting on the terrace of the Hotel Santa Caterina in Amalfi. It was unseasonably cold. He had on his blue coat, and pieces of peanut were clinging to his lips. He smelled different: of cellars where there's lots of dancing and no ventilation. There was a gravy stain on his white summer trousers, and his hands trembled like fledglings that were trying to fly away but kept falling back.

Mehlman had crisscrossed Europe with three steamer trunks and a huge bag of unopened mail. Now he'd taken up residence at the Santa Caterina, where he'd finagled a room with sea view at half-price, because the season was somehow refusing to get underway.

He used to travel with his private secretary, but the secretary ran away.

When I first showed up, Mehlman had refused to see me. "Go away," he'd shouted, "can't you see the state I'm in?"

I felt like leaving right then. I hadn't traveled all that way to be snapped at. But when I talked to my mother on the phone, she said, "Stay there, he'll change his mind." And the next morning at breakfast he had indeed changed his mind.

"What you've got on," he said, "you should throw away."

Two waiters were staring somberly at the gray sky. The season was three weeks late in coming. An Austrian asked in bad Italian, "When will there be a train going south?"

"There are no trains here," the waiter said in English. "If you want to go south you'll have to take a taxi." The waiter moved over to our table. "Am I right in assuming that you will be paying today, Mr. Mehlman?"

Mehlman nodded, and the waiter said, staring at the sea, "Yes, once a guest has settled in, there's no getting rid of him."

The bag full of unopened mail was under the breakfast table. Mehlman rummaged through it, pulled out a bill, glanced at it, then tore it into tiny pieces. "They can't find me anyway," he said, "and when they finally do, I'll have been dead for a long time."

He wiped a little jam from his lips and ordered a glass of whisky. The waiter tried to walk away, but Mehlman stopped him. "When I was your age," he said, "I had hair too, and you should have seen it."

"Life races along," the waiter said, and kept staring at the sea.

The hair Mehlman still had was white and stuck out in all directions.

"It's been almost a year," he said.

"What?" I asked. "What's been almost a year?"

"Since my secretary disappeared."

The Austrian got up. "So are there any taxis around here going south?" he asked in a loud voice.

All the people having breakfast looked at him. There weren't very many of them; there were more waiters than guests.

An elderly gentleman sitting at the window with at least five foreign newspapers in front of him said in a mannered voice, "I've been coming here for thirty years, I know more about this place than the staff do. If you need a taxi going south, I'll find one for you."

A woman at the buffet, who was struggling to slide a slice of pineapple on to her plate, shouted, "My parents used to come here, and I'm telling you, don't go south. There's nothing south of here, only poverty."

But the Austrian wasn't in the market for unsolicited advice. "If I want to go south, that's my business."

"Precisely," said the gentlemen with the newspapers. "And if you require a taxi, you should talk to me. I know everyone in this village." He looked around triumphantly, and when no one said anything he went on. "When I was sixteen my Latin tutor said, 'Henri, most people are dead, do not wake them.' But I paid him no heed, I have waked them wherever they were to be woken."

"Should have let them sleep," Mehlman mumbled. The lady who was still struggling with the slice of pineapple resumed her favorite motif: "Further south the poverty starts. I've been there, first with my parents, then five years ago on my own, and nothing has changed."

Mehlman was slowly spreading jam on his bread. I don't believe he was actually planning to eat the bread at all.

"I don't want to wake up," the Austrian said. "I want to go south, I need some warm sun. I have a bad back."

A few of the waiters had already started setting tables for lunch. It seemed to me that a number of guests did nothing but sit here all day, waiting for the next meal, returning to their rooms only after dinner. Maybe they went downstairs to the games room between five and six, to play a little table tennis.

"You have to die before you spend all your money," Mehlman said. "Not the other way around, otherwise you're just a burden on people. And they don't quite deserve that."

Robert G. Mehlman is my father. Even though, during sudden fits of rage, he has denied that. "Me, your father?" he would shout. "You know what your mother's like!"

When I was born, Robert G. Mehlman was at the peak of his glory. He was more than a major talent. But within five years there wasn't much of that glory left, and my mother sometimes compared him to a bunch of roses that had been left in a vase too long without water.

Probably the only reason I was conceived was because my father, for once in his life, felt he had to keep a promise. Because my begetters were in the midst of a crisis and didn't know what they were doing. But the important thing isn't *why* I was conceived, the important thing is *that* I was conceived. Even though my father would deny that as well. "Every detail is important," he would say. "Nothing must escape our attention."

But, of course, it's not like that. Many details are unimportant. Most details are unimportant. The important thing is that I was born on a cold January day in a hotel on Long Island.

At the outset of the pregnancy, my parents had discussed the advantages of having an abortion, but those discussions lasted so long that by the time they were done it was too late for any abortion. My mother, who was bent on having a child, had suddenly fallen prey to doubt. Giving birth seemed like a nightmare to her, but so did an abortion, and she decided in the long run that, as far as nightmares go, giving birth was the more bearable of the two.

My parents had taken a few days' vacation at Montauk. My father liked to work in hotel rooms. The contractions started earlier than expected. They wanted to go to a hospital, but it was too late. Someone fetched a midwife, but there wasn't much left for her to do.

During the birth my father got drunk in the hotel restaurant, which had an ocean view. According to the bill, which he saved and gave me on my fourteenth birthday, he paid that evening for two bottles of Chianti, four glasses of grappa and two bottles of champagne. I suspect that the Chianti and the grappa were from before my birth, the champagne consumed afterwards.

That same evening, it seems—although readings differ on this point—he asked one of the waitresses to marry him. My mother wept, I shrieked like a banshee, the midwife slapped my buttocks and, two storeys down, my father was proposing marriage.

*

During my circumcision, my father fainted. It wasn't because of the blood, though, or because he couldn't stand the thought of my being in pain, it was just a convenient moment for him to faint. A girlfriend of his, someone my mother couldn't stand and who she referred to as The Empty Vessel, had showed up for my circumcision as well. My mother had apparently shouted: "If that Empty Vessel shows her face around here, the circumcision is off!" But by then The Empty Vessel had already settled in nicely on the couch.

Not long after that, my father fainted. They brought him to with sweet red wine. And my grandmother, who had developed a vitality in the face of death paralleled by very few of her contemporaries, shouted that they should be careful because my father was a very sensitive person. When he came to, my father did his best to keep The Empty Vessel and my mother separated. I see my circumcision as the first in a series of minor and less-minor catastrophes, although my mother in particular seems to have been convinced that a child would have a healing and calmative influence on my father.

While the doctor was putting the knife to my dick, my mother whispered, "Where do you get the nerve to invite that Empty Vessel? Don't you have any respect for me?" And my father whispered back, "This isn't the right moment. Let's talk about it later." But then, that's what he always whispered.

David, a good friend of my father's, an old school buddy, tried to calm them down, but it was no use. "It's hard to summon any sympathy for your situation," it seems he whispered in my father's ear. "What have you gotten yourself into? Why do you let them walk all over you?" At which my mother apparently shouted, "Shut up, David, don't make him any crazier than he already is."

And so my parents became bogged down in an argument over an empty vessel, and I was being circumcised.

*

The first few years of my life we lived in New York. It was my father's idea to name me Harpo. And because my mother wanted me to have a normal name as well, my middle name became Saul. Harpo Saul Mehlman, that's me.

On the birth announcements, my father had printed: "Harpo Saul Mehlman announces his entrance into the world and gives you little kisses," which my mother felt in retrospect was hardly an appropriate text.

That it is absolutely inhuman to name your child Harpo goes without saying. Of course there are any number of other inhuman names, but they don't get much more inhuman than Harpo.

My father was working on his magnum opus at the time, my mother was a practicing partner at a day clinic for psychiatric patients. Her most famous patient was the man who talked to the wall, on the assumption that the secret service could hear him. When the secret service didn't react to his messages, he became destructive. That's how my mother met him. She wrote her dissertation about that man. Thanks to my mother, he discovered that he'd spent twenty years talking to the wall for no good reason. That was too much for him, and he threw himself down an elevator shaft. Which pretty much put a damper on my mother's post-dissertation party, seeing as he was supposed to be the guest of honor. Afterwards she wrote a couple of articles in which she questioned the wisdom of helping people rid themselves entirely of their delusions.

My father always distanced himself from psychiatry. For years, however, he did go to a therapist three times a week—for no other reason, he said, than to make the therapist laugh. If the therapist laughed at least once, the session was a success in his eyes. Shortly after his divorce, following a session in which he failed to make the therapist laugh even once, my father abruptly stopped his therapy and went into a deep depression.

My mother knew, by the way, that my father was using his therapist as a guinea pig for the stories he later wrote down and sent out into the world. And, understandably, she had qualms about the ethical validity of using a therapist to that end. But my father considered it a stroke of genius. Besides, he said, the end justified every means.

When it came to Robert G. Mehlman, my mother said, psychiatry was bound hand and foot. Anyone else would probably have taken this as an insult, but my father saw it as a compliment. "When I meet the therapist who can cure me, I'll put him in my will," I heard him say on several occasions. And then he'd drum his fingers on the tabletop.

He believed that any therapist who treated him intensively for two consecutive years would end up in the madhouse himself. According to my mother—who had, after all, spent almost twenty years with him under the same roof—that was, for once, not far from the truth.

In the morning my father would work, in the afternoon we would go to the movies. During the first ten years of my life I spent almost more time in movie theaters than anywhere else. We'd often see more than one movie on the same day; some movies we saw two or three times.

Those are my earliest memories: my father and I running from one movie to the next, while my mother cured patients who talked to the wall.

*

My father was a writer. My regard for literature and writers is even lower than my regard for men. Anyone growing up in a restaurant kitchen will probably feel differently about restaurants as well. And the son of a glassblower will never be able to see glass in the same way an innocent hobbyist does.

Everyone thought my father was working on his magnum opus, and that I was busying myself with piles of toys on the floor in front of him, but in fact he was writing letters. Letters to me, letters to the gas company, letters to the bank, letters to The Empty Vessel, letters to people he believed were out to pull a fast one on him, letters to strangers he'd met in bars and whose addresses he had somehow wangled out of them.

Later, when his publisher grew tired of the deadline for his magnum opus sliding towards the horizon, my father decided to publish his letters to me, under the title *Letters to Harpo*. Without, by the way, asking my permission.

His first letter to me was written when I was almost five months old.

"Dear Harpo,

"By the time you read this I will be an old man, probably bald, and that will be the least of the indignities in store for me. Perhaps I will not even be spared having hair grow on my back. Now, even though you're less than five months old, I would still like to urge you to lunch well when you grow older. A lunch break of an hour and a half is no luxury, but an essential requirement for human life. Whatever terms of labor you agree to later on, insist on at least a ninety-minute lunch. A long lunch breaks the day in two, and believe me, that's the least you can do; the days are long enough as it is.

"Here I must stop, because your mother will be coming home any minute, and one must at least create the illusion of having picked up a little and having, as promised, taken off one's shoes when entering the house in order that the cleaning lady may not have mopped in vain. That, too, I would like to pass along to you now: mopping is always in vain. Remember that, and the rest will come of its own accord."

That was the first of about five hundred letters to me which my father, when he later fell on hard times, put up for auction, promising that he would buy them back for me in a few months' time.

*

When I turned six, my father began taking me with him to cafés, bars, coffeehouses and hotel lounges, where we met people. Almost always women.

One time we bought a dress for a woman. She had long brown curly hair, and she threw her arms around my father every five minutes. I was supposed to call her "auntie."

We went into a lot of shops. Everywhere she tried on dresses. I got sick of it. I wanted to go home. My father said, "Pay attention, this is informative."

Later, as we were walking home, I asked, "Why did you buy that lady a dress?"

"Didn't you notice?" my father asked. "She was desperately in need of a summer dress."

That day my father wrote to me:

"*Dear Harpo,*

Today we bought a summer dress for the woman your mother calls The Empty Vessel. Someday you will discover that this woman is no vessel, and also a great deal less empty than your mother supposes. Of course your mother has a few good reasons for calling this woman The Empty Vessel, but I can come up with a few good arguments to the contrary. That, too, you will probably discover someday.

"There are people who think I shouldn't take you along when I buy dresses for The Empty Vessel. Besides the practical matter of what I would do with you otherwise, however, I can assure you that no matter what therapists may someday try to make you believe, you had a wonderful time today. You climbed in dress racks, butted into changing rooms where women were trying on expensive clothes,

and charmed old ladies as though you would someday make that your profession.

"There are also people who think I shouldn't buy dresses for The Empty Vessel at all, whether you're with me or not. My accountant, for example. Only three days ago he wrote to me: 'My dear friend, as you will have noticed, your revenues are not what they once were. Mightn't it be wise to adapt your consumptive behavior to fit this new situation, which is doubtless of a highly temporary nature?'

"Dear Harpo Saul, if you ever get a letter like that from your accountant later on, promise me you'll go on buying summer dresses like your life depended on it. I hope, of course, that you will be spared such letters, or that you will have no accountant whatsoever, or at least one who doesn't stick his nose into your consumptive behavior.

"You're sleeping in the room next-door right now, at last, but not before you smeared vanilla ice cream all over the curtains. Won't that be fun when your mother gets home? She's been busy all day trying to cure patients of their delusions. What a life. Fortunately I informed her early on that she is to keep her hands off my delusions, and yours as well. Should you have any. I'm not positive you do yet. I suspect you do. Whatever the case, she has solemnly sworn to keep her hands off our delusions.

"Four tender little kisses, two on your feet, one on your navel and one on your forehead."

*

That evening, during dinner, I told my mother we had bought a dress.

"Oh Jesus," she said, "for The Empty Vessel again, I bet."

It was the first time I'd ever heard my mother mention The Empty Vessel. Her going into a rage about The Empty Vessel during my circumcision was something I'd heard about only from my father. She sometimes spoke of "that troll" and "that woman," but she was always referring to one and the same person.

"Why do you take our child with you when you go to The Empty Vessel?" my mother shouted, pushing away her plate of mozzarella. It's fair enough to assume she was eating mozzarella, because that was her favorite appetizer, and she ordered it almost every day.

"What else am I supposed to do with him?" my father shouted. "You want me to drop him off at the mental institution? The boy has enough mental problems at home."

"I don't want our child to meet The Empty Vessel," my mother went on imperturbably, and she pinched my father on the arm, hard.

"They didn't meet," my father said triumphantly. "The Empty Vessel pretended the child wasn't even there."

"That's even worse," my mother shouted. "Children shouldn't be ignored. Who does she think she is, not paying attention to Harpo!"

All of this served as an indication that my parents, despite their relatively elevated social positions, were not quite right in the head.

"Did that woman ignore you?" my mother asked.

That woman had been completely absorbed in picking out a dress, but it didn't seem prudent to me to mention that. "Not too much," I mumbled.

"I don't want the child and The Empty Vessel ever to meet again," my mother said, and pinched my father's arm for the second time. So hard it left a bruise.

Then my father said in a loud voice, so the whole restaurant could hear, "It's a miracle that more healthy, intelligent people don't think they're the living Christ."

*

During the years my parents lived together, we had, I believe, one meal at home. We ate in restaurants, bars, subway stations, coffeehouses, bowling alleys, movie theaters, parks, athletic facilities, stations, trains, planes, hotels, but never at home. My father had stuffed the kitchen full of books, papers, newspaper clippings and magazines, and he used the oven to store his dictionaries.

Once, when yet another of my mother's patients had committed suicide, she begged my father to let her cook, just once, because it calmed her down. My father refused, and my mother said, "Try and stop me." Upon which she began melting butter in a pan, and my father had a nervous fit. He picked me up and ran downstairs. While we were standing on the sidewalk, my mother opened the window and threw a couple of his books down, with one hand. She had the pan of butter in the other.

"Don't do it, Mama," I screamed, "don't do it, please don't."

My mother was at least as pigheaded as my father. Once she'd decided to throw something, there was no stopping her.

One time she caused my father serious bodily harm by throwing a key ring at his head. Another time I saw her drill a big hole in a dictionary with a knife.

Without saying a word, my father picked up his books and put them in the downstairs hall, with a note: "Property of Robert G. Mehlman. Please don't touch."

In the cab on the way to the movie theater my father said, "Aggression is not only an animal phenomenon, but also a human one. Your mother went to school for six years to learn to deal with human aggression." Then my father squeezed my hand hard and said, "Six years of school to deal with human aggression, do you realize what that means?"

From the moment I realized that my parents weren't quite right in the head, and that I was the only normal one in our family, I felt responsible for them. Although my upbringing was not particularly religious, that evening I wrote a letter to God in which I explained that my parents had named me Harpo, that they threw books out the window, that they weren't right in the head without realizing that themselves—in brief, that His help was sorely needed. Later that evening my father found that letter, and used it. The way he used everything.

That evening my father wrote:

"Dear Harpo Saul, sweet little crazy son of mine,

"Apparently it is the will of the Almighty that all Mehlmans grow up in a madhouse. I grew up in a madhouse, and now you're growing up in one too. It won't surprise me if, should you ever have children of your own, they grow up in a madhouse as well.

"You mustn't worry too much when your mother occasionally throws books out the window, not even if you read this later and vaguely remember a certain evening when she opened the window and my books came fluttering down like autumn leaves. Books are relatively harmless things to throw out the window; remember, she could have thrown furniture or costly vases. What's more, books can survive a fall of forty feet, while people usually don't. You must understand that many of your mother's patients throw themselves down elevator shafts, or take an overdose or toss themselves in front of a subway, and that's not something you can brush off lightly. Even though I've explained to her many times that there's no stopping someone who's bound and determined to throw himself down an elevator shaft.

"I met your mother in an all-night delicatessen. She was working her way through college, I was a potential suicide, although I kept that to myself. Back then I didn't do much besides walk around and write letters, which I almost always sent registered mail, because I lived in the delusion that the postal service would lose them. That's how we met. I'll tell you the rest some other time.

"Many years later, when I was drinking coffee in a New York café with a television anchorwoman who had flown eight hours to ask me questions I couldn't answer, I introduced her to your mother. When your mother got up to go to the ladies' room, the anchorwoman

leaned over and whispered in my ear, 'She's not the love of your life, is she?' I didn't know what to say for a moment, then I replied, 'No, of course not, the love of my life is you.'

"*Tomorrow we're going to buy you a pair of sandals, so you can parade down the street like a little prince. Because that's important.*"

*

A couple of times each year, Grandma Mehlman would come to visit. She'd take up residence at the Sheraton, a two-minute walk from our house. When they'd give her a room at the front, she would complain about the noisy traffic. When she was put at the back, she complained about the noisy neighbors. During the day she would clean our house or baby-sit for me and complain that my mother was a lousy housekeeper, and that it was just like her son to marry a slattern.

I never met my grandfather. Apparently he was a famous tennis player. My grandmother always spoke of her husband as the famous tennis player, Aron Mehlman. But in reality he never made it past 268th in the world rankings. When he saw that he was about to be bumped out of Wimbledon in the first round again, he lost his self-control, climbed over the net and attacked his opponent, a young man from Chile, with his racket. When his opponent tried to run away, my grandfather fell to the grass and sank his teeth into the man's leg. The Chilean had to be taken to the hospital with a split lip and a wound to his calf, and the tennis federation suspended my grandfather for life.

At a press conference, my grandfather later claimed that the tennis federation had put narcotics in his tea and that he was the victim of a conspiracy. It was the only time he ever made the front pages, with headlines like "Tennis Player Turns Mad Dog."

Whenever anything bad happened to him later in life, he would always shout, "Ha, I bet the tennis federation could tell us more about this."

My father grew up with the myth that his father was an important and famous tennis player. Until he found out that his father had never made it past 268th in the world rankings, but still told checkout girls, "I'm Aron Mehlman, the famous tennis player from the Thirties."

Fortunately, by the time my father wrote his first real book, *268th in the World*, which rocketed him to fame, my grandfather had been consumed by dementia. He sat in a chair by the window, and the world went by. Thanks to dementia, he never had to read how, in *268th in the World*, his son portrayed him as a tyrant and a mythomaniac who always told his family when they went to a restaurant, "Tell them I'm Aron Mehlman, the famous tennis player from the Thirties, and I don't like charred potatoes."

My grandmother always said, "Sure, that book, they call it literature. I wouldn't know about that. It's too gloomy for me. People already have enough gloominess in their own homes. But whatever it is, it's a pack of lies. Your grandfather was the Borg of the 1930s. The McEnroe of the interbellum, that was your grandfather. A graceful player. He simply floated over the court."

Then she'd pick up her sponge and start cleaning again. My grandmother believed that happiness could be found in total neatness. So she waged a lifelong battle against dust, bacilli and other germs. My grandmother was obsessed with dust and death. During her one-month stay in New York, she would lie on her deathbed almost every other day. At least six times each visit we had to call the ambulance, and countless were the times we took her to the hospital for no good reason.

Tennis, understandably enough, interested her as well. Whenever we saw a tennis match on TV she'd say, "Oh, but your grandfather was better than that." She never said a word about the incident. When I asked her about it one day, she said it was a lie.

My grandma's house was packed with trophies from obscure, bush-league tennis tournaments of the 1930s. On the living room wall was a huge painting of Aron Mehlman in action. And hanging on the wall in the hallway were five tennis rackets. The strings had long since sprung, the wood was decaying, but they stayed there. Her house looked like a tennis museum.

In addition to dust, death and tennis, bringing down disgrace on your own family was one of her great interests. Many times I heard her say to my father, "Do something about those shoes! Do you think Aron Mehlman would have walked around in shoes like that? Don't be a disgrace to your family." She was always telling my mother, "Do something about your hair, are you trying to drag our family through the mud?" And to me she'd say, "Do your best at school, don't ruin a good name."

When my grandmother came to visit for a few weeks, I always had the feeling, bordering on absolute certainty, that the best thing you could do was crawl under your bed and stay there, or lock yourself in the closet. Suicide, after all, would only have blemished the family reputation.

"Oh sure," she often said, "people think your father's really something. But your grandfather, now he was really somebody. The famous tennis player, Aron Mehlman, that's where you come from."

The year she died, when madness had her in its grip for good, she had a big sign hung on her front door that read: IN THIS HOUSE ONCE LIVED THE FAMOUS TENNIS PLAYER, ARON MEHLMAN. Underneath it, she'd left the other sign hanging: PLEASE WIPE YOUR FEET.

*

The last time Grandma Mehlman came to visit, she brought her whole wardrobe with her. She'd come to celebrate her birthday. In the taxi, she told us, "The date of birth in my passport is wrong, I'm actually five years younger."

She grabbed my father by the arm and said, "You know what you should write about? About how the tennis federation poisoned our lives, that's what you should write about."

My father was working on his magnum opus at the time, and I don't believe he had any intention of awarding the tennis federation a role in it. "I'll think about it," he said quietly.

Each year she brought more luggage, so this time she'd reserved a suite. That's where we celebrated her birthday. There was a big cheesecake, because that was her favorite. I had to sit on my grandmother's lap. She stroked my hair, which was much redder than it is now.

"Harpo Saul," she said. She always called me Harpo Saul. As if just plain Harpo wasn't bad enough. "Harpo Saul," she said, "if you only knew how the tennis federation ruined our lives, if you only knew."

"Enough already with that tennis federation," my father said. "Let's not talk about it."

This is how Robert G. Mehlman himself, in *268th in the World*, portrayed my grandfather and grandmother:

"I'm always envious of children whose parents experienced real victories, real successes or, for my part, real defeats. Children who grew up in the shadow of something real and palpable.

"The first thing I learned was playacting; everyone in the Mehlman family was an actor. Everything that happened within the four walls of our home was to be kept top secret. As far as I knew, family secrets and professional secrets were synonymous terms. That's why, when my father would return home in the evening and remain standing in the vestibule, wearing his fur hat, his cigar in his mouth, his briefcase in his hand, waiting for my mother to take his cloak, no questions were to be asked. 'Other people wear coats,' he'd say, 'but I, I wear a cloak.' As if cloaks were somehow of a higher status than coats. His life was ruled by a remarkable order, unintelligible to others. He would walk from the vestibule to his desk, open the top drawer, to which only he had the key, pull little cream-colored envelopes out of his inside pocket and place them in the drawer. He never said much. At most, only: 'I'm home.'

Or: 'Did anyone call?' Then he would sit down at his desk, still wearing his fur hat. He often left it on until right before he went to bed. There were even days when he showed up at breakfast with his fur hat on. He was plagued by a permanent sense of cranial draft. Many were the times I heard him shout, 'You could catch your death in here. Close the door.' Wherever the famous tennis player Aron Mehlman went, there was a draft in his head.

"When people asked, 'What does your father do?' I was supposed to say, 'My father is a famous tennis player from the Thirties.' I was an actor who struggled with his lines, who had nightmares about his lines.

"My father ran a courier service. He delivered all kinds of things to people's homes: money, jewels, horses, weapons, and he asked no questions. The man who picked me up after school, who charmed other parents with his small talk, who enquired politely about trivialities, didn't exist. My father was a figment. It wasn't the war that had come between my father and the absolute top, not as so many people often claimed. It was the fact that he had bitten his opponent in the calf, before the eyes of the umpire, a handful of photographers, and at least four hundred spectators.

"Everyone has a past that's gone by. That's more painful for some than for others. But my father had a past that didn't even exist.

"When he would arrive home at night with his briefcase, a cold cigar in his mouth, the fur hat on his head, a heavy leaden cloak on his shoulders, all I knew was that we were to ask no questions. Not: 'How did it go?' Not: 'Where did you go?' Not even: 'Did it go well?' Questions only make sense when there's a chance that you'll receive an answer. For Aron Mehlman, answers were a mortal danger.

"He had dedicated himself to forging what may perhaps be the most difficult thing of all to forge: your own past.

"Countless times I said to him, 'But no one knows who Mehlman is, no one even cares.' He would always brush that off. As if I were too young to understand what people cared about. 'Tell them anyway,' he'd say.

"I believe that, even then, I unconsciously understood what I was able to formulate only much later: there is only one way to compete with a myth, there is only one way to escape a myth, there is only one way to keep yourself from playing an eternal bit part in some-one else's myth—that is to create a myth of your own, to become your own myth."

*

All this, as I mentioned, my grandfather never had to read. But while we were celebrating my grandmother's birthday, there in the suite of the Sheraton, she started on about it again.

"As if the tennis federation hadn't hurt us enough," she said to my father, "as if that wasn't enough. You had to come along with that book of yours."

My father was standing at the window and mumbled, "Later, some other time. This isn't the right moment."

My mother blew out the candles.

Grandma Mehlman walked on high heels, even though her feet barely fit in shoes anymore. It took her two hours each morning to apply her makeup. With her face powdered white, she looked like an escapee from a carnival float where the crew's assignment had been to look as much like the Grim Reaper as possible. The more sharply she sensed the end approaching, the greater became her need to be a diva. The wife of the celebrated Aron Mehlman. To shine one last time. When you saw her on the street, you saw a huge overgrowth of red hair, and beneath that a skinny body squeezed into a dress so tight it made her look even skinnier. Shiny black lace-up boots to complete the effect. A striking sight, there can be no contesting that.

I was still sitting on her lap. My grandmother was listing the prices of the articles of clothing she wore. Everyone was doing their best to listen with interest.

"Harpo Saul," she said suddenly, "you're the last of the Mehlmans."

The powder on her face looked like peeling paint.

"She used to say that to me all the time too," my father said. "Don't pay any attention."

He was still standing at the window, a glass of champagne in his hand. No one else was drinking champagne. My grandmother was having sweet red wine, my mother a glass of water, and I didn't like champagne. I still don't, actually. It's not something I favor.

"Harpo Saul," she said again, "you should be taking tennis lessons, I think you could be one of the greats."

My father closed the window with a bang. "Harpo Saul is not taking tennis lessons," he said firmly. "Boxing lessons, karate, Sumo wrestling, all fine by me—but no tennis lessons."

My grandmother put me down and waved her arms furiously. A cloud of powder rose from her cheeks. A hoarse screech came from her throat. "So what if I want him to take tennis lessons?" she shouted. "So what if I say he has the soul of his grandfather. Your loving father, God rest his soul, who spent his whole life doing nothing but working his fingers to the bone to make sure you had everything you need. And what thanks did he receive? That you told nasty lies about him in dirty books. That child is taking tennis lessons."

I watched as my grandmother and my father fought over whether I was going to take tennis lessons. My grandmother was quite good at being beside herself.

Finally, she put on her hat. It was bigger than the biggest wagon wheel. That hat barely fit in the taxi. We were going to the theater for her birthday. She was wearing gloves, because brown spots had appeared on the backs of her hands of late and she wanted to hide them from the outside world.

As soon as we'd taken our box seats, she fell asleep. I was sitting on my father's lap. The musical didn't interest him. He whispered, "It's almost over."

During the intermission, my grandmother woke up. More hoarse sounds came from her throat. I caught the phrase "tennis lessons." The wagon wheel on her head, she pushed her way to the buffet and ordered a glass of water. When she'd finished her water, she said in a loud voice, "This is so incredibly boring, Robert. How much did you pay for these tickets?"

That is how we celebrated my grandmother's last birthday.

*

"Dear, naughty, and from time to time completely unmanageable son of mine," my father wrote that night, "your grandmother turned eighty-two today. We went to the theater and, although she slept through most of the performance, she seemed to enjoy herself reasonably well. When I turn eighty-two (I don't think I'll make it, but you never know—when I was eighteen I thought I would commit suicide at twenty-three, I was still a poet then and twenty-three seemed the best age for a poet to die, but all this aside), when I turn eighty-two, will you take me along to the theater, or to one of those nightclubs for young people where they play music too loudly, so that I'll be forced to turn down my hearing-aid and spend the whole evening staring into a half-empty glass, thinking about triumphs I missed by a hair's breadth?

"Harpo, until further notice, your father is the boss, would you please keep that in mind? Sometimes I get the impression that you think you're the boss, and that is truly a misconception. If you start believing that, then there is something wrong with the way we're raising you, although I wouldn't have the slightest idea what, and your mother doesn't seem to know either, even though she went to school for that. From me you mustn't expect much in the way of upbringing, I was barely brought up myself, but your mother was educated in that respect, so don't try to take us for a ride.

"When other people are around, you could at least summon up the courtesy to pretend that I'm the boss. Being a writer no one in New York has ever heard of is no great pleasure in itself, but if people are forced to watch as I'm pushed around by my four-foot-two son, I soon won't be able to show my face at all. Let's agree on this: I'm the boss, your mother is the boss, and you're not!

"So don't think you can jerk me around. I am capable of terrible things, rest assured of that. Sometimes I close my eyes and think: Oh God, I would rather have rats in the house than a son. But then I open them again and think: How wonderful it is that you're around, sweet, unconscionable, miserable, sensitive, and beautiful little Harpo of mine.

"P.S. You're going to be more handsome than your father. Another of those things I can't stand."

*

"To Mr. R. Mehlman. Please call 212-573-9653. I have a package with me from the Netherlands that should be handed to you personally."

In front of me is a piece of cardboard. In black magic marker, someone has written a note on it. The handwriting is graceful. The telephone number no longer exists. They found the piece of cardboard in my father's hotel room in Sabaudia. He didn't like to throw things away. That he didn't frame this one, though, is really something of a mystery. During the last few years of his life, he had everything framed. Beer coasters with notes on them, signed frontispieces, linen napkins with a few words scribbled on them. In fact, once I even received a framed pair of socks in the mail.

Now the time has come for me to tell you about The Empty Vessel—the manuscript, that is. Not, in other words, about The Empty Vessel who was sometimes referred to as "that woman."

Not about The Empty Vessel who they say ran my father—financially and, to hear my mother tell it, physically and mentally as well—to rack and ruin.

The last time I asked my mother about it outright—it's no longer such a touchy subject with her, these days she lives with a Russian who's working on a non-allopathic cure for schizophrenia—she said, "No, of course not. It wasn't that one empty vessel, and not all the other empty vessels either. And it wasn't the circumstances that finally ruined him either. Although circumstances always play a role. Within psychiatry, you see, it's quite hard to speak of inevitability." She looked thoughtful for a moment, then said, "But that probably applies outside psychiatry as well."

Having said this, she took my face in both hands, as if trying to hypnotize me, as if by holding me that way she could unravel the mystery of why people do what they do, as if everything would become clear if she only held me long enough. Finally she said, "You look so much like your father."

I still don't know whether that was a compliment, or something closer to a curse. Not even now, now that I've read the manuscript.

2

ROBERT G. MEHLMAN
The Empty Vessel and Other Pearls

PRINCESS FAIRYTALE

Two men had been in my house all morning, trying to clean the chimney. One of them had a bandanna tied around his head, the other was almost bald. I understood from what they told me that my chimney was a problem case. After three hours, the chimneysweep with the bandanna said, "The wind blows right into it, there's nothing we can do about that."

I know nothing about chimneys. It was my wife's idea to have the chimney cleaned. She was in Vienna for a conference about dreams, which is why I was stuck with her chimneysweeps. My love of fireplaces has its bounds, but my wife is possessed of many inexplicable desires.

"Yeah," the chimneysweep with the bandanna said, "we could always mount a ventilator on the roof, then your problems would be over. Then you just push a button and the chimney draws like there's no tomorrow. But that's going to cost you."

A ventilator on the roof, that had to cost a fortune. And there were no fortunes left, the fortunes were gone. Even if I'd had the money, it would definitely have meant being stuck with the chimneysweeps for a few mornings.

My wife would have been quite pleased with a chimney that had a powerful draw instead of one the wind blew into, but the prospect of being stuck with the chimneysweeps seemed insuperable.

For a moment there I considered calling my wife and asking her advice, but a chimney was too trivial a reason to bother someone taking part in a conference about dreams.

"Well," I said, "I'll think about it."

The chimneysweeps began taking the plastic sheets off my furniture, and I was suddenly overwhelmed by gloom. They had covered the whole room with plastic sheets, then they'd spent three hours in the chimney, but it had all been for naught; the chimney still didn't draw.

"We'll be in touch real soon," I told the chimneysweeps. As if there was something I had to make up for.

"Take your time, think about it," one of them said. "A ventilator wouldn't be a bad idea, the wind blows right into it."

When they were gone, I called my wife's hotel. "The wind blows right into the chimney, we need a ventilator on the roof, but it's going to cost a fortune," was the message I left behind. I had to repeat it three times, and even then the receptionist asked, "What is it exactly the wind blows right into?" It seemed to me like a nice message to find when you came back after a whole day of talking about dreams.

After that I read a letter sent to me by a professor from a university in Paris. "Dear Sir," he wrote, "perhaps you recall that, during your residency in Paris, a number of students and teachers worked on a translation of your story entitled 'Shoe Polish.' You attended several of those translation sessions. Would you allow us to print the translated story in our university magazine? Unfortunately, we cannot offer you any payment."

The letter was a couple of weeks old. I felt the time had come for a reply.

"Dear Professor," I wrote, "how are you? My memory is excellent, thank you very much. Of course I have not forgotten the translation sessions held during my stay in Paris. I may never forget them. I haven't forgotten you either. After leaving Paris, there have been no other translation sessions. Attending the translation sessions you led was a great inspiration to me. Of course I grant you permission to print my story 'Shoe Polish' in your university magazine. Too bad there can be no payment, because medicines are expensive. To say nothing of a chimney that draws."

*

I met my wife on a Thursday in spring, long before I knew a thing about translation sessions. I had no idea they even existed. It was late in the evening. A few hours earlier I had eaten dinner at the home of a vague acquaintance. She had made me a macaroni casserole with blue cheese that was not a complete success. The failure was due largely to the blue cheese. My vague acquaintance was quite upset by that. I wasn't all too stable myself in those days, but I still said a few times, "Meals sometimes don't turn out the way you want them to, it's no big deal. It happens to the best of us." Comfort doesn't lie in original phraseology. Comfort lies precisely in clichés, although of course it helps a lot when you pronounce them with a sincere look on your face.

Later that evening, or should I say early the next morning, I met my wife. I was working at an all-night delicatessen in Amsterdam. She came in and said, "Could I hide here for a little bit? There's someone after me."

I was working alone that evening, and I'm not much of a hero.

"Sure," I said. "You can hide here. Is it cold outside?" She shook her head. She stared at a piece of vegetable quiche, while I kept one eye on the door and wondered what I would do if some brute aggression accidentally focused on me. Back in those days I always thought aggression was going to focus on me. One of those things you call down upon yourself without meaning to.

"Do you want me to call the police?" I asked.

She shook her head again.

"Do you make that yourself?" she asked, pointing to the vegetable quiche.

"No," I answered truthfully, "but we can warm it up for you." A large part of my work consisted of warming things up. I was quite good at it.

"It'll just take a few seconds," I said to my wife-to-be. And together we stared at what was left of the salmon salad. I thought about the man who was after her, and about how soon I might be crawling across the delicatessen floor in search of my teeth. I don't know what she was thinking about. There is no such thing as foreshadowing.

I wiped my hands on my apron and weighed the words I might be about to say. But if you weigh your words too long, nothing comes out of your mouth; before you know it your life is over, and you haven't said a thing.

I wanted to live, but I didn't know how. Working at an all-night delicatessen seemed the perfect way to find out. Looking back on it, working at the all-night deli turned out to be grander and more compelling than going to translation sessions. Which, in retrospect, does constitute an advantage.

Fifteen minutes later, when the man who was after her still hadn't come in, I sold my wife-to-be a second piece of vegetable quiche. I was hoping the creep would show up at some point, though, otherwise I'd be stuck with her all night and I'd have a hard time closing the shop. She wanted to eat her second piece of vegetable quiche right there in the shop too.

"Fleeing works up an appetite," I said.

She agreed, with her mouth full. She seemed about to eat everything in the shop. I wasn't too pleased about that, about her eating there, because it made a mess and I'd have to clean it all up. But my boss had said I shouldn't stop people from doing that. "If they want to eat it here," he'd said, "let them eat it here. That's good for turnover. Otherwise they'll just go to Barbarella."

Only years later did I realize that maybe there wasn't any man after her that evening, that maybe she was just a little confused. I know from experience that there are lies you keep telling right up to the bitter end. Not because being found out would be such a disaster, but because there are some illusions you don't want to end. They're often very minor illusions, but those minor illusions can be so lovely.

That evening she was wearing a short skirt, my wife-to-be. It looked like a Scottish kilt, but without the brooch, and she had on high heels. I haven't seen her in high heels for years. Back when I met her, though, she was going through a period when she wore high heels all the time.

"Boy," she said after she'd devoured her second slice of vegetable quiche, "that tasted good."

"Yeah," I said. "Listen, if you want me to call the police anyway, I'd be glad to."

"Don't bother," she said, and paid for the quiche. She was getting ready to leave.

"Is the coast clear?" I asked.

She looked out the window and said, "Yeah, he's after other women now."

"Goodbye," I called out, and started cleaning the two ovens, because that was the first thing the boss looked at when he came in in the afternoon. Whether the ovens were clean. He didn't seem to care whether mice had been nibbling at the chips, as long as the ovens were clean.

A couple of days after that first encounter, she came into the deli again. This time she wasn't fleeing from some creep. She said,

"I came back for some vegetable quiche. Could you warm it up for me?"

"Sure," I said. "That's what I'm here for, to warm things up."

And so she became a regular client for our vegetable quiche. She almost always stopped by in the middle of the night and ate her quiche standing up. On rare occasions she would take off her shoes and say, "There, that's easier."

I thought she was awfully nice, but that business about the shoes I never did understand.

She never complained about how I did my job, about the quiche being too cold or the beer too warm or the milk too expensive. Almost all the other regulars complained about something, mostly about the prices. Even the bums who came into the deli complained that it was warmer outside than it was in there, and that they broke their teeth on our bread. We saved our stale bread for the bums.

Once, one of the bums tried to clip his toenails in the shop. But I told him, "Listen, this is a delicatessen, not a shoe store." But I let my wife-to-be do whatever she wanted. Walking around on high heels all the time couldn't have been very pleasant.

Sometimes we passed a little information back and forth. You couldn't really call it having a conversation. But that was how I found out she was studying to become a psychotherapist.

I'd never thought of psychotherapists as women who stood around in their bare feet in all-night delis, devouring slices of vegetable quiche. And not once a week, no, but three or four times a week. Maybe that was my own ignorance. Back then I hadn't met very many psychotherapists.

One evening, after she'd come in a bit later than usual—it had been a very quiet evening—I asked, "Could I go into therapy with you?"

A strange question, I admit. I didn't have much to say in those days. That is, I had a lot to say, but it didn't come out right. Shyness, probably. I weighed words that shouldn't have been weighed at all. Anyone else would have said, "Would you like to catch a movie with me sometime?" Or something along those lines. But I said, "Could I go into therapy with you?"

She was working on her last slice of vegetable quiche. Some nights she drank a beer along with it, but that evening she'd only asked for a glass of water.

"So what's wrong with you?" she asked. As if the therapy had already started, right there in the delicatessen.

I wiped the counter with a cloth, then stuck a fork in the last two fishcakes. Only throw things away when mold starts growing on them, that was the boss's philosophy.

"Oh, well," I said, "everything, really."

*

The day two chimneysweeps swept my chimney in vain and I vowed to myself never to attend another translation session, The Empty Vessel came into my life.

I know people who insist on trying to see the ineluctable hand of fate in every series of coincidences. I have never been able to do that. The world has always reminded me most of a psychological experiment in which the guinea pigs, for the purposes of the test, are never told that they're guinea pigs. What would happen if we made that girl get cancer? How will Mehlman react if we let him run into The Empty Vessel? Sometimes I wished I could pull up a chair in that cubicle where they sat, observing us, running through long checklists of our customs and behavior. But maybe that cubicle was empty. Maybe it was like acting in front of a movie camera with no film in it.

That day, as I was walking to the coffeehouse where I had breakfast every morning, I thought about how my wife sometimes did writing sessions with her patients. And I thought about a crocodile-leather belt I'd been planning to buy, until I saw the price tag. The girl in the shop had done everything she could to convince me of the immortality of crocodile leather. "You'll give up the ghost before this belt does," she'd said. That sounded good to me. After all, *something* had to be immortal. If I was God, I suppose I would have chosen crocodile leather too. And I thought about my Sidney Brochstein cycle. Sidney Brochstein was a restaurant critic. My editor, Frederik van der Kamp, had called me and said, "Robert, this Sidney Brochstein cycle of yours is depraved."

"What are you talking about?" I said. "Could you be a little more specific? What do you mean by depraved, do you think I'm depraved?"

Memories of that conversation failed to cheer me, so I started thinking about translation sessions and my time in Paris.

I sat down at my usual table in the coffeehouse, close to the restroom, and opened the newspaper. It was a perfectly normal afternoon, the afternoon The Empty Vessel came into my life. Nothing unusual, not a foreshadow in sight. Chimneysweeps don't foreshadow anything, do they?

In the past I have occasionally claimed that you can only see fate as ineluctable when you suffer from a chronic lack of fantasy, when you close your eyes to all the possibilities left unexplored. I don't know whether I'd make claims like that anymore.

At the coffeehouse, I actually had to ask for my coffee and orange juice. The young man waiting on tables hadn't been working there very long. Before him it had been a young woman, Evelyn, but she had disappeared overnight.

I studied the stock market reports in the paper, even though there was a good chance that I owned no stocks anymore. I had lost track of my financial situation. Nevertheless, I decided that the purchase of a crocodile belt was a justifiable one, in view of the immortality of its leather.

In departure from my normal routine, I ordered a second cappuccino. Now that I was going to buy that crocodile belt, a second cappuccino was no sweat. I reflected on the article about Svevo I had to write later that day.

I looked at a little boy in a stroller, who was too fat already, and suddenly I realized how much I liked sitting there, drinking coffee and reading the newspaper, and how at that moment I wouldn't have minded at all having to sit there like that forever. But the editor was waiting for my article on Svevo. And there were debts, debts that had always been there but that had suddenly all started ticking at once, like so many time bombs. Of course the honorarium for the piece about Svevo would only be a drop in the bucket, but when debts start ticking like time bombs, every drop is welcome.

If the paper hadn't been waiting for my article about Svevo, I might not have gone home at all, and everything would have been very different. But thinking in that way is almost like giving in to the desire to see coincidences as more than just coincidences, to see links where no links exist.

I got up, paid for my two coffees and the orange juice, and thought of an opening line for my article on Svevo. Before I left, I bent down to say goodbye to the little fat boy in the stroller. His mother smiled at me. As she should have, of course; little fat boys in strollers are none too popular.

I still had absolutely no idea how I must live, but I'd got better at pretending. What could I say about Svevo? Why Svevo? Why me? And for whom or what had I got myself into such deep debt? For the thankless.

I stood there and wrote on my little notepad: "He went bankrupt on the thankless." I'd started drafting my own obituary around that time; if there's one thing you should never leave to others, it's your own obituary.

I had once told someone that writing was a profession like any other. Some people sold shoes, others wrote. I could no longer make that claim. Writing was a form of cannibalism. First you devoured life, down to the last scrap, then you spit it up. For the writer, life was a tainted mussel. One that was all green and slimy, it was already in your mouth, but you could spit it up just in time, before the food poisoning really kicked in.

From the coffeehouse I walked to my local newspaper stand, where I bought fifty dollars' worth of scratch-off lottery tickets. At crucial moments I fell back into my old, familiar cannibal's role. I had discovered scratch-off lottery tickets about four months before that, and I'd decided that when it came to manual therapy, very little could beat the scratch-off lottery ticket. Sometimes, when I had to go out to dinner with my wife's colleagues, I'd buy about a dozen tickets for everyone. I'd hand them out after the main course. I always enjoy seeing what scratch-off tickets bring out in a person. Besides, it saves conversation; scratching people don't talk.

*

A few days after my request to go into therapy, she came back to the all-night deli. She said she wasn't officially allowed to give therapy yet, but if I really wanted, she could try. I said I really wanted.

She suggested we do something practical. "Maybe we could bake cookies," she said, massaging her left foot. "Have you ever baked cookies?"

"No," I said, "I never have. My mother bakes things sometimes, but never cookies."

She didn't smoke as far as I knew, but my wife-to-be always smelled of cigarettes and parties. It was a penetrating odor that clung to her. Back then I liked to think it was the smell of existential loneliness. Existential loneliness is a lot of hooey, of course. But not the smell, that really exists.

Sometimes I'll still catch a whiff of it. The smell of smoke, sweat, a hint of urine, the smell of parties that have gone on too long, the hostess long retired but the last die-hards making no move to leave. Some never leave, at least not until half a lifetime later.

And so we baked cookies. First we did the shopping, then we baked cookies in her kitchen. It wasn't a fancy kitchen, but this was about therapy, and she had those eyes that always looked at me lovingly when she asked for a slice of vegetable quiche, that made me feel as though she was asking for something very different. For tenderness, for attention, for a kiss on the forehead—God only knows what went through my mind, there in my all-night deli.

We didn't talk much. We focused on the cookies. I thought her house smelled of existential loneliness as well. I myself smelled of fish and vegetable quiche. Later, both those smells were buried under the aroma of freshly baked cookies.

I'd never realized that baking cookies could be as exciting as climbing Mount Everest, or a first, cautious kiss. I discovered then that happiness wasn't some idea that could only exist in the past, or in a future that I'd furnished sloppily while waiting for customers in the all-night deli. It could also exist right here in the present, with hands sticky with dough and sweat that trickled down everywhere, because the oven had turned her little kitchen into a hothouse.

"We should do this more often," I said. "It helps, I can tell."

"Yeah," she said, "I think it's doing you some good."

Finally we went outside and handed out the cookies to passersby. We'd baked enough to feed an orphanage. When the cookies were all gone, we said goodbye. "I'll see you at the deli," I said. The words I'd been meaning to say had escaped me. I'd weighed them too long again.

Cookie-baking proved a successful form of therapy. My wife still does it with groups of patients. Healing is an illusion, but baking cookies is good for them. "It gives them the feeling," she explained to me, "that it's possible to regain control over their lives."

"Why?" I asked. "What's one have to do with the other?"

"Well, they finally do something that works out," she said. "Finally something goes right."

*

I sauntered home. I'd won five dollars on one of the scratch-off tickets; the scratching itself had taken at least twenty minutes. The nice thing about it was that you made contact with other people who were standing in the shop, scratching their tickets. After a while you got to know the other scratchers. There arose something very like camaraderie. Suddenly it seemed to me that to spend the rest of my life scratching tickets would be no disaster at all.

Writing, of course, was the best possible way to avoid living, while still maintaining the illusion of being in the midst of it, of life, of experiencing it to the fullest. And all the time you yourself are secretly the one pulling the strings. This loneliness, too, had a smell: the smell of grenadine cocktails that have stood on the table too long and gone sour. In fact, all loneliness had a smell, which is what makes loneliness bearable, being able to sniff at it like a dog.

I stopped by the post office to check my post-office box, but there were only a few wayward reminders that I didn't take home anyway.

The euphoria of the manipulative writer may be even shorter-lived than that of the erotomaniac. As soon as the person being manipulated has surrendered, has come under one's sway, and the distinction between person and character has been almost completely wiped out, it's over. Nothing else comes to take its place. After that nothing *can* take its place. Except a story.

For months I'd been working on a story about a manipulator, but I couldn't finish it. About a man who gives lessons in love, or rather, lessons in seduction. All his female students learn something from him, but he learns nothing from them. His greed merely increases. And so the lessons he gives are both his salvation and his downfall.

Waiting at the crosswalk, I ran into an old lady I knew from the coffeehouse. I said, "Were you on vacation? It's been so long since I've seen you."

"They took out half my upper jaw," she said. She opened her mouth wide; she wasn't ashamed to show her wounds.

"That's terrible," I said. And she said, "You could always have picked up the phone and called. That's what it's for, you know. How's your wife?"

"Good. She's in Vienna, at a conference."

*

The morning my wife left for Vienna I'd walked into the bathroom; she was in the tub, scrubbing her legs with a sponge. I went to the mirror to shave, but couldn't find my razor anywhere.

"Oh," my wife said, "I guess I used it to shave my legs."

"Fuck," I said, "why don't buy your own razors? It's disgusting to shave with the same razor you use to scratch the hair off your legs."

"So I suddenly disgust you, do I?"

"No. It's just that I want my own razor. If you're too lazy to buy your own, stop shaving your legs. Nobody looks at them anymore anyway."

She dropped back in the tub. The water splashed over the sides. Indeed, we had a nasty argument about a razor the morning she left for Vienna.

"You're a kind of stone," I said, "that I have to roll up the hill every day."

"Thank you very much," my wife said, "thanks for phrasing it so succinctly once more," and went on scrubbing her legs.

*

Coming around the corner into my street, I suddenly remembered the article about Svevo. It had to total about two thousand words. I'm very adept at counting words. My wife sometimes said, "If you were only as good at counting your money as you are at counting words."

41

In the downstairs hall, right in front of the door, I found a piece of cardboard. Garbage in the hall is nothing unusual, sometimes homeless people sleep there, and I was about to kick it aside when I saw something written on it. I bent down.

"To Mr. R. Mehlman," I read. "Please call 212-573-9653. I have a package with me from the Netherlands that should be handed to you personally."

I wasn't expecting a package, it had been a long time since I'd expected any packages at all. The telephone number didn't ring a bell, and there was no name on the piece of cardboard either. As if a telephone number alone was good enough these days. It was the piece of cardboard in particular that fascinated me: Why not a sheet of paper, a grocery receipt, or even a napkin? Why a piece of cardboard?

That day went by like many other days that year. I watched a movie, a thriller, then I worked on my article about Svevo. Halfway through I discovered that I actually had nothing to say about Svevo, but I felt it would be impolite, on the day of the deadline, to notify the editor of that fact. By the time I'd finished the article, prose felt like an affliction, like hemorrhoids but then worse.

In front of the fireplace I found a flashlight the chimneysweeps had forgotten. I furnished myself with a minor distraction by writing them a letter.

"Dear chimneysweeps," I wrote. "You left your flashlight at my house. When can you come and get it? I would also be quite pleased to bring it to you, if only you would tell me where your offices are located."

The only address on their bill was a post office box. Rather puzzling for a firm that had "reliable chimney service" printed on its invoices. For a moment I considered writing a book entitled *Letters to My Chimneysweep.*

Then I remembered the piece of cardboard in my inside pocket. I poured myself a glass of calvados, which, after a moment's hesitation, I tossed down the sink. Then I dialed the number on the piece of cardboard. I had to repeat my name a few times. The young man on the other end of the line seemed to have no idea what I was calling about. "You're not trying to sell anything?"

"I want to pick up a package," I said emphatically. "I have nothing to sell."

Whether salvation existed at all was very much the question, but if it did it seemed to me not unlikely that it was to be found in a package with lots of foreign stamps on it, and the stubs of customs forms. Probably, yes, in a package that had been torn open at customs and then slapped back together with tape.

I explained the whole story to him one more time.

"Oh," the young man said, "call back later this evening."

"Perhaps you could ask him to call me back," I said, and left my number. I'd had my fill of begging for packages I'd never asked for in the first place. Then I called my wife in Vienna. Everything there was going well. Most of the speakers were boring, but a psychiatrist from Rome had said something interesting. That evening there would be a party but she wasn't planning to stay late.

"And what about you?" she asked.

"I'm all right," I said. "I'm going to write a book. *Letters to My Chimneysweep*.

"That's good," she said. "It's about time you started something new."

"*Letters to My Chimneysweep*," I repeated, to see whether she'd get it this time. Did she really think I was serious?

"Take care," I said, then poured myself another calvados, which, after a moment's hesitation, I dumped down the sink as well. This one I'd sniffed at a little.

During dinner at a little French restaurant where lots of older, single men came, I thought about *Letters to My Chimneysweep*. Maybe my wife was right, maybe it wasn't such a bad title after all. She had good ideas sometimes.

She'd once told me that I would blend in perfectly with the other patients in a clinic, and that the only reason I'd never ended up in one was because I had her to talk to all the time.

In all the years she'd worked at the day clinic for the mentally ill, she found out one day, not a single patient had been cured. At best they'd been able to make the patients' problems manageable, but the slightest little thing could bring on a major relapse. One patient who'd seemed to be doing very well, for example, had been found late one evening running naked through the Holland Tunnel. The police picked him up and took him to a hospital. I'll admit, at night I sometimes walk around my own house in the nude, but there's a difference between the Holland Tunnel and your own house.

"Recovery is an illusion," my wife said one morning while she was waiting for her cappuccinos.

The two of us often went out the door together, early in the morning. We'd walk to the coffeehouse where I always read the morning paper. She would order two cappuccinos to go, in plastic cups she took with her when she went to her loonies.

I was the first one up, because she always slept through the alarm. I'd let her sleep another fifteen minutes while I read through the letters I wanted to answer that morning. Then I would seize her by the shoulders and shake her and yell, "The loonies are waiting, the cry of the loon has sounded, they need you." That woke her up.

"If recovery is an illusion," I said, while she was still waiting at the counter for her cappuccinos, "then your patients' only real problem is that they were ever born."

"Yes," she said, "that's your problem. That you were ever born."

*

For a period of about three years, I spent all my waking hours at the all-night deli. At a certain point I started going straight from home to the deli, and from the deli straight back home. I made the occasional attempt to enter a café, a movie theater, the home of an acquaintance, but it almost never got beyond an attempt.

When I started dreaming about the price of fishcakes, of salmon salad, of the vegetable quiche and the satay, I realized it was time my life took a different turn. But I didn't know how to do it. I had shinnied up a tree and now I was afraid to climb down. High amid the branches I looked at other people and occasionally I warmed something up. Shouting for help, I felt, would be unseemly. So I acted as though there was nothing I wanted more than to sit in that tree, as if that were my goal in life.

*

During dinner at the little French restaurant, I leafed through a magazine. In my inside pocket were about twenty scratch-off tickets, but I was saving them for after the coffee.

My wife's patients were referred to as "clients" and were paid a nominal fee to come to the day clinic, thereby creating the illusion that they were actually employed. I had thought about writing an article, a virtuoso treatment of the parallels between a day clinic for psychiatric patients and a commercial enterprise. I told my wife about it, but she said, "Maybe you should put the virtuoso treatment on hold for the time being."

I also had the idea of writing a story about a man who falls in love with his psychiatrist, and decides to feign schizophrenia. He does it so convincingly that everyone believes him. Even the experts. So the man figures: well, if everyone believes me, maybe I should just keep it up.

While I was having my coffee and calvados, of which I drank only half—I'm a man of enormous self-control—I started talking to a man who was wearing glasses that had only one earpiece. He came to this restaurant almost every day. He talked to me about a political crisis, and I listened passively, as I usually do when talk turns to politics. That was fine by him. He'd reached the age where he could only tolerate having other people around when they listened to him.

"Care for a few scratch-off tickets?" I asked when he'd finished talking.

He was thrilled.

"You always lose," he said, "but I enjoy doing it." As we scratched we carried on an intimate conversation about the price of homeopathic virility capsules. He had no health-care package. It was, all things considered, a pleasant evening.

I was already in my pajamas when the phone rang. I answered, because I thought it was my wife. She calls at the weirdest times when she's traveling.

"Am I speaking to Robert Mehlman?"

"Yes," I said, turning down the music a little.

"I'm calling about the package I need to give you."

"Oh yeah," I said, "you're the one," and suddenly I was reminded of the chimneysweeps.

"When could I give it you? Tomorrow?"

"Tomorrow would be fine."

"Maybe we could meet at the Museum of Natural History, if that's not too much trouble. I work there. Of course, I could always come by your place."

"No, no," I said. "I'll come to the museum, it'll be a good excuse to go there again."

We agreed to meet the next afternoon at three, in the museum café.

"Could I ask your name?" I asked.

"Rebecca," she said. "Oh, and before I forget, there's more than one café in the museum, let's make it the Garden Café."

On the back of the chimneysweeps' invoice I wrote, "Garden Café, 3 o'clock, Rebecca."

Only after I'd hung up did I realize that, in all the years I'd lived in New York, I had never been to the Museum of Natural History. My wife had said any number of times, "You should go there sometime, it's wonderful," but I'd always told her, "No, it's not my kind of thing, I don't like dinosaurs."

*

By two o'clock I was already at the museum. A class of schoolchildren arrived along with me.

"Are you here for the butterfly collection as well?" asked the woman at the ticket desk.

"No, I'm here for the Garden Café," I said quietly. As if that were something I should probably be ashamed of.

She gave me a tag to wear around my wrist, so I could move freely through the museum all day.

I had no intention of spending an hour waiting in a café for someone I didn't know, so I wandered past the sharks and zebras. Stuffed sharks and stuffed zebras, that is. Or maybe they were plastic models; my layman's eyes couldn't tell the difference.

That morning I'd called the chimneysweeps and told them I had decided not to go for the ventilator on the roof. They were extremely disappointed.

The museum was bigger than I'd expected. At the dinosaurs, I ran into the schoolchildren again.

"This was a very nasty animal," I heard the teacher say. I stood there with the children and looked.

At a quarter to three I thought: now I can rightfully appear at the Garden Café. But by five to three I still hadn't found it. I asked several museum guards, but they didn't seem to know either.

For a moment there I was afraid it didn't even exist. That this was all a hoax. The piece of cardboard, the telephone call, the Garden Café. Consulting a floor plan, though, I finally found it. The café was almost deserted. There was only a family with seven children, all speaking Portuguese. My wife and I had been to Lisbon together once. Romantic town, Lisbon.

I sat down in a corner where I had a view of fish behind glass. I recognized a couple of the sharks; I'd seen them earlier in the day, and when I'm in a museum I always read the nameplates very carefully. There was another animal in there with them that looked a lot like a giant turtle. Then, suddenly, I sensed that the woman with the package had been there for a long time already, that she was observing me from behind one of the dimly-lit displays. The most dangerous psychiatric patients are out on the street, I'd heard my wife say more than once. And experience had shown that loonies were drawn to me like bees to honey.

I looked at the fish-behind-glass again.

"Don't you think they're pretty?" the waiter asked.

"They're definitely big," I said, and ordered the cocktail of the month. I decided I'd leave as soon as I'd finished it. It's not prudent to respond to messages on pieces of cardboard you find lying in the stairwell.

Halfway through my cocktail—which was absolutely disgusting—a woman came into the café carrying a plastic bag. She walked right up to me, but even if she hadn't I could never have doubted for a moment that this was the woman with a package for me.

"Sorry I'm so late," she said. She took off her coat and sat down. The briskness with which she'd crossed the café and taken off her coat had something strange about it. Something that wasn't quite right, or, in any case, something peculiar. She was no sooner seated than she began rummaging through her purse, then lit a cigarette. All this she did just a little too quickly as well. It made me think of an actress who did exactly what the director told her, but in a higher gear.

We looked at the fish. She inhaled greedily. Her face reminded me of a troll.

"I'm Rebecca," she said, and we shook hands.

It wasn't that she was small, she was actually taller than me, but the first thing I thought of when I saw her was a troll. Not an unattractive troll, but a troll nonetheless.

"Would you like a cocktail of the month too, or something else?" I asked.

"White wine, please," she said.

I flagged down the waiter.

I'd attracted quite a few loonies in my life. A woman once wrote to me to say that her daughter had to get married. After writing back and forth a few times, I received a letter from the woman's psychiatrist saying that she had no daughter, and that for the sake of the therapy it might be best for me not to answer her letters. The last letter I received from that woman said, "The male nurses in the asylum are much better looking than the ones at the day clinic. Besides, in the asylum they at least know how to crack down on troublemakers, and they're not afraid of a little physical contact." I asked my wife whether that sounded familiar, whether that was how asylums really were, but she said she'd only worked in day clinics.

I tried to visit an asylum once, because I was curious, but they wouldn't let me in.

*

Rebecca lit another cigarette. She smoked like a person who'd rather die today than wait for tomorrow. If I kept a diary, I could have written, "Today I met a troll who wants to die." But I don't keep a diary.

We looked at the fish.

"You like fish?" I asked.

"I'm doing research."

"For school?"

"For a biologist."

I nodded as though that was exactly as I'd thought, and then, just to break the silence, I said, "They also have some very lovely dinosaurs here. And a butterfly collection."

"I spend the whole day in the stacks. That's why I'm here, I have to look up something."

49

Perhaps she didn't like dinosaurs either. I could imagine that. A butterfly collection, however, seemed to me just the thing for young women. Dead, yet still romantic.

For a moment I considered asking whether anyone had ever commented on the fact that she looked a bit like a troll. It's better to simply come out and ask questions like that, that's been my experience. It all depends on your choice of words. The right choice of words can render bearable the most uncivil remarks.

She drank the same way she smoked. A bit too hurriedly. I didn't want to let her sit there with an empty glass, so I ordered another white wine. Then I looked at the plastic bag and she said, "Oh yeah, the package."

"It's pretty bulky," I remarked.

All of a sudden I had no desire to take that package home. Maybe it was something I'd be expected to read and comment on, maybe it was something even worse than that.

I was reminded of a letter I'd once received. "Dear sir, two years ago at Christmas time I sent you my book. Your silence speaks volumes. As you have treated my book, so shall I treat your books. Yet I would still appreciate a message from you to indicate whether you can endorse the form and content of my novel." After some rummaging around, I finally found the manuscript at the back of the bookcase. I returned it immediately, with a friendly letter. "With this message I would like to let you know that I am not in the habit of endorsing novels by third parties. I would recommend that you send the book to as many publishers as possible. Thank you for the confidence shown in me."

"You're not secretly a writer, are you?" I asked.

"Not secretly, and not unsecretly."

She put the bag on the table.

"I have a friend," she said. "She's an artist. And she makes sculptures of people she's seen on television. She made a sculpture of you, and when she heard that I was going to New York she said, 'Would you give him this?' That's it."

I looked at the plastic bag.

"What is it your friend does?"

"She makes sculptures of people she sees on TV, she takes classes in it, at night. During the day she works in an office."

"She takes classes to learn how to make sculptures of people she sees on TV?"

"No, to make sculptures in general."

I glanced at the bag again. The melancholy that had hit me the day before during the chimneysweeps' visit came back now, but twofold.

"Is it a nice job?"

"What?"

"Your friend's office job."

"I think so. She answers the phone."

I ordered another cocktail of the month, no longer caring whether they were drinkable or not.

"And what's in that bag, exactly?"

"A sculpture she made of you. I already said that."

"I haven't been on TV for a long time."

"Last year. You were on that quiz."

This reply, too, came a bit quickly.

"You're right," I said. "I was on that quiz."

Again I had the feeling we were being spied on from behind the display cases full of fish. Perhaps this whole encounter was being filmed. I had the feeling I'd walked into a trap of my own making. The only problem was, I'd made it so long ago that I no longer knew for whom it was set, or why.

My cocktail arrived.

"For one dollar you get a third one," the waiter said.

"All right," I said.

I still didn't have the courage to open the bag, even though it lay there on the table so invitingly.

"Why people she's seen on TV, if you don't mind my asking?"

"She has psoriasis; she doesn't want models coming to her home."

I stirred my cocktail with a straw. A superfluous gesture, for there was nothing left to stir.

"She also made a sculpture of the weatherman."

"The weatherman?"

"The guy on TV who predicts the weather. That one's in a gallery now, and she sold it for five thousand guilders."

Weathermen. So that was the category I was running in these days. And now, over to Robert G. Mehlman for tomorrow's weather. Maybe it would actually be a relief only to have to talk about the weather.

"But she wanted a writer in her collection, and she thought you had a good head. She also likes striking noses."

"Did that weatherman have a striking nose, too?"

Rebecca shrugged, and lit yet another cigarette.

A striking nose, a female psoriasis patient, a troll, and on top of that the chimneysweeps—it was all just a little too much. I felt a slight headache coming on, but I had to finish my cocktails.

"What I don't understand is what I'm supposed to do with it." I pointed at the plastic bag.

"She always makes three statues. One of them is for the model. But it was a little too expensive to mail it all the way to New York, so when she heard I was going she said, 'Would you take it to him? It's a present.'"

"A present. How nice," I heard myself saying. I reflected on the chimneysweeps again, and on the fact that becoming a weatherman could very well constitute the salvation I was looking for.

"My smoking doesn't bother you, does it?"

"Not at all."

I looked at the woman sitting across from me. It couldn't have been a coincidence, her sitting there across from me with a sculpture made by a psoriasis patient. This had all been planned for a long time. The only thing I didn't know was what she wanted from me, and why she wanted that from me, of all people. Maybe she didn't want anything. Maybe she only wanted to help her friend.

*

My wife says that the inability to surrender control is a sign of weakness. People who want to be in control all the time don't really live. I have remarked to her that she herself put a great deal of effort into trying to give her patients back a bit of control over their lives, or at least the semblance of some control. But she didn't think that was a good argument. Life isn't a novel, she said, you can't control everything. This was something we'd disagreed about for years. I felt that life really was a novel, a bad one perhaps, a boring novel, maybe even one of those detective novels where you know who did it by the time you get to page ten, but a novel nonetheless.

"Are you working hard?" Rebecca asked.

It had been a long time since anyone had asked me that.

She had long brown curly hair. They looked like pin curls. She should have worn her hair up. Every time she bent over, her hair brushed the dust off the table.

"I just had the chimneysweeps in," I said as nonchalantly as possible.

"Are you working on a book at the moment?"

I don't like questions, I prefer asking them myself.

"It's called *Letters to My Chimneysweep*." I couldn't come up with a better title.

"Is it about someone who's very lonely?"

I hadn't thought about that yet, but it seemed there could be no harm in affirming that. A weatherman was, of course, also a very lonely person. *Letters to the Weatherman* wasn't such a bad title. Especially if the weatherman wrote back. Maybe a romance between an older woman and the weatherman. The older woman writes, "I'm your biggest fan, I can't sleep without seeing you. The

53

news doesn't interest me at all, but I stay awake for you." And slowly something beautiful blossoms between the lady and the weatherman.

"I won't keep you from your work any longer," she said. She looked so grumpy. I couldn't tell how old she was.

"No, Rebecca," I said, "you're not keeping me from my work. Not at all."

Her pack of cigarettes was empty. She looked around, undoubtedly in search of a vending machine. My wife's patients weren't allowed to smoke at the day clinic. During the lunch breaks, monitors walked around to make sure they lived up to the rules.

The family with seven children had gone, we were the only ones left.

It's hard to find something to say when you're surrounded by stuffed dinosaurs, a few sharks and a cocktail of the month. The silence bothered me, it reminded me too much of the all-night deli and of dreaming about the price of fishcakes by the unit, salmon salad by the ounce, bags of barbecue chips, vegetable quiche and milk.

In my mind I formulated a sentence on the subject of the butterfly collection. I had to at least try it out; I couldn't imagine that Rebecca wasn't interested in the butterfly collection. And if not in butterflies, then certainly in scratch-off lottery tickets.

She leaned over a little. I saw clumps of mascara sticking to her lashes.

"I have ugly hands," she said.

Another silence fell. This one lasted a bit longer than the first. I looked at her, thinking I'd misunderstood her. Maybe it was only my imagination, but I thought I saw tears in her eyes. Of course the smoke could also have been bothering her.

"And ugly feet," she added.

I looked at the fish again, I searched for a text, but the fish didn't hand me any text. I couldn't even come up with a quote, even though I'm usually ready with a quote. What I said at last was pretty inept: "So why don't you wear gloves?"

She looked at me in disbelief, as if now she was the one who'd misunderstood. Her eyes were still full of tears. My eyes were smarting too, from the smoke and dust.

The house where my wife lived when we met was always smoky too. That was because she lived with a woman who chain-smoked. One day the woman fainted on the toilet and started a small fire that was relatively easy to contain. That's why my wife-to-be came to spend the night at my place. Because her place was always full of smoke. That night she swore a few times that she would never again live with a woman who chain-smoked, or a man who chain-smoked either, for that matter. I didn't find that particularly romantic, because she said it just when I was looking around for a condom.

*

Rebecca was busy with her lenses.

"Take your time," I said, because that's one of those things you have to do carefully.

There was a lens balanced on the tip of her index finger, and she was trying to put it back in her eye.

"Maybe you should visit the butterfly collection anyway, they say it's world-famous."

She nodded absentmindedly. Clearly, butterflies and dinosaurs were one to her. To me too, actually.

"My wife has tried to drag me along to the dinosaurs a few times, but she never succeeds."

"You have a wife?"

I nodded.

"Nice."

"What?"

"To be married."

"Yes, it's okay."

Her lenses were back in place now.

"And your wife likes dinosaurs?"

"Well, I wouldn't say that, but she has broad interests."

The morning we'd fought over my razor, my wife had asked me, "Why is it that everyone around you sooner or later ends up feeling like an ant?"

I replied, "Because I'm an ant."

"They're like catcher's mitts," Rebecca said.

"Sorry, I was thinking about something else there for a moment."

"They're like catcher's mitts, my hands."

For the first time, I actually looked at her hands. Catcher's mitts was putting it too strongly. "Better than having psoriasis," I said.

She looked at me, and I could tell that she felt differently about being blessed with catcher's mitts for hands.

I thought again of the story about the erotomaniac I'd started on a long time ago, but never finished.

On a napkin I wrote down the name of a restaurant. It was on impulse, a strange impulse.

As far as I could remember, I'd never carried on a conversation about ugly hands. Other ugly body parts, okay, but not hands.

"If you get hungry later on," I said, "come to this restaurant. I'll be there from about eight on. Even if you only want to eat cookies or fruit salad, you're still welcome."

Then I picked up the bag from the table. It was heavy. The statuette must have been in bronze. "Ciao," I called out.

My farewell was neither polite nor charming. But I was afraid to get caught up in a never-ending conversation about ugly body parts.

In the cab home I thought about a romance between the weatherman and the older lady, so I wouldn't have to think about all those other things.

A few months earlier, a German journalist had interviewed me at length. It was the last interview I'd given. He had typed out all the questions beforehand. One of those people who don't leave anything to chance. He'd done a lot of background research and knew what he was going to hear; he only wanted to have it verified.

When we were finished, he said, "You're quite charming." For a moment there I thought he was going to kiss me. He put away his tape recorder and his microphone and smoked another cigarette.

"Are you actually interested in power?" he asked me suddenly.

I looked at the ashtray, the pack of cigarettes, his hands.

"Power," I said. "Yes, I suppose so." And then I added, "Who isn't?" And I laughed charmingly. To put my own words in perspective, maybe even to play them down.

"Power is a two-edged sword," the journalist said, and shook my hand. "But it's not too repulsive for you to wield?"

"There isn't much I find repulsive," I said, and walked out of his life.

When I returned home from the Museum of Natural History, I stood in front of the bookcase for a while. I looked at the top shelf, where my own books were, along with their translations. At other moments I had always felt a certain satisfaction in looking at the spines, but now it was as though I'd found the physical remains of a long-distant affair. A postcard you'd written, but for some strange reason never mailed. The text on the back of the card suddenly disgusts you, and you wonder how you could ever have believed it.

*

By the time she arrived, I'd stopped expecting her. I was working on my dessert, a fruit salad, to at least maintain the appearance of doing something healthy.

I had put the statuette, unopened, plastic bag and all, in front of the fireplace. Not that I planned to burn it, but it seemed wiser not to open it. My wife was better at that kind of thing. She always said, "Just send them a thank-you note. Even if it's only one sentence."

The season of receiving presents was over, thankfully. The season of reminders and warning notices had begun. The statuette from the psoriasis patient would do nothing to change that. In fact, you could divide my life into epochs: the all-night deli epoch, the scratch-off-lottery-ticket epoch.

Rebecca was soaked to the bone.

I asked the waiter for a towel.

"Dry your hair first," I said.

She had the kind of hair that held rain. My hair held rain too.

"Do you always eat alone?" she asked.

"What do you mean?"

"You've got a wife, don't you?" The way she said it made it sound as if she didn't believe a word of it, as if it was only some excuse I'd made up, as if I'd invented a wife.

"Yes," I said. "But she tends to work late."

"Don't you mind that?"

"There's nothing I can do about it. There, your hair's dry now."

She looked at me grumpily.

I asked whether she wanted something to eat.

"What's good here?"

I recommended the risotto.

She ordered a plate of risotto.

*

The night my wife stayed at my place, that time the female chain-smoker had caused a minor blaze, I asked her the next morning, "Is this part of the therapy?"

She looked at me in the semidarkness. We were sleeping under rough blankets that she'd pulled up around her, as though she was cold. "Maybe," she said. "I'll have to think about that."

After a brief silence, she said, "I've never slept with anyone who works in an all-night deli."

"No," I said. "I can imagine. There aren't that many all-night delis in Amsterdam."

"I didn't know you could laugh so hard with someone who works in an all-night deli."

"It's a miracle," I said. "Maybe we should stay together for all time."

Everything could be therapy, I realized. Baking cookies, fucking, maybe even eating vegetable quiche in an all-night deli.

Later we sat around drinking orange juice and coffee, until she said, "I really have to go now. I have to go to the hospital."

"Yeah," I said. "I have to go to the deli later on." And again I thought about the prices of the things I sold. Prices I repeated in my mind like a mantra. As if a mantra could prolong the euphoria.

When I came back that night, I found a pair of her panties behind my couch. We'd slept on the couch, because I hadn't changed the sheets on my bed for the last five months, and I felt that tourists deserved better than that. Because I'd decided that's what we really were, my wife-to-be and I. Tourists. She was a tourist in my all-night deli, and I was a tourist in her student flat, although of course I was also a tourist in my own deli.

In those days I saw it as Man's highest calling to be a tourist. Life itself as a three-week safari to Kenya. And it all looked better in the brochures; up close the giraffes were a disappointment and the tour guides were all on strike, but a one- or two-day holiday romance was always a possibility, and the guitar-playing wasn't bad either.

My discovery meant she had left, in high heels but no panties, to attend a practical at the hospital. What a remarkable psychotherapist she'll make, I thought. I considered taking the panties with me to the all-night deli and giving them to her the next time she came in for a piece of vegetable quiche, but I decided against it. It's important not to mix business with your personal life.

*

"Why do you look so grumpy?" I asked. Maybe Rebecca was in pain, I thought, or maybe she was incurably ill. Although personally I felt that death was no reason to go around looking grumpy. Maybe I was a disappointment to her. In real life. If so, I felt she should just come out and say it. For a moment there I had the urge to say, "You're a cute little troll," but the situation seemed too precarious for outbursts of that nature. A person burdened with ugly hands and feet had no desire to hear outbursts concerning the similarities between herself and a troll.

She looked at me without explaining why she looked so grumpy, then went back to her risotto.

My wife had hung a note on the refrigerator that said, "There's smoked breast of duck in the fridge. Please either eat it or throw it away."

While looking at Rebecca, I suddenly realized that I had neither eaten the smoked breast of duck nor thrown it away. I don't open the refrigerator very often. In fact, I'd recently suggested that we get rid of the fridge altogether. It had been a hard day. One of her patients had thrown himself out the window. He'd thrown his furniture out the window first. Not that he had a lot of furniture to throw: two chairs and a coffee table, no more than that. Then he'd jumped. And he had been doing so well. But that happens fairly often. Once people have decided to put an end to it all, things suddenly start going well. I asked my wife, "So why did he have to throw all the furniture out the window? What was the point of that?"

"Rage," she said. She didn't say much else for the rest of the day. I believe it was the same day she went out and bought that smoked breast of duck.

"I want to eat alone tonight," she said. "You go to the restaurant." The next day she bought one of those mini-bar refrigerators and put it next to the bed. "In case you actually get rid of the big fridge," she said.

From that day on, we had separate refrigerators.

*

Rebecca wiped her mouth and laughed. I'd been sitting across from her in silence, watching her clean her plate. Maybe I should have passed out scratch-off lottery tickets. There were still drops of rain falling from her hair. She should actually have been called Zaza, or Froufrou, or Mimi or Sisi. Or Yalta, that would be a good name for a troll, too.

"I look grumpy because models always do."

I picked a grape out of my fruit salad.

"Models?"

"Models, when they do fashion shows. They always look grumpy, haven't you ever noticed?"

I thought about a sponge being rubbed back and forth over a leg and my wife saying, "If you think I'm a stone you have to roll uphill every day, then maybe I should go away."

"Yeah," I said. "Now I get it." But it was a lie. I didn't watch fashion shows very often, and when I did, I didn't pay attention to the models' faces.

"I figured, 'If I look grumpy, people will think I'm a model.' But I guess I was wrong about that."

"I didn't think you were a model, but that doesn't necessarily mean anything. I don't usually think people are models."

I picked another grape out of my fruit salad, held it in my hand for a moment, then put it back. It had a brown spot on it. Was she serious about this, or was she just trying to see how I'd react? Sometimes I said things just to see how people would react. When I'd told my wife that, she'd started crying.

"What are you crying about?" I'd asked her.

"About what you've made of yourself," she said.

So people made things of themselves. The way writers made books and filmmakers made films, people made things of themselves. And what I'd made of myself was apparently something to cry over.

"So what else do you do, beside bringing statuettes to New York for psoriasis patients?"

A young Chinese man came to take our plates. Usually I ate here with my wife, but these people were discreet.

"I fail to function," Rebecca said.

I leaned back in my chair. My wife always ate without making spots on the tablecloth, but no matter how I tried, I always spilled things. This time I counted three big spots. And a couple of smaller ones.

"How can you tell?"

"Oh, everyone says so." Her intonation and the way she moved her shoulders seemed to suggest that I'd asked a stupid question.

I'd arrived at a strange point in my life. Chimneysweeps had left a flashlight in front of my fireplace, I'd written them a letter, I had even offered to bring the flashlight back in person. My wife was in Vienna, we had separate refrigerators, my debts were growing by the minute and I was sitting across the table from a woman who claimed that she had ugly hands and feet and, to make matters worse, that she failed to function. Maybe it was time to go home. To call it a nightmare would be putting it too strongly, but at the very least this was a dream I needed to wake up from. The only problem was, for a long time already I'd had the feeling that life itself was something you needed to wake up from.

I didn't go home. Instead, I said, "Functioning is acting as though."

A piece of fatherly advice, rolling off my lips of a late evening. Along the lines of: anyone can do it, chin up, love, it's just puppet theater for grownups.

She nodded, as though she'd heard that one before. "Well," she said, "I'll probably never make a great paramour."

Had I heard her correctly?

"That's not what I meant," I said. "I was talking about functioning."

"Do you function?" Rebecca asked.

I said, "I can't complain," and pretended to be removing a spot from the tablecloth. Death hadn't reached out and touched me yet:

I'd seen a few people around me dying, some of them quickly, others more slowly. But my own death wasn't on the agenda quite yet, though on several occasions my own wife had told me how short-sighted it was to think that. The more time I spent with Rebecca, though, the more I got the feeling that Death would come and touch me soon.

"Don't you think people look better when they smile, not counting a few exceptions here and there?" I asked. I looked at her, my head tilted to one side, a slightly ironic smile on my face.

Maybe she was a femme fatale in training, but maybe the training hadn't been very good and I was sitting at the table with an incompetent femme fatale who was still part troll. She was probably only what other people wanted to see in her; some people are like that, they take on the color of their surroundings, and I didn't know what I wanted to see in her. At least, not yet.

Rebecca didn't share my views on smiling people. She said, "It's really true, models always look grumpy."

If all loneliness has a smell, what did this smell like? I sniffed, but I couldn't smell anything. My nostrils were stuffed up. A cold coming on, or one that was just going away. I didn't keep count. Colds came and went.

"A Frenchman once said to me," I said, "that the only thing a man wants is to make a woman smile." That was nicely said. A lie, but a nice one, one that could elevate your life to a higher plane for a few seconds.

"Oh," Rebecca said, "I've never met a Frenchman like that."

A few tables away, grated cheese was being sprinkled over a plate of pasta. We both watched with interest.

"Do you know him personally, that Frenchman?" Rebecca asked.

"He disappeared from my life," I said. "But the fruit salad here is very good, they make it fresh every day."

There were no stuffed fish to look at here. No butterfly collections, no dinosaurs either. Only a little grated cheese, two dozen scratch-off lottery tickets in my inside pocket and a handful of old people, regulars who I'd already looked at sixty times. Some of them I saw going downhill from week to week. If your own life was going downhill from week to week, would you notice that too?

Rebecca pushed her spoon around in the fruit salad she'd finally ordered. "May it serve you well," I'd told her. "Tonight it's on the house."

"Where did you learn to use your knife and fork like that?" I inquired.

"At an English boarding school," she said. "The meat was disgusting, but they did teach us table manners."

"What kind of meat was it?"

"I have no idea, but it was disgusting."

"And did they beat you? With a cane?"

"No, but I had to stand in the corner pretty regularly and stare at the wall."

"Ah," I said, "that sounds familiar."

My wife had patients who spent the whole day staring at the wall.

An older couple were struggling to get up from the table. Two waiters came and dragged the man through the restaurant to his taxi. His wife carried his cane. I like to surround myself with invalids and others in a state of decay. It makes one's own situation so tolerable.

My wife had called that afternoon. Her speech on the concept of *non compos mentis* had been well received. It was rather a strange topic for a conference about dreams, but it happened to be her specialty. She'd published a number of articles on the subject.

The day she left, she'd asked if I'd look at her speech. I crossed out a few superfluous words and broke a few sentences in two.

"Is it clear enough?" she'd asked in the cab on the way to the airport.

"Yes," I said, "perfectly clear. If I ever murder you, I'll have myself pronounced *non compos mentis*. I should be able to swing that, don't you think?"

She didn't laugh. Her speech was precisely about whether mental incompetence could be quantified. Was a person who planned his crime carefully by definition mentally competent? Did the entire concept of mental incompetence have any substance at all outside the courtroom? As we were walking to the gate, she said, "Sometimes I have the feeling that the patients are there for the psychiatrists, rather than the other way around. I mean, where would I go every morning if it wasn't for the patients?"

"Yes," I said, "that's a good question."

*

I watched Rebecca wipe her mouth. She did it with exaggerated care. She still wasn't saying much.

She was wearing the same clothes she'd had on that afternoon. I had changed and brushed my teeth. After that I'd made a few changes in the article about Svevo and sent it to the newspaper. It still wasn't good, but better than it had been. If I ever get around to writing my memoirs, *The Story of My Cowardice* would be a nice title.

"You sure ask a lot of questions," Rebecca had said earlier that afternoon. "Do you always do that?"

"I always do that," I said. "I can't help myself."

Now that I wasn't saying anything anymore, she was quieter than ever. She was absorbed in her napkin, she looked at it like she was seeing a burning bush. I needed to invent a name for her. Zaza had already been taken, and so had Zouzou, but it needed to have that sound to it. A story about a woman who becomes absorbed in her napkin, a woman and her hands.

"I once had a relationship with seven men at the same time," Rebecca said suddenly. She had another cigarette in her mouth. At least she was saying something. Silence reminds me so much of death. And of popping pimples.

"Seven men. That's a lot. It must have kept you pretty busy. How many disciples were there again?"

I ordered another bottle of wine, she was drinking so quickly. With my left hand I felt around in my inside pocket for the little bundle of scratch-off lottery tickets. Pious Jews kiss their prayerbooks after use, I had made a habit of kissing my lottery tickets beforehand. Even heathens need their idols.

"Twelve disciples," she said. "I went to Sunday school."

"I've never read the New Testament. Have I been missing anything?"

"You can borrow one from me."

She slid her chair back and crossed her legs. "Before my lovers came over, I always scrubbed the house with an abrasive sponge."

On my left pinkie was a piece of loose cuticle which I removed.

"Did they all come over at the same time?"

"No, one at a time."

"But you're saying you received them in a clean house?"

"They already had dirty homes of their own."

I pulled off another loose piece of skin.

"Were they the product of dirty homes?"

Rebecca thought about that. "I believe so, yes," she said. "They almost all complained about their wives, how their wives let the place go to pot."

My mind was drifting. I was recalling how I had sat with my own wife in this same restaurant, not so very long ago, and she had told me about a movie with Marcello Mastroianni in which Mastroianni gave a woman an orgasm.

"Every man," she had said, "should see that movie."

"Me too?" I'd asked.

"Yes," she'd said, "you too."

That evening we'd got awfully drunk in a hotel bar, along with an old, balding pianist. We'd applauded so loudly for him that he'd come over to our table.

At the time I'd mentioned something to my wife about how maybe I should stop writing and become a restroom attendant. In a nightclub or a striptease joint. One of those men in tuxedos who pass out towels and smile and even spray a little aftershave behind the customers' ears, so they won't smell too suspicious when they get home.

"You should do whatever you feel like," my wife had said.

When we got home in the middle of the night, that was the last time we'd had sex. The next morning I found one of my wife's shoes and her pantyhose on the stairs. I had laughed a great deal about that, but now I could no longer remember exactly why I'd laughed so hard.

"That's right," Rebecca said, "six of them were married and one of them was living together." She began messing with a bobby pin in her hair. She was wearing it up now, that afternoon it had been hanging down in long strands along her face. One of her eyes was a little sore looking.

"Another bottle of Gavi de Gavi, Mr. Mehlman," the waiter said.

It's nice when waiters know your name. It may even be one of the most important things in the world. That women forget your name, you can learn to live with that, as long as waiters remember it.

One bottle of Gavi de Gavi cost seventy dollars, and my first-quarter revenues had been a bit disappointing. That was putting it euphemistically. I'd sold forty-six books, for which I'd receive 137 guilders and 54 cents. Frederik van der Kamp had said, "Count your blessings. Last quarter you were still in the red."

Rebecca knocked over her first glass of Gavi de Gavi. There goes twenty bucks, I thought. Being rich is unimportant, the point is to make sure people think you're rich.

"Cheers," I said. "To you, Rebecca."

"To you," she said.

*

I stopped talking again. I was remembering how, long ago, my wife had come into the all-night deli. With a girlfriend of hers, a psychiatrist in training. They were so loud and cheerful, it was like they'd won the lottery. They even started dancing, right there in my deli. To the music on the Top 40 station, because we had that playing all night.

"I'm not sure the boss would like this much," I said, and warmed up two pieces of vegetable quiche without having to be asked.

The girlfriend who was studying to become a psychiatrist had penetrating blue eyes. She examined me while she ate her vegetable quiche. "Do you do something else," she asked, "or are you a fulltime all-night-deli attendant?"

"Actually, I'm a fulltime all-night-deli attendant."

"Actually?"

I told her that, in my leisure time, I was working on a book entitled *268th in the World*.

The girlfriend with blue eyes paid for the quiche and said, "Weird title. Why?"

"Every answer is a lie," I said, and counted out her change. Slowly, because I liked counting out change, even when there were a lot of customers waiting. No matter how minor, a transaction is a transaction, and you should make the most of it.

"I still want to know," said the girlfriend of my wife-to-be.

"Okay," I said. "Then I'll give you the prettiest answer."

She put the change in her pocketbook. I saw pictures, one of a baby too, I believe.

"Why the prettiest answer?" she asked, looking at me like she was inspecting a side of beef. "Why don't you just explain it the way it is?"

"If everything's a lie, one should choose for beauty, don't you think?"

They put their shoes back on. They'd taken them off, which I still didn't understand, but I'd stopped commenting on it.

"Where are you two going?" I asked.

"To do a little more dancing," said my wife-to-be.

"Then wait," I said. I wrapped up a few broken fishcakes and some pieces of quiche, and added a couple of bags of chips.

"Here," I said, "take this. Dancing won't keep hunger from the door."

*

We drank another bottle of Gavi de Gavi. Rebecca's drinking was becoming more avid all the time, and her replies more terse than ever. In fact, she wasn't producing any sound at all now. The last thing she'd said was, "Can't you stop talking, not even for a second?"

That's when I gave her half the scratch-off lottery tickets, and we both started scratching, most peacefully.

After I had received my first-quarter revenues statement, I called the publishing house.

"What is this?" I said. "Forty-six copies sold and four hundred and twenty-seven copies returned? What's this supposed to mean?"

"Well, we've reached a certain saturation point," my editor said. Officially his name is Frederik van der Kamp, but I'm supposed to call him Fred.

"Saturation?" I shouted. "Who's saturated? You think I'm saturated with a hundred and thirty-seven guilders and fifty-four cents? Have you ever heard of anyone who could live on a hundred and thirty-seven guilders and fifty-four cents a quarter?"

My editor admitted that he had never heard of anyone who could do that. "But you have other sources of income, don't you? What about your lovely wife?"

I shut him up quick. I don't like other men talking about my lovely wife.

"So publish a paperback edition of my first novel," I said.

"We've already done that."

"Well, then make it a luxury edition."

"We've already done that, too."

"So make a movie out of it," I shouted into the phone.

"That's been done, too," my editor whispered.

"Well, think of something!" I shrieked. "Make it a children's book or a comic book, or have you already done that too? Or, better yet, have it printed on curtains. Then people won't have to take the book to bed with them, they can read the curtains. When they've finished one book, they can hang new curtains. This is a million-dollar idea. Believe me, the future of the literary book lies in drapery." Then I hung up and paced the room for a couple of hours.

The next morning there was a message on my machine from the head of the board of management. He said he appreciated my idea, but he didn't think the market was quite ripe for literature printed on curtains.

I called back right away.

"Mr. Moesman can't come to the phone right now," the receptionist said.

"This is Mehlman," I said, "Robert G. Mehlman, and for me Mr. Moesman can always come to the phone."

"Oh, Mr. Moolman," she said. "No one told me that. I'm sorry, but I really can't put you through."

"Young lady, I don't know your name, and I don't even care what your name is, but you may have heard of *268th in the World*? Have you ever heard of that?"

She admitted to having heard of that.

"Precisely," I said. "I wrote that book, which is why you're going to put me through to Mr. Moesman, because otherwise this could very well be your last day with this organization."

She put me through.

"Mr. Moesman," I said.

"Call me Paul," he said. "To you, it's Paul."

"Paul," I said, "you claim the market isn't ripe for literature on draperies, but I wanted to tell you that the market is ripe for anything. For anything, you hear me?"

"I'm in a board meeting right now, Robert, let me call you back."

"What do you people expect me to do?" I shouted. "What am I supposed to do? Open a grocery store, is that what you expect me to do? Open a grocery store around the corner?"

"Let me call you back, Robert."

I hung up, and two minutes later my editor called. "Listen," I told him, "you know better than I do that selling books is a struggle. But I'm telling you, selling my books is a full-scale nuclear conflict. Tell that to your salespeople."

He promised to pass the message along, but he didn't think it would help much.

"Arm them, as far as I'm concerned," I screamed. "Until now we've been able to sell my books unarmed, but if we can't do it the easy way, then we'll do it at gunpoint. You can't keep a Mehlman down that easily."

"Listen, Robert," my editor said soothingly. "You're one of our most respected authors, but we can't work miracles. We've reached a saturation point, but I'm sure the new novel will change all that. People are really waiting for a novel: another collection of stories or a couple of poems, that just doesn't cut it."

I felt myself growing nauseous. The eggs I'd had that morning were working their way back up.

"A new novel? I can't wait that long. A hundred and thirty-seven guilders and fifty-four cents, you can't even buy dessert here for that."

"But Robert," my editor said in a tone that sounded like he'd joined an association for the propagation of Oriental medicine, "we've already paid you two advances. A third advance just isn't realistic."

"Not realistic?!"

The eggs were now balancing on the back of my tongue.

"Let me tell you what's not realistic! That I start a grocery store here around the corner. Or a second-hand clothing shop—is that what you people want? That I sell my own wardrobe and then call up all the women I've ever bought clothes for and say, 'You know that dress I bought for you last Christmas? Well, I need it back. I'm opening a second-hand clothing store.' Is that what you call realistic? At the end of this month I have to pay American Express fifty thousand dollars, and I'm already two months behind, you understand? And then I'm not talking about all my other debts. Is that realistic?"

Then I hung up, because I had to get to the bathroom fast. My whole breakfast came up. Scrambled eggs, coffee, orange juice.

I waited for two minutes, then called my cardiologist. My arms were hurting badly, and my mother always said that pain in your arms was a sign of a coronary on its way. She knew what she was talking about; half her family had died of coronaries, and they were always complaining about pain in their arms and other parts of their body. One of my great-uncles had even bought a new house in order to be closer to his family doctor, that's how often he went in.

After I'd called the cardiologist and made an appointment, I sprayed a cockroach to death. I had to spray for three minutes before the thing died.

*

Rebecca was looking at me and smiling. Now she was smiling. At least that was something.

"What were you thinking about?" she asked.

"Oh," I said, "about my work. Nothing important. How would you like to go to Atlantic City with me tonight? We'll go down by car and be back tomorrow morning. If you want, I can even have you dropped off in front of the Museum of Natural History."

When you're standing with your back to the wall, the best thing is to go full speed ahead. I'd spent half my life with my back to the wall, and I'd always gone full speed ahead. I didn't see any reason to change my tactics now.

Rebecca thought about it, or acted like she was thinking about it.

An acquaintance of mine went bankrupt four times in his life. When he went bankrupt for the third time, he wrote to me:

"I hope this letter reaches you before my note does. My attempt has failed. Pills and champagne proved insufficient.

"When you're young, bankruptcy still has the air of adventure. Bothersome as it may be, there's still something exciting about it, and far at the back of one's mind the prospect of making a comeback is always present. But at my age, going bankrupt is nothing but a disgrace. A feeling of shame and failure that won't let itself be eradicated, not by drink or antidepressants. Even when you're asleep, the disgrace won't go away. Your whole life seems to have been reduced to the bankruptcy, to the day they came to pick up the property they'd seized, to be auctioned off for a fiftieth of what you paid for it.

"My bank accounts have been frozen. Tomorrow they'll apply for the injunction: a subpoena has also been filed against me. This despite the fact that I am the one who taught all these people who are now taking me to court how to spell their own names, how to eat with a knife and fork. I am definitely doing something, no, many things, wrong."

That letter made such an impression on me that I learned it by heart, maybe as a sort of charm.

When that same acquaintance went bankrupt for the fourth time, another suicide note arrived. "Practice makes perfect," the first line read. I waited for another letter to say that this attempt had failed as well, but the letter never came.

"Atlantic City," Rebecca said. "I don't know."

"It's kind of like Las Vegas, but smaller. And we almost broke even with those lottery tickets. That doesn't happen very often."

"Almost broke even." She laughed derisively.

"Believe me, I know all about scratch-off lottery tickets."

"I don't have any money to gamble with."

"But you like gambling, don't you? Anyone who's had something going with seven men at the same time must like gambling, right?"

"I don't have any money, I'm broke."

"How broke are you?"

"Real broke. Have you looked at my shoes?"

She showed me her shoes. There were holes in them the size of matzo balls. All good people were broke, it seemed, and they spent money that wasn't theirs to spend.

"If you don't have any money, we can gamble with mine."

She smiled. "Okay, let's do that."

My side of the tablecloth was covered in spots and twenty used lottery tickets. It looked quite festive.

"Rebecca," I said, "life is wonderful, don't you think?"

It wasn't that I was ashamed of my wife finding out that I'd earned only a hundred and thirty-seven guilders and fifty-four cents in the last three months. She'd understand that. The problem was more that, with her salary, we could pay the rent, the gas (which we never used), the phone bill, and buy a pair of shoes and maybe a couple of bottles of milk, but no more than that.

It's not easy getting used to snack bars when you're accustomed to eating in the finest restaurants. We'd been living on borrowed money for the last six months. Or, to put it more accurately, we'd been living on six different credit cards.

I hadn't told my wife any of this. I adhered to the old-fashioned standpoint that women should spend money and otherwise not worry about it. Someone had once referred to me as a failed macho. But my old-fashioned standpoint had many attractive features as well. The illusion is everything, and, perhaps even more important, the illusion can be bought.

I had to write a new book, not a collection of stories or a book of poems, but a novel that would allow me to pay my debt to American Express and to VISA. And then there was the back rent for the last six months that had to be caught up on. The mere thought of it made me gag. As a child I'd had to gag often as well. I tried to figure out how much money I'd save if I stopped eating, except for a little yogurt, but I couldn't.

"Okay," Rebecca said, "let's gamble."

She had little round wrinkles on her neck.

"Yeah," she said, "I spent a lot of time practicing in front of the mirror, but nothing helped."

Was she talking about looking grumpy? Did you have to practice that? I thought it came naturally.

"I tried wearing rings, but nothing helped, they didn't even fit around my fingers."

I leaned over and examined her hands with interest; maybe I'd overlooked something. Aesthetically attractive they were not. But aesthetics were nothing but an agreement. Or were they biologically determined?

If I paid the minimum monthly charge on all my credit cards, I would have to live to the age of four hundred and seventy in order to pay it all back, I'd figured that out.

"Do you always talk about your hands all the time, when you're around men?"

"No," she said. "Normally, I never talk about it. You're the first. In fact, I never talk to men much."

"You don't?"

She shook her head. "We never get around to it."

The Infertile, maybe that was a good title. But not a title that would solve my problems with American Express. People wanted to read about fecundity. "Negative titles don't sell books," people had assured me on numerous occasions.

Again I thought about the story I could write about Rebecca. It would be a beautiful story, because through her I could say everything I still had to say. A story about someone who couldn't stop talking about her monstrous hands.

"And all this because of your girlfriend with psoriasis," I said laughing. "Excuse me for a moment."

I got up and walked to the front of the restaurant, where they sold cakes and ice cream as well. The Japanese manager greeted me from behind the counter.

"I need to make a phone call," I told him quietly. "Someplace where I won't be disturbed."

He led me to a little room beside the kitchen. An old man wearing spectacles was in there, doing the bookkeeping, and he didn't even look up when I came in. A pencil was trembling in his hand.

Maybe everything would finally start rolling now. You couldn't go on until you died with the idea that life was something that still had to start rolling.

"Dial nine first," the Japanese manager said, and left me alone with the bookkeeper. I'd spent a fortune in this restaurant, and at least that was paying off.

*

Two days after she'd first spent the night at my place, my wife-to-be showed up in the all-night deli. I still had her panties at home. She didn't ask about them. She took off her shoes and massaged her feet and ankles. She'd recently started a daytime job working with juvenile delinquents; at night she danced to forget the delinquents. Those were her own words. I would never refer to people as juvenile delinquents. One evening I'd taken the bull by the horns and asked her, "What kind of work are you doing now, now that you're almost finished with school?"

"I work for the justice department," she said, "with juvenile delinquents."

"Killers?" I asked, taking her vegetable quiche out of the oven.

"Thieves," she said. "Rape, other violent crimes."

"Aren't you ever scared?"

"No," she said, "not really. It's all a matter of establishing trust."

Later, when she was getting ready to leave, I said, "I'm actually a juvenile delinquent myself."

That made her laugh. Back then I wasn't confident about my jokes. I still hadn't found a form into which to pour my jokes. I hadn't found that form yet. Now I have. These days I'm fairly confident about my jokes. That confidence is a trap, but by the time you realize that it's too late.

When she came back a few evenings after that, she was cheerful. She'd had, or so it seemed to me, an extremely enjoyable evening at a discotheque. Her hair was hanging loose.

"So," she said, having taken barely two steps into the shop, "so you're a juvenile delinquent."

"Yes," I said, "that's what I am."

Maybe that was my innocence, that I truly believed I was a juvenile delinquent.

These days you could no longer call me juvenile, at least not with a straight face. From a juvenile delinquent I've been transformed into a delinquent. If you've always thought of yourself as guilty, sooner or later you'll probably adapt your deeds to match the thought.

"So what's a juvenile delinquent doing working in an all-night deli?" she wanted to know.

"This is merely a disguise," I said. "The white apron, the plastic gloves, all a disguise."

She laughed loudly. She was probably drunk. It's confusing to think that the woman who once entered the deli drunk would, when asked years later why she was crying, say, "Because of what you've made of yourself." It's almost beyond belief that those two women are one. But still, that's the way it is. Denying it is useless, metaphysical ploys equally so. Reality may be unknowable, but it's not that unknowable.

The color of her hair has changed of course; she wore her hair differently back then, had a different look in her eye. She sleeps at night now, instead of dancing. And I quit my job at the all-night deli long ago. I'd found a form for myself, for myself and for my jokes, and I'd continued to wallow in it. Like a bath you never get out of. You don't even bother to slash your wrists, you just lie there, and every once in a while you add a little water to keep from cooling off. Your skin starts peeling away, but you don't even notice.

"But I write nice stories, don't I?" was what I'd said the evening she'd cried about the person I'd made of myself. I had never realized that the person I'd made of myself was something to cry about.

"Nice stories," she repeated, "there's more to life than nice stories."

I had no idea what she meant. If there was more to it than nice stories, I'd never found out about it. If nice stories were not the length and the breadth of it, then that had escaped my eagle eye.

*

The number I dialed was that of my friend and personal secretary Josef Capano. I didn't really have any friends, but the term "personal secretary" alone didn't quite cover it. And acquaintance wasn't the right word either.

The bookkeeper worked on imperturbably. Nothing seemed to interest him, nothing but his books.

Capano had once earned a lot of money dealing art, but the work of the artists he represented had unexpectedly diminished in value and taken his fortune down with it. After that he had entered the service of a wealthy old actress who believed that a life without a secretary wasn't worth living, or was at best incomplete. When the actress ended up in the hospital with a liver ailment, Capano began doing odds and ends for me. Although I'd known him for quite some time it wasn't completely clear how he got along, but I felt that was none of my business.

When it had rained at night, he would go by expensive restaurants in New York the next morning and say, "I left my umbrella here last night." In that way he would collect about forty umbrellas, which he later sold.

He also did catering for wealthy ladies, who were all crazy about him. He took the most expensive bottles of wine home with him in plastic bags and sold them, or he drank them himself when he was feeling somber, which was fairly often.

He also had any number of good addresses to do his purchasing. He would go by a baker and pick up day-old cookies for free. When dinner was over, he would say to his clients, "And now for the cookies, the best cookies in New York. I paid ninety dollars for these, but you have never tasted anything so divine."

And the people would nod and say they had never tasted anything so divine.

"And they mean it from the bottom of their hearts," Capano explained to me. "They think about all the money they paid for those cookies, and they taste divine."

Capano felt he did absolutely nothing immoral. On the contrary, in fact. He said, "I make people happy, how could anyone call that immoral?"

I'd seen with my own eyes that the people to whom he catered loved Capano like their own son. The illusion of care, dedication and love was what mattered. Capano offered the top-of-the-market in the very product people need most desperately: deception.

I admired him because he seemed able to live on air alone. Or, as he put it, "I live from the street and the wind at my back." That seemed ideal to me. One time, during lunch, he told me, "When people stop laughing, the time has come for them to die."

*

"Josef," I said, "this is Robert. I'm at St Ambroeus'. I need you."

He started laughing. Capano's laugh was catching.

"I'm at St Ambroeus'. With a woman. I need a stretch limousine to take us to Atlantic City."

"Again?" he said.

"Listen," I told Capano, "the chauffeur has to act as though he drives only for me. You get it? As though he's my personal driver."

That made Capano laugh even harder. "Do I know this woman?"

"No," I said, "you've never seen her before. I barely know her, I don't even know her last name."

"Well, it would be better if she didn't hear my real name," Josef Capano said. "What should I call myself?"

I had to grin when he said that. That people should ever ask me what to call themselves.

"Michael Baumgold," I said. I'm usually very good at inventing names.

"Michael Baumgold," Capano said. "That's a good one. And the two of us speak only English together."

Capano was born in Antwerp, but he'd worn out his welcome there and escaped to New York. Now he was busy wearing out his welcome in New York. Some people see it as their task in life to wear out their welcome.

"One other thing," I said. "If this chauffeur drives only for me, I should know his name. How am I going to find that out?"

"I'll give him a note to hand to you," Capano said. "I'll be over there within an hour."

"And please, not a filthy limousine, make it sort of a new one."

"Robert," Capano said, "have I ever arranged a filthy limousine for you?"

"No," I said. All the limousines Capano had arranged for me through the years went driving by in my mind. It looked like a funeral procession for some big Mafia don.

"All right, so don't insult me."

"And bring a few cigars with you."

"Why cigars?"

"Maybe she likes them. Some women like to smoke cigars in the middle of the night. I want to be prepared for all eventualities."

"It's your dime, right?"

"And a few rubbers, just to be safe, and anything else you think I might need."

Capano sometimes did my shopping. I knew that if a bag of oranges cost two dollars, he would charge me eight. But I didn't mind, because he made me laugh. People who make you laugh are rare. Besides, I didn't care how much money I handed out, because it all comes back again. If not tomorrow, then the day after. If not the day after, then the week after that. That's how it had always been; it wasn't until about a year and a half ago that suddenly, almost imperceptibly, that all changed.

The bookkeeper didn't even look up when I left the room. The pencil was still trembling in his hand. I went back to the table.

"We'll go in an hour. My chauffeur's coming to pick us up."

"You have a chauffeur?" Rebecca asked.

"Of course," I said. "How could you get along without a chauffeur?"

"Did you like the statuette?"

"I haven't unwrapped it yet, it's still beside the fireplace. Your friend won't mind, will she?"

She shook her head.

"My mother," she said, "thought you looked awfully pale the last time she saw you on TV. She wonders whether you take good care of yourself."

"Your mother?"

"When she heard I was planning to look you up, she said, 'Take this along for him.'"

Rebecca slid a little box across the table. It was sloppily wrapped in Christmas paper.

"How thoughtful," I said.

I unwrapped it.

They were pills. "Winter Stamina," the label said, "vitamins and minerals, one hundred coated tablets."

"That's certainly nice of your mother," I said. "Does she take a lot of pills herself?"

"Oh, lots, and she wants me to go to the acupuncturist."

"Why?"

"To help me quit smoking. She smokes like a chimney herself, even though she's been to six acupuncturists, but she wants me to go, too."

"Do you see your mother a lot?"

"Three times a year, the less often the better. But she gave me her old coat."

I examined the instructions on the box of Winter Stamina tablets. "Healthy and fit, all year long," I read.

"Please tell your mother I said thank you," I said, but Rebecca didn't reply.

Once again I thought about *The Infertile*, and about the silent woman across from me, about the scratch-off lottery tickets, and about a crocodile belt I could wear until I died, and finally I asked her, "Are you infertile?"

It's important to make your questions sound as natural as asking, "Do you know what time it is?" The question has to take the other person by surprise, but at the same time they should think, "Why hasn't anyone ever asked me this before?" That's how natural the question should sound. My conversation exists by virtue of a lack of clarity. Haggling over a suitcase without knowing what's in it.

"Me? No," she said. "I've had a few abortions. That means I'm not infertile."

"Ah," I heard myself say. "That's good."

*

St Ambroeus' was emptying out. The personnel were hoping we'd leave, but I had to wait for Capano and my limousine.

"Why the abortions?" I asked.

"I was careless."

"With men?"

"No, with the pill."

"Ah, with the pill. I guess you can be careless with that too." I put a leftover piece of chocolate in my mouth.

"Are you always so careless?"

What was I careless about? About people, maybe even about life, as though it was a room I mopped without bothering to turn on the light.

I imagined having to look at those monstrous hands all the time, even when they were old and even more monstrous, and that one day I would have to say something about that. I was quite lucid, I knew exactly what was important and what wasn't. Monstrous hands, that was important.

But so were checks with strange pictures on them. Not just blue or green checks. Ones with fish on them, or cherubim, or cats. For a few dollars more you could get checks like that. That was very important. In any case, it was something that cheered me up a great deal. About ten days before I'd met The Empty Vessel, I'd ordered checks like that. I'd ordered a set of every picture they had. I was drunk when I ordered them, and when they arrived a few days later—I order everything EXPRESS—I got drunk again. Simply at the sheer thought that I now had enough checks to last me all my life. I had checks with motorcycles on them, with birds, with horses, with cartoon characters. There were so many of them that I had to empty out one of the kitchen cupboards to store them all. I was happy. When my wife came home, I opened the kitchen cupboard and said, "Look, enough checks for the rest of my life."

"You're out of your mind," she said.

*

"So you have a fireplace?" Rebecca asked.

I nodded. "My wife insisted on a house with a fireplace. The fireplace clinched the deal."

She laughed, Rebecca did, brushing back a strand of hair to reveal a few little pimples on the left side of her forehead.

Perfection is repelling, at least to me, it's precisely the semi-perfect, the unfinished, the scar that attracts. Perfection is absolute, and therefore already dead.

"Yeah," Rebecca said, "some women love that, a fireplace."

"Vitamin C: 60 mg," I read on the back of my present.

"Rebecca," I said, "this isn't the time to talk about fireplaces. Let's talk about you."

"About me?"

"Yes," I said. "How are you doing?"

*

A few days after I'd heard that my quarterly revenues had amounted to a hundred and thirty-seven guilders and fifty-four cents, a man from the bank called and wanted to talk to me about my VISA card. "Could we do this some other time?" I asked. "I'm in a meeting right now."

But the man from VISA was clearly the kind who never goes away once he has a foot in the door.

"When would you like me to call back? In an hour? Or maybe at the end of the afternoon?"

"Well, all right, let's do this now," I said.

"Are there problems we can help you with, Mr. Mehlman?"

As soon as people want to help you, you can be sure you're being threatened.

"Help? What do you mean, help? I'm fine, thank you."

"You're speaking to Steve Williams. We've had a look at your account, and we noticed that it's been three months since you paid your bill. Or have we overlooked something?"

Had they overlooked something? What kind of questions were these? Of course they hadn't overlooked anything. They'd overlooked nothing. They did this to bait you, asking whether they'd overlooked anything when they knew perfectly well they hadn't overlooked a thing.

"I don't think you've overlooked anything, Mr. Williams," I said. "I'm waiting for an advance."

"An advance?"

"A payment, in fact. I'm a writer. The money should be coming in any day now, and when it does I'll pay you right away. I've been a customer of yours for years, and in all those years I've never paid my bills on time; I've paid them too early. Too early, do you understand?"

"We're aware of that, Mr. Mehlman, we're aware of that. And we'd like to thank you for placing your trust in us."

"I don't place any trust in you." It was one of those mornings when I didn't trust anybody.

"Oh, I'm sorry to hear that."

"There's nothing for you to be sorry about, I didn't mean it personally."

"We're actually quite eager to know when we'll be seeing your payment."

"When you'll be seeing my payment? I just told you that. I'm waiting for an advance."

What kind of payment could you see? Real money couldn't be seen at all, real money was invisible.

"Could you name a date?"

"A date? What do you take me for? A thief? A crook? A credit-card hustler, someone who doesn't pay his bills, a criminal?"

"Mr. Mehlman, we don't take you for anything at all. We only note that you haven't paid us for three months, and it's our duty to warn you that, as from today, you can no longer use your card until we have received payment."

"Mr. Williams," I said, "I assure you that payment will be made within a week. Within one week. I'm a writer, a successful writer, and I'm expecting an advance. You know how publishers are, they shift their assets around until they can't even find them anymore.

Everyone else comes first, and the writers are all the way down at the end of the line. And you know why? Because people still believe that poverty results in better art. It's insane, but that's what people believe. If you say that bloodletting cures cancer, they'll tell you you're crazy, but if you claim that riches interfere with the artistic process, everyone just nods sagely."

"Well, Mr. Mehlman," I heard him say, "I wouldn't really know about that." He sighed. Of course it was his job to call defaulters, day in, day out. Mr. Williams was probably on the verge of going insane; what else could you do when you spent eight hours a day, five days a week, reprimanding defaulters? But I didn't want to be a dime-a-dozen defaulter, I wanted to be a very special one, a defaulter Mr. Williams would remember for the rest of his life.

"Mr. Williams," I said, "don't you like art?"

I heard him sigh again.

"Nah," he said. "What I really like is fishing, or playing baseball with the boys."

I'd wangled a personal confession out of him. Once you have one personal confession, even more can be wangled. Every conversation is actually an interrogation. Every good conversation, that is. I held the telephone between shoulder and ear and poured myself a calvados. I sniffed at it, but then poured it down the sink anyway. I'm a master of self-control. And talking to a man from the bank early in the morning with a glass of calvados in your hand, it looks so shoddy.

"Mr. Williams," I said, "within ten days I'll pay everything, everything I owe, the interest, the fines, the whole shooting match. Agreed?"

"Agreed," he said. "As long as you realize that, until that time, you won't be able to use your card. I'm sorry," he added quietly.

I had triumphed. I was sure that, to Mr. Williams, I was no longer just one of the defaulters he'd had on the line that day. That's why he'd added that "I'm sorry" so quietly. That evening, when he got home, he would say to his wife, "Today I had a defaulter on the phone, but he was completely different from all those other bastards who can't handle money. So civilized, he wanted to talk to me about art. Mehlman was his name."

I had five more credit cards, so not being able to use one wasn't such a disaster.

"Thank you for placing your trust in us, Mr. Mehlman," he said again before he hung up. He probably had to say that, maybe he'd get fired if he forgot to thank defaulters for placing their trust in VISA.

On a scrap of paper I scribbled, "I am a defaulter." Then I poured myself a calvados, which I actually drank. Now that I was a defaulter, I could no longer afford to pour glasses of calvados down the sink.

I called my German publisher, but he was on a trip. When my calvados was finished, I called my accountant in Amsterdam.

"Sylvia," I said, "good afternoon. This is Robert. Could I speak to Maurice? It's rather urgent."

It took a long time for him to come to the phone.

"Good morning, Robert," Maurice said. "How are things in New York? Has spring already sprung?"

"Not really."

If you ask me, he'd been drinking again.

"Things aren't too great here, financially speaking. I've lost a credit card."

"Where, on the street? Was it stolen?"

"No, not on the street. It's been blocked. I was too late with my payments."

"Yeah, the banks are strict," I heard him mumble. "And they're getting stricter all the time."

He was really drunk. When you're not drunk yourself, you can tell right away when someone else is.

"Listen," I said, "I want to sell my shares and have the money wired to my account in New York."

"But Robert, you liquidated all your stocks and bonds a couple of months ago, don't you remember?"

"Vaguely. Very vaguely. Isn't there maybe a little share lying around somewhere, though, one they maybe forgot to liquidate?"

"No, Robert, your entire portfolio was liquidated a few months ago, at your own behest. Shall I ask Sylvia to fetch your dossier?"

"No, forget the dossier. What am I going to do? I need money."

"I'm your accountant, Robert, not a pawnbroker. And I warned you about this a long time ago."

"Listen, Maurice, they think I'm a defaulter. You hear that? A defaulter. Mr. Williams just talked to me on the phone for about twenty minutes. I'm not a defaulter, and I have no desire to be called up by people who do nothing all day but call up defaulters."

My accountant coughed. "But Robert."

"Don't I pay you a quarterly fee to tell me how to manage my money?"

"What if you wrote a collection of short stories about defaulters, or edited one?"

I blew up at that. "A collection of short stories about defaulters? Maurice, I don't need you to tell me what I should write or what I should edit! I'm not going to edit anything. I'd rather die than edit a collection."

"Well, it's almost Easter, time for meditation."

"Every time there's trouble you start talking about meditation."

"In times of trouble, I've meditated a great deal myself."

My accountant was loony. I needed money badly, and he was raving about meditation.

"You're not an accountant, Maurice," I shouted, "you're a father confessor."

*

"But isn't it boring to gamble with other people's money?" Rebecca asked. She popped a bonbon in her mouth.

"Just forget that it's someone else's money. Then it's not boring, then it's actually pretty exciting. Money makes ugly men handsome."

Another bonbon disappeared between her lips.

"And women?"

"What?"

"Does money make women pretty too, money?"

"Oh yeah, money makes everything pretty."

The subject didn't seem to interest her particularly, because right away she asked, "Do you believe in a heaven?"

"Yes, I do. Except that, for people like me, heaven would be hell."

We went on like that for a while, discussing heaven and hell and The Pearly Gates, until Josef Capano came in. He was looking good. He'd slicked his hair back, and in his right hand he held an old-fashioned attaché case.

"Mr. Mehlman," he said in English, "your car is at the door. These are the items you requested."

I opened the attaché case. It contained a bottle of champagne, two glasses, cigars, household utensils, a family-sized package of prophylactics and a camera. One of those cameras you can throw away after use.

Capano winked.

"Wait, let me introduce you," I said. "Rebecca, this is Michael Baumgold, my personal secretary."

"Hello, Michael," she said, and shook his hand.

"Oh, before I forget," Capano said, "your regular driver has been taken ill. I've found a replacement. His name is Anthony."

"Thank you, Michael. Would you care to join us for a glass of wine?" There was still half a bottle left.

"No, thank you," Capano said, "I'm on duty. I must be going. Have a wonderful time in Atlantic City, Mr. Mehlman."

He was already heading out the door.

"I'm going to need new toothbrushes tomorrow," I shouted after him.

He came back to the table. He bowed his head a little and said, "I'll take care of it, Mr. Mehlman."

"Six of them," I said, "all different colors." Once I creep into a role, I really creep into it well, sometimes so well that I can't get out of it anymore.

Capano disappeared without a word.

It was, I realized suddenly, precisely such little charades that made me happy. The moment I started believing in my own carefully staged reality, that was the moment of euphoria. The moment that the story you've thought up runs away with you. The moment you sense that someone has finally seated themselves across from you at the chessboard, that you're no longer playing against yourself. That moment, that's the moment of euphoria.

My wife once explained to me that the brain naturally produces all kinds of drugs. And she had the feeling that the factory in my head was working around the clock, that I should be careful that someday the reactors didn't blow up.

"A peculiar man," I said to Rebecca, "but an excellent secretary. In fact, you really can't get along without one, don't you think? I find it so depressing to do my own shopping. Shall we be going?"

"Sometimes it can also be very beautiful, shopping, when you do it with your beloved."

"No," I said, "there's nothing beautiful about that. The most beautiful thing is to have a woman drive you to bankruptcy, that is, if you're going bankrupt anyway. I mean, imagine you went bankrupt because you'd put all your money in some steel mill, and the steel mill suddenly went bust. I once advised my mother to buy antique silver, and she never recovered. Financially, yes, but not mentally."

At the cloakroom she tried to put on her coat, but the hatcheck girl was too quick for her. I always gave the hatcheck girl a big tip.

"They help you into your coat here," I told Rebecca. "You mustn't do it yourself. Otherwise that woman has nothing to do. That would be sad."

She nodded as the hatcheck girl draped a tattered raincoat over her shoulders, and I thought about my wife telling me that people produce drugs in their own heads. "Psychiatrists believe," she said, "that everything can be solved medically. A lot of it is a question of chemistry, but not everything, and not all chemical questions can be helped with pills alone."

We went outside. I could sense that people were looking at us. At this restaurant they were too discreet to show what they thought of their customers. The chauffeur held the door open.

"Jesus," Rebecca said.

It was indeed a new limousine. A very new one, in fact. There was a waterbed in the back.

Capano was insane. Tomorrow I'd call him and say, "Josef, I didn't ask for a limo with a waterbed in the back. Just a limo, no waterbed."

And he would reply, "But I thought you'd like the waterbed. You have a bad back, don't you?"

"There's nothing wrong with my back!"

"Oh, but that girl had a bad back, right?"

"No, she doesn't have a bad back either. No one here has a bad back. I asked for a limousine and I got, for I don't know how much money, a waterbed on wheels."

"What's a dollar or two here and there? I thought a waterbed would be fun for you. It's not something you do every day, drive around in a waterbed on wheels. How many people have ever lain on a waterbed on wheels?"

That's how our conversation would go tomorrow, because dozens of conversations between us had already gone that way.

Of course, what had happened was that one of his friends had said, "Hey, Capano, I got a waterbed on wheels for you, isn't that something for that guy you know? That Mehlman, he's got money coming out the wazoo, right?"

And of course Capano had replied, "It's exactly what he needs, I don't understand how he got along without one all these years." Because that offer fell within the category of the ones you couldn't refuse. That's how I got stuck with a waterbed on wheels.

"Is that a waterbed?" Rebecca asked, and pushed in the mattress with her hand, like she was testing to see whether it was real.

"Yes," I said, "that's a waterbed."

"I've never seen anything like it."

Neither have I, I wanted to say, but instead I said, "Yeah, you have them these days. Once you get used to it, you don't know how you ever got along without one."

I sort of half crawled to the other end of the limousine and said, "Tony, we're going to Atlantic City." Then I whispered, "Where's the button to close the window?"

"In the back," he said, "where she's sitting now." He had a two-day beard, and otherwise looked like he hadn't slept for a long time.

I crawled back and closed the tinted window that separated the front seat from the back of the limo. He couldn't see us now, not unless this car was equipped with closed-circuit video.

I had no idea how much this limousine had cost me, which was just as well: if you're out to have even a little bit of pleasure, those are the kinds of things you're better off not knowing. For just a moment my thoughts flashed to Mr. Williams and the defaulter I had become. In fact, I'd been a defaulter all my life, with a brief interbellum when my books were suddenly selling well and I was paying my bills on time. But soon enough I'd found myself in debt deeper than I could ever write my way out of.

"Good morning, Robert," read the scribbled note Josef Capano had put in my hand. It seemed safe to me to read it now. "It's early April, and you're still an animal. I have, from some distance, already observed the young lady in question. Teeth finer than Jesus' own, and hair on her head that looks like it came straight down from heaven.

"This is pretty much the end of the line for your bank account if you keep this up. Here are a few costs I incurred on your behalf:

Cigars $50.

Tip cigar merchant $5.

Household items (including rubbers) $25.

Cab fare $16.

Camera $8.

Champagne: a present.

Champagne glasses: stolen for you from a bar, so you're allowed to break them.

Have a good time. Don't spend it all in one place. Shall I open a savings account for you, or does that question come a little late?

You're a people-eater, you know that?

Regards, Josef Capano."

I tore the note into tiny pieces and stuffed the pieces into the ashtray.

When it turned out that antique silver had become almost completely worthless, my mother had shrieked like a suckling pig. That's the way people are: give them one bit of bad advice and they'll never let you forget it, while the twenty bits of good advice you gave them are forgotten forever.

I had, in fact, only one investment strategy. When a company was doing poorly, I bought shares. The worse a company was doing, the more money I put into it. As soon as I read in the paper that a big company was having problems, I called my man at the bank and told him to buy, as though I was an expert. Which I am, of course. I believe in the law of scarcity. When everyone wants apples, buy pears. When everyone wants to climb the mountain, go down the other side. If everyone is looking for happiness, go in search of misery, and if everyone is stretching out his arms to God, go drink tea with the devil. In fact, I was the same way with people; the more trouble they were in, the more interest I was able to show in them.

"Have you had a lot of luck in your life?" I asked Rebecca.

She looked out the window. Maybe she was thinking about it.

"No," she said, "not much."

That sounded good, people without much luck in their lives could still count on beginner's luck. Beginner's luck was a way station I'd passed a few years back.

I opened the champagne. We drank half the bottle. She went and lay on the waterbed and I stayed on the seat. A cello concert was playing on the classical music station. It was raining. Rebecca slept and I thought about my blocked credit card, and about the five other ones that hadn't been blocked yet, and about Rebecca's seven men, and about my wife's speech on the concept of *non compos mentis.*

Then I thought about the day my wife-to-be had come back to pick up her panties. There were about fourteen pairs in my house by then. She had a little suitcase with her, which she set down beside the couch. She stuffed the panties into a plastic bag. I didn't ask what was in the suitcase. Panties went, suitcases came, life was a riddle that couldn't be solved. We still drank a good deal, but we'd stopped mixing everything together.

"How's it going with the juvenile delinquents?" I'd asked.

"Good," she said. "Are you pleased that I finally came to pick up my panties?"

"Well," I said, "they didn't really bother me. Are you moving in?"

"Would you like that?"

"Yeah," I said, "that would be nice. It's no all-night deli, but I can warm up all kinds of things for you."

"I'll have to think about that," she said.

We didn't need anyone but ourselves, we slept a lot and after that we warmed up food. We also made soup from packages, and we laughed about everything. But still, I can't remember any of that happiness. It was there, I know that for a fact, but it's a blank spot in my memory.

*

Rebecca had fallen asleep, the cello concert played on. I must have fallen asleep too, because a telephone started ringing in my head. When I answered it, I had the bunko department at American Express on the line. A while back they had, indeed, sent me a letter which I still hadn't answered. Rebecca snored. I'd read about people who heard their partners snoring and suddenly lost all interest in sex. Snoring has never repelled me, it's the inhuman sounds that repel.

I thought about that evening in The Russian Tearoom, the evening I'd considered becoming a lavatory attendant. They'd been predicting snow. The clouds were low. A Russian alto was singing melancholy songs. She had a lousy voice. I was fascinated by the two backup vocalists, though. One of them was little, the other one was huge. And they were having such a good time.

"Fiction has no consequences," I'd said, and my wife asked, "Please, could we talk about something else?"

Intimacy without consequences is a deceitful form of intimacy. That, I told my wife, was my specialty. Lying until the pieces looked like intimacy, creating intimacy that never had any consequences, intimacy that was an intimation and nothing more. And which, finally, when the smokescreen of words had lifted, would remain nothing but a footnote to a life story. And if by chance it turned out to be more than just a footnote, it would always leave the sour taste of swindle in the other person's mouth, the way deceitful intimacy happens to taste. The rage and hatred that welled up once you'd found out how deceitful the intimacy was, they would have the same flavor as well. One day, the ones who'd been swindled would say, "Life tastes like tainted tuna fish. But, once you get used to it, there are worse things."

Halfway to Atlantic City I opened the tinted window, so I could see the driver. "Tony," I said, "could you stop at a gas station? I have to pee really badly."

My coat draped over my head, I ran into the shop. There was only one toilet, and it was occupied. I bought something to drink. Maybe it would be good to stay right here, with the cup of lukewarm tea I'd purchased, and to ask Tony to drive back to New York and drop off Rebecca in front of the Museum of Natural History. Then, tomorrow morning, she could continue her research, of which—despite a twenty-minute explanation—I still could make neither head nor tail. Maybe that would be more than good, maybe that would be the best. For all involved, as it's put so nicely. I would leave a note for her, saying: "Going to Atlantic City was a mistake. Hope you still had an enjoyable evening. Thanks for everything." Or words of that nature.

"Could I borrow a pen and paper?" I asked the cashier. It seemed to be an unusual request. She rummaged around in a cardboard box and finally came up with a ballpoint pen and a paper napkin. A napkin would do just fine.

"Dear Rebecca," I wrote. "Going to Atlantic City was, on second thought, a mistake. Hope you still had an enjoyable evening."

"Do you have another napkin?" I asked.

I wasn't satisfied with my text. The message was clear enough, but it needed a little more in the way of aesthetics.

Then the door opened. Rebecca had left her raincoat in the car. The few steps from the car to the shop had soaked her to the skin.

"Jesus Christ," she said, "why didn't you tell me it was raining?"

I crumpled the napkin with my note on it and used the second one to hold my plastic teacup. "You were sleeping so soundly, probably because of the waterbed. Would you like a cup of tea?"

She shook her head and yanked on the toilet door, but it was still locked tight. Her hair was only half up now; when you stood close to her you could smell sweat, old sweat. What was she doing here, for god's sake, here in this gas station? She should have been lying in bed, dreaming about something, probably a man or an abortion. What was I doing here? How was I supposed to explain this?

I was a man in an all-night deli and I fell in love with a woman who came in all the time for vegetable quiche. I became a writer, not unsuccessful, but the debts piled up. Some people have trouble controlling their rage, others have the same problem with their money. And one day, when my wife was in Vienna for a conference, I went to Atlantic City with another woman, one with ugly hands and feet. I'd better not tell anyone about this. They would say I was crazy.

"No, I don't want any tea," she said. "I've got such a weird taste in my mouth."

In Europe it was almost seven o'clock. Another hour, I figured, and my wife would be waking up. I needed to write something so I could pay off my debt to American Express. Something that would make money fast, because American Express was running out of patience, but what went fast? An article about Svevo wouldn't get me there.

"I really feel like gambling now," she said. "At first I wasn't sure whether I wanted to, but now I do. My whole body's tingling with it. Do you also play blackjack?"

"Only roulette. I don't want to entertain the illusion that I can influence the game."

"You don't?" She shook her head in disbelief.

I ordered another cup of tea. Not because it was so good, or even because I was thirsty, but because I wanted to have something to do while we stood there waiting for a toilet door that wouldn't open.

I tried to imagine that I was taking part in a conference about dreams. I'd taken part in conferences about literature, once I'd even held a short speech about taboos in literature. The delegates, writers all, had reacted to my story with mild assent. After I was done, a Slovenian had shouted, "Exactly, let's forget about taboos, literature isn't a nursery school!" I couldn't remember his name, so I looked up his picture in the program booklet. He looked completely different in real life. According to the program, he lived in a remote castle and had won a prize for a book of poetry about horses. The book, unfortunately, was available only in Slovenian. But the Slovenian had a stenciled English translation, which he handed out to anyone who showed even the slightest interest.

I was interested. Stenciled literature has always enjoyed my interest and warm support.

One evening the Slovenian said, "Yes, writing poetry is lovely, I can't deny that, but actually I'm a gambler."

"I play blackjack sometimes, when I've got money," Rebecca said.

"You do?"

I didn't believe a word of it. I no longer even believed there was a statuette in that bag I'd toted all the way home from the museum. Rocks probably. Or a bomb.

"You're a time bomb," my wife had said one evening when she was cleansing her face. "I can't live with you anymore, I can't take the stress."

"Listen," I said to Rebecca, as I leaned against the door of the cooler, "how about if we get married?"

*

I reached out to caress her cheek, but she grabbed my hand and pushed it away. As though she thought the gas station wasn't the right place to let me caress her cheek. Maybe it didn't have anything to do with the gas station. Maybe she just didn't want me to caress her cheek, as a point of order. Or maybe I should just have said, "Your sweat sure smells nice." It's the little things that comfort people. And you have to comfort them before you touch them. You have to make them believe that everything will turn out fine, that everything will be all right, as long as they let you touch them.

I yanked on the toilet door again, but it still wouldn't open.

"What's with the toilet?" I asked the cashier. "Is there someone in there?"

"If the door is locked, there's someone in there."

"I understand that, but the door's been locked for a long time, maybe someone's died on the toilet."

"No, not on the toilet," she said in a voice full of amazement.

"That happens sometimes, people die on the toilet."

"The cleaning crew gets here at seven, they have a key."

I looked at Rebecca, but she didn't seem worried about the toilet. Maybe she was thinking about my proposal.

In some magazine I'd read that an entire series of fatal errors are needed to make a plane crash. One fatal error is never enough.

"Do you have another toilet?"

The cashier shook her head. "You'll just have to be patient."

"Patient." I laughed. In this rain, peeing up against a tree in the parking lot seemed fairly unappealing.

"Come on," I said to Rebecca. We ran back to the car. Tony was listening to waltzes on the radio.

"So what's he going to do while we gamble?" Rebecca asked.

"Him? Oh, he'll go to sleep. Or he'll do some gambling too."

We got to Atlantic City a little after two. I woke Rebecca. She was lying on the waterbed in the back of the car, snoring softly.

"Which casino do you want to go to?" Tony asked.

"It doesn't matter," I said. "Any casino will do."

He drove us to Bally's. It still hadn't stopped raining. Actually, it seemed to be raining even harder.

"What time would you like me to come back?"

"Four-thirty," I said. "Or make it five, that's even better."

We went into the casino. It was almost empty. I'd never been in a casino at that time of night.

"The machines make so much noise," Rebecca said.

"You get used to it."

There was a telephone next to the cash dispenser. I called the people at MasterCard. I was put through to a friendly young lady, I gave her my credit card number and all the other information she asked for. I also made a joke that didn't make her laugh. I was allowed to withdraw a maximum of five thousand dollars. "That will have to do," I said. When all the formalities were over, she wished me luck.

I couldn't help grinning. A young lady from MasterCard wishing me luck. "Thank you," I said. "Lots of luck to you, too."

We walked past the roulette tables. Rebecca took my arm. Most of the tables were deserted. Apparently there were more people who wanted to sleep at night than people who wanted to gamble.

It took us a little less than two hours to run through five thousand dollars. You couldn't really say Rebecca was very lucky. She lost money like there was no tomorrow, but I don't think blowing five thousand dollars really fazed her. When we were down to the last two thousand, she became so nonchalant that I couldn't stand to watch.

"So where's your wife now?" she asked suddenly.

I'd asked the cocktail waitress for a calvados, but they'd never heard of that at Bally's.

"My wife," I said, sliding a few chips back and forth across the table, "my wife is in Vienna, at a conference. About dreams." I laughed, the way people laugh when they have nothing more to say but are afraid of the silence.

"Oh," Rebecca said. "She does something with animals, right?"

"No, with people. Where did you get that about animals?"

"Because of the dinosaurs she kept trying to drag you to all the time."

"Well, not all the time," I said. "It was once."

Rebecca glared at me, hard. "You didn't make all this up, did you?"

"What?"

"This business about having a wife, and about how she tried to drag you to see the dinosaurs."

"No, of course not, why would I make that up?"

I looked at the chips in Rebecca's hand. Something had to happen, I had to press my luck, this was urgent. What was I going to lay my money on? I'd already tried my phone number, my zip code, my birthday, Rebecca's birthday, her mother's birthday, the dates of her abortions. So what was left? My mother's concentration camp number. Maybe that was an idea. Maybe my mother would make me lucky. After all, *she'd* been lucky.

"Wait a minute," I said to Rebecca. "I'll be right back."

Never before had I had such a fine sense of what my wife meant when she said that people's heads contained little drug factories. My head felt like it was housing a steam engine that had been stoked up a little too far.

I found a phone booth close to the exit, and placed a collect call to the Netherlands. It took a while. The man at the phone company switchboard hadn't been working there very long, or else he was half asleep. At last I got my mother on the line. I heard them asking her whether she was prepared to accept the charges. Fortunately, she said yes.

"Mama," I said.

"What time is it in America, are you dead?" she shouted.

"No," I said, "not yet. I just needed to ask you something."

"Why aren't you in bed?" my mother said. "It's the middle of the night over there. I was just getting ready to take a shower."

"Listen. What was your number at Auschwitz?"

"Is that why you're calling me in the middle of the night? Are you out of your mind?"

"For me it's the middle of the night, for you it's morning. I can decide for myself what I do in the middle of the night, can't I? I'm a grown man now, Mama."

"Where are you?"

"I'm in Atlantic City."

"Where's that? Is it a dangerous place?"

"What was your number? Hurry up, this is urgent, there are people waiting, they need to make calls too."

"You think I know my number by heart? By the time I got there they'd stopped tattooing it on people's arms. We got a sign around our neck. What do you need that number for?"

"Do you still have that sign?"

"It's upstairs."

"Go and get it, then. This is urgent."

"So why do you need my Auschwitz number all of a sudden?" my mother shouted. "What's happened? Where are you? Are you sick?"

"Hurry, hurry, hurry," I shouted. "Go get that sign, before it's too late, there's a whole crowd of people waiting here, I need your number, maybe it will bring me luck. You should never have taken off that sign, maybe you would have had more luck too."

"Hurry, hurry, hurry! Is that any way to talk to your mother?"

"Go get that sign or I'm going to die!" I roared.

I heard her lay the phone down on the table at last.

Three minutes later she was back.

"I almost couldn't find it," she said.

On the back of a pack of chewing gum, I jotted down my mother's number.

"As long as you don't use my Auschwitz number in those books of yours," she shouted at last. "That number is worth more than everything you've written put together."

"No, no," I said. "I'm not going to use it for those books. I need it for something else. I'll explain later." Then I hung up.

I ran to the toilet, the pack of chewing gum still in my hand. There I barfed up all the cocktails I'd had that day. After that I washed my face and thought about my wife, who was probably busy packing her suitcases right now.

Rebecca was sitting at the table, exactly as I'd left her. She was smoking. The pile of chips had halved itself again.

"Where were you?" she asked.

"Puking," I said. "Can't you smell it?"

"No," she said. "I can't smell anything."

My mother's Auschwitz number didn't bring us any luck either. On the contrary; after that the situation went downhill even faster.

When we had only five hundred dollars left, Rebecca said, "Actually, it's really boring."

Beside us was a Japanese man with a big signet ring. He wasn't having much luck either. He had a pencil stub he was using to make complicated calculations in a little pocket diary, but it didn't seem to help much.

"What's boring?"

"Gambling," Rebecca said.

We went looking for a bar.

"Five thousand dollars is nothing to you, right?" she asked mischievously.

"Oh, no," I said. "To me, five thousand dollars is nothing."

I put my arm around her. This time she didn't push it away. It wasn't an erotic gesture, or even a suggestive one, it was more along the lines of deceitful intimacy. But, at that moment, it seemed to me that my whole life fell within that category.

We had to cross half the casino to find a bar. Most of the gaming tables were deserted. Here and there men were sweeping up cigarette butts and other garbage.

"Hi, I'm Peter," said a carefully coiffeured young man. "I'm your bartender for the evening. What will it be?"

My wife had started taking dance lessons. A few weeks before Christmas she'd come home and said, "I'm going to take dance lessons, I want to learn to tap dance."

The next day I went with her to buy tap shoes. I didn't ask why. I never asked why. If she wanted to learn to tap-dance, then I'm sure she had a good reason for it. Her lessons were on Sunday afternoon. At first I went down a few times to pick her up after class.

"Did you know you can make five different sounds with tap shoes?" she told me once when I picked her up. "Do you want to meet our teacher?" I shook my head. At home she put on her shoes and made those five different sounds, but I couldn't hear the difference.

Now, at the bar in Atlantic City, someone was tap-dancing in my head—only I didn't know who, and I didn't know when the performance was going to end.

Rebecca just sat there, a cup of coffee with too much milk in it on the bar in front of her. She stared at me without a word. As if neither of us could believe we were really sitting here.

"You're not the most stimulating company," I said.

"No," she said, "you're not either."

She slid off her bar stool and said, "I'm finished." I'm not sure, but I thought I saw tears. Was there someone tap-dancing inside her head too?

I wiped black moisture from Rebecca's cheeks. They were tears. Lots of tears, in fact, a whole deluge that had washed away the residue of black makeup from her skin, and makeup of other colors as well. After a while there was a mud puddle running down her cheeks.

"I'm falling apart," she said.

"Don't fall apart," I said. "I'm already doing that for both of us."

*

When I stopped working at the all-night deli—they fired me—I lost track of my wife-to-be. She was doing a lot of traveling at the time. Until one day I ran into her at the post office. She was working behind the counter.

"What are you doing here?" I asked. For a moment there I was too startled to remember why I'd even come into the post office.

It was during a period that I sent a lot of registered letters. I registered them to lend the letters a certain urgency. I didn't feel that, as far as urgency went, I could rely on my words alone.

A few days later I ran into my wife-to-be at a shoe store close to my house. "This can't be a coincidence!" I shouted, without knowing what else it could be.

We'd exchanged a few words at the post office, but that was all. An all-night deli is apparently more intimate than a post office.

When I ran into her that time at the shoe store, I asked, "So what was the next step in that therapy?"

She was with her mother.

"I'll have to think about it," she said. "Come by the post office sometime. I'm going on vacation for a month, but I start in October again." While she was waiting for them to bring her the right size, she asked, "Do you mean you're still not feeling any better?"

Her mother looked at me suspiciously; if I'd been her mother, I probably would have done the same.

"Not really," I said. "At least, not that I've noticed. Are you still going to move in with me?"

I once heard her tell Josef Capano, "Sometimes he's not completely normal. What I mean is, he's nuts, only no one notices." That was three years after we'd first met in the deli, and I never asked whether she really meant it.

According to Josef Capano, my wife was a fairytale princess. He always said, "How's the fairytale princess?" But he never said that when other women were around.

Rebecca had climbed back on to her barstool. The milk in her coffee had formed a skin. I ordered her another one. Peter asked if everything was okay, and whether there was anything else he could do for us. I said everything was fine, and when he had withdrawn discreetly I put my arm around Rebecca and said, "It's not that bad."

But maybe it really was that bad, what did I know about how bad it was? I had no idea.

"It's fatigue," she said. "I didn't get enough sleep."

It suddenly occurred to me that, in all the years since I'd met my wife, very little had changed. Of course there had been my discovery that I had little talent for true alcoholism.

I glanced over at Rebecca. She looked like she'd just woken up. I suddenly regretted having left the camera in the limousine. Women are at their prettiest when they've just climbed out of bed. Maybe men are too.

*

In the early days of that winter, David, who had once typed out my first short story "Green Tea" on his father's typewriter for me, said to me during a copious lunch, "You're past your prime; maybe you should accept that."

He had also loaned me the money to buy stamps to send that story to literary magazines.

"Past my prime!" I shouted. "What do you mean, past my prime? Being past your prime means you've been at your prime, but I haven't been anywhere, so how can I be past it? Past what?"

"Don't scream like that, Robert," he said. "I'm not stating a fact, I'm just suggesting that you may be past your prime, and if so that you should simply accept it. It would make you happier."

I slammed my fist on the table. "Has it made you happier? I'm not completely out of my mind. You were past your prime at fifteen, David."

"Might I draw your attention to the fact," he said, so quietly that I had to lean across the table to hear him, "that I was the only one willing to lend you money to send your story "Green Tea" into the world, and that it was typed on my father's typewriter, and that I was the one who encouraged you to write about that crazy tennis player?"

"That crazy tennis player was my father, I don't want anyone calling him crazy. Especially not you, David."

That evening, when my wife came home, I said to her, "You won't believe what David said to me today. He said I'm past my prime. How can I be past my prime? I've never even been anywhere."

"You've been with me," said my wife, the fairytale princess, and she put another log in the fireplace that, even back then, didn't draw too well.

"Okay, but that's not what I'm talking about."

Sure, maybe they were about to relinquish my Sidney Brochstein cycle to the bargain basement, but that wasn't being past your prime, I felt. Being past your prime was a lot worse than that.

*

"Rebecca," I said, "tell me the truth. Why did you leave that piece of cardboard in my stairwell?"

More skin had formed on her coffee.

"I had to give you that package, and I thought maybe we could go out and have some fun."

"What made you think we could go out and have some fun?" I was holding on to her arm. I didn't know why I was doing that, but it suddenly felt like an urgent question to me.

"I'd read one of your books."

"Which one?"

"*268th in the World*."

I let go of her arm.

*

"You used to say you didn't care whether your books went to the bargain basement," my wife said. We were waiting for a taxi to take us to a restaurant.

Our life carried us from restaurant to restaurant. With brief lay-overs in movie theaters, bars and coffeehouses, and in our house, which was a hotel without room service.

"My books used to be in the top ten, and not for six weeks or twelve weeks either. No, for sixty-eight weeks."

We'd finally flagged down a cab.

"You should be thankful when David tries to tell you the truth," my wife said.

"I am thankful. Only it's not the truth. I'm not past my prime. Besides, I picked up the tab at lunch. I'm telling you, *he's* past his prime."

"Don't get wound up," said the fairytale princess. "Obscurity passes over no one."

"All I'm asking is if obscurity could possibly wait for about ten years, until my finances have been straightened out, then obscurity can strike. Why does obscurity have to be in such a hurry?"

Later, at the restaurant, the fairytale princess said, "Maybe you should stop writing about Sidney Brochstein."

I ordered another cocktail. Normally I don't drink cocktails, but suddenly the idea appealed to me very much.

"You," she said, "have started to look a little too much like Sidney Brochstein yourself."

I couldn't believe my ears. "How can I look like Sidney Brochstein? He's a character in a book. In fact, I created him myself."

She thought about that. We were sitting in the same restaurant where I would dine with Rebecca one evening. Or should I say: dined the evening before?

"Sidney Brochstein is someone who does his best to hate himself; hating yourself is so easy," said the fairytale princess.

"What do you mean, easy?" I said, slamming my fist down on the table.

"Happiness," said the fairytale princess, "is the ability to exist for your own sake. You can't do that. You only exist for an imaginary audience. Just like your mother."

"I could puke all over you, you know that, all over you and all over your snappy bits of wisdom."

"Yeah, go ahead," she said.

After that we didn't say anything for about twenty minutes. But when the bill came, she started in again. "If you want to use me, the way you've always used me, then this time at least credit me in your book. You want to know everything about me, and later on I read my answers word-for-word in your stories, word-for-word. Sometimes you don't even bother to think up one word of it yourself."

"What do you mean?" I said, signing my name to something without even looking; apparently, I'd already given them my credit card. "You want me to write an acknowledgment? 'With thanks to the fairytale princess'"?

"You know what's wrong with you? You're a bargain-basement kind of guy, you were born in the bargain basement. You've called this down on yourself."

"Aha," I said. "Well, thanks, that should keep me going for a few years."

*

The receptionist at Bally's Park Place Casino Resort was addressing us with exaggerated friendliness. As if it wasn't five-thirty in the morning. As if there wasn't any makeup running down Rebecca's face. As if my own face didn't bear the telltale signs of the bargain basement.

"A room for one night?" she asked.

"Maybe two," I said. "We're not sure yet."

I'd given Tony a big tip and sent him back to New York.

I handed the receptionist a different MasterCard; this one had a four-thousand-dollar limit, and I hadn't used it for a long time. Then we took the elevator to the eighteenth floor. The room had a view of the ocean. And of the boardwalk. It was still raining.

Rebecca walked around looking at the room as though it was a house she was planning to buy. She opened closets. "There's no mini-bar," she said.

"No," I said, "they never have them in casinos. They don't want you to stay in your room."

There were two beds, I sat down on the one by the window. Some blue and green light from the neon signs was coming into our room.

"Do you want anything else to drink? Shall I call room service?"

"Some water," she said.

We had to wait fifteen minutes for a bottle of mineral water.

We didn't say a word. I looked out over the deserted boardwalk. The only person on it was a man in a raincoat, walking around in circles like it was summer and he was out enjoying the sunshine.

After she'd finished her water, Rebecca took off her shoes and said, "I stink."

"It doesn't matter," I replied, "we're pretty far apart."

Once Rebecca had locked herself in the bathroom for a shower, I went back downstairs.

"Where can I make a phone call?" I asked the receptionist. She was the same one who'd just checked us in.

"Behind you," she said. "But there's also a telephone in your room."

"No, no, thank you," I said. "This will be just fine."

My mother was already quite old when she bought herself a dog. To keep her company. She stuffed it full of vitamins, because she said it had eaten nothing but junk at the animal shelter.

I said, "It's a dog, Mama, you have to feed it dog food."

But she gave it cucumber peels. Peels she'd first used on her face, because cucumber peels kept the skin young.

One evening she called me.

"The dog and I have something in common," she said.

"What's that?" I asked.

"We're both survivors," she said.

As it turned out, she wasn't too right about the dog being a survivor. It hadn't survived more than three months on the rabbit food my mother fed it.

I never saw the dog, but she'd sent me pictures of its grave. I know it's a strange thought, but while I was standing there in front of the pay phone in the foyer of Bally's Park Place, I suddenly wondered if anyone would take pictures of my grave.

I waited while the hotel in Vienna put me through to my wife's room. It took a long time. I stood there listening to waltzes for four minutes. Finally I got my wife on the line.

"Robert," she said, "Robert, is that you? I've been trying to call you at the house the whole time, but you didn't answer."

"No, I'm not at home."

"So where are you?"

"I'm in Atlantic City."

"What are you doing there? In the middle of the night?"

"Looking around, observing people, the usual."

"Listen," she said, "when I tried to pay my hotel bill, my credit card was blocked."

I felt myself wobble, a dizziness that started in my head and slowly worked its way down.

"Blocked. Which one did you use?"

"The MasterCard."

"Yeah, maybe it's over its limit."

"How can it be over its limit? We agreed that I was the only one who would use the MasterCard, and I never use it. It was so embarrassing, this psychiatrist from Rome had to lend me the money, I didn't even have enough cash with me. If he hadn't been there, I might be in jail right now."

"No, they wouldn't do that so quickly."

"How can a credit card suddenly be blocked? What's going on? This has never happened to me before. It was an incredibly painful situation, six other psychiatrists were standing around me and I couldn't pay my hotel bill."

"I thought the conference was paying for the hotel."

"Not the extras."

"Was it so much? What did you order, anyway?"

"You know, it adds up; a dinner, the bar, room service, the cleaners. Before you know it you've got a bill of a couple of hundred dollars. Who are you in Atlantic City with?"

"With that French guy."

"What French guy?"

"The one from the restaurant."

"Oh, Gérard."

"Yeah, Gérard."

"So why did he go to Atlantic City in the middle of the night?"

"He wanted to see what it was like."

"Wanted to see what *what* was like?"

"Life in a casino in the middle of the night." I cleared my throat.

"Don't you have another credit card with you?" I asked.

"No, I just told you that. Why don't you ever listen?"

"I am listening, I'm just a little tired, it's the middle of the night here."

"Then you shouldn't go gambling in the middle of the night."

"I'm doing research."

"So how's the research coming along?"

"It's coming along. What are we going to do about your money?"

"I've got my bank card with me. I can try to get some money with that. Do you think there's still anything in the account?"

"It's your account, so there's probably still something in it. I never touch it."

"Are you having fun in Atlantic City?"

"Yeah, it's coming along well."

"You sound tense."

"I am tense. It's the fatigue."

"Do we need to spend less money?"

"No, there's no reason for that. Everything's fine. Everything's great. When are you going to Basel?"

My wife had friends in Basel. She was going to visit them. My wife had friends all over the world.

"This afternoon. I'm leaving for the airport in a minute. That psychiatrist from Rome is giving me a lift."

"Oh, that's nice. Give me the number of your hotel in Basel."

I wrote the number on the back of an old receipt.

"It'll be all right with the money," I said. "It will be fine."

"And with everything else?"

"That too."

"Really?"

"You're my Princess Fairytale, right?"

"Am I?"

"Of course you are. But I have to go now, I'll call you in Basel. Lots of kisses."

"Lots of kisses," my wife said, "lots and lots of kisses."

The receptionist smiled when I walked past. "Good night, Mr. Mehlman," she said.

In the elevator there was a man who put his hands in his pockets and pulled out handfuls of chips. "Luck really exists," he said. Then I went deaf.

THE BUS DRIVER AND HIS WIFE

Rebecca was sitting on the bed, her hair still wet. She'd put her clothes back on, and she was holding the remote loosely in one hand.

"Are you leaving?" I asked.

"No," Rebecca said, "I'm looking for the news."

"Why, has something happened in the world?"

I walked over to the window. It was still raining.

"You stayed away so long," Rebecca said. "I thought you weren't coming back."

I opened the little box of winter stamina tablets and swallowed three of them.

"Be sure to give your mother my regards," I said.

"I told you, I almost never see her."

I sat down in a chair and pulled off my shoes.

I'd had an affair once with a woman who worked at the coffee-house I went to every morning. Maybe it wasn't exactly what you'd call an affair. We didn't have much to talk about. But on second thought, maybe that's the mark of an affair, that you don't have much to talk about.

Her parents were from Puerto Rico, she had a son of about nine, another son who was one-and-a-half, and fat legs.

Sometimes we met at the Sheraton, where my mother always stayed when she came to New York.

At first I used to give her presents, later on I started bringing presents for her children. The oldest of the two was a shy boy with beautiful eyes. For the baby I brought bibs and rattles.

In a different, perfect world we might have eaten cheese fondue together, but in this somewhat less than perfect world we fucked. Her name was Evelyn. I almost never called her Evelyn. In my mind, she wandered around nameless.

She wasn't what you'd call a beauty, but I've rarely met anyone who could touch as well as she could. Her touches had what I wished my words always had: they were charged. You had the feeling her hands could explode any moment, because there was too much longing in them.

I liked to look at her while she got dressed afterwards, and I liked her black boots too.

She knew the fairytale princess, because she made cappuccinos for her. The first thing she always asked was, "How's your wife?"

I probably wasn't her only lover. I never asked about that, but sometimes she'd make some comment about other men, almost a slip of the tongue. Of course, she might have been doing that to make me jealous.

One time she said, "If you lived in my neighborhood, I could cook for you."

We would gossip about the other regulars at the coffeehouse. She was good at imitating people, so good that tears of laughter sometimes rolled down my cheeks.

It was through her that I found out that the owner, an extremely fat man, had once spent four years in prison. When he got out, he went straight to the best restaurant in New York and ate himself silly. Six hundred dollars' worth.

From that day on, I saw the owner of the coffeehouse through different eyes. I saw him in the best restaurant in New York, sitting among all those chic, wealthy people, and him all alone at that table, eating himself silly, to celebrate his freedom.

I didn't want to enter her world, and she didn't want to enter mine. It would have been impossible anyway. Our worlds were separated by a forty-five-minute subway ride, but the distance couldn't be spanned.

I'm not sure whether she even wanted to know more about me. Maybe secretly, at times, in some lost hour. Maybe she was too smart to show that she wanted something she knew wasn't there to be had. But she was no longer eighteen, she wasn't naïve, and above all, she seemed to have her imagination under control.

Sometimes, when I came in with my wife, she'd write a message for me on the back of the bill, then tear it up discreetly once she'd seen that I'd read it. "Come by, I need to talk to you, I'll be here till four." Those kinds of messages became more and more frequent. After a while it seemed like she needed to talk to me every day. The perfect affair is an illusion. Supply and demand rarely, maybe never, balance out. You'd have to be deaf and blind to think that your supply is in perfect balance with demand.

I guess I must have been deaf and blind there for a while. In order not to feel anything, I'd been deaf and blind. At first I'd taken her to the expensive restaurants I always went to myself, but when I noticed how uneasy that made her feel I started taking her to cheap bistros, where it was dark and where the burns on her arms were harder to see. I never asked her how she got them.

At a certain point we stopped eating altogether. We didn't have time to eat, we only had time to fuck.

In order to meet her growing demand, I perfected my lying. I raised it to a higher plane. The fucking disappeared from view behind layers of clever talk. Persuasiveness is a matter of choosing the right words. Perhaps ethics is really a matter of choosing the right words. My ethics, in any case, had been brought back to a matter of wording and rhythm, the handmaidens of persuasion.

My stories on behalf of the daily practice of making love to Evelyn achieved rare heights and, I must admit, left my fiction on behalf of newspapers, literary journals and short-story collections far behind. Every story I told the fairytale princess was more incredible than the one before.

I'd been having the most fantastic adventures, while in reality I had been fucking in a hotel room. Funny and touching stories I entertained my wife with during dinner. Sometimes I thought: this is so good, I should really write this down. But I never got around to it.

Lying became a fulltime occupation; even the food I ate was a lie. It had long ceased being anything as banal as an alibi, it had become a means to keep the world, which refused to obey my rules, at bay.

I gave my wife a notebook for her birthday. When she heard a nice sentence, she could jot it down. In that way the stories I told my wife served a twin purpose; they put her mind at ease, and they provided me with material.

The affair wound down the way wars wind down. First you have the big bold headlines on the front page, then the headlines grow less bold, then the story moves to page nine, then to the section for foreign updates, and then suddenly the war has disappeared from the news altogether. As though the war no longer existed, as though the war had never been.

It was like that with us, too. We'd never talked about it, but one day we didn't go to the Sheraton anymore. And not to the other hotels either. Sometimes, when it was quiet at the coffeehouse, I went back behind the counter and helped her put pies in boxes.

All that was left of our affair were looks, a hand resting on an arm, a nicely wrapped present for her son pushed across the counter on a warm Saturday afternoon. Jokes only the two of us could get. A hand through my hair, quickly, when no one else was looking. Sometimes, when I came in in the morning and saw her, I would get an erection. My memory is, in part, located in my balls.

I don't know whether my wife ever noticed or suspected anything. Whatever the case, she never said anything about it, never even hinted at it.

She was awfully fond of my lover, as a waitress that is. The fairytale princess said, "She's the best. No one can make cappuccinos the way she does." Both of us tipped my lover heavily.

When the three of us were together, I never felt ill at ease. Maybe because the roles were so clearly defined, and because we both stuck to that. My lover knew exactly what she could say when my wife was around, and she never crossed that line.

Sometimes she'd ask, "Is your wife coming in today?" If I shook my head, she'd take me outside and start to talk. With increasing frequency, she spoke Spanish to me, as if it didn't matter whether I understood her or not, as if the only thing that mattered was that we were together, without my wife, and that for a moment we were something more than a customer and his waitress.

My lover never showed her feelings, if she felt anything at all. Let me put it this way: she couldn't permit herself to show her feelings, which is why I never found out anything about those feelings. Which, I suppose, was just as well with me.

Sometimes I felt a little regret at not having made a greater contribution to her happiness, but that's the way it goes with regret. Regret doesn't stick, regret is a sieve everything drips right through.

*

Now I took off my shirt, and my trousers as well, and lay down on the bed closest to the window.

Rebecca was still searching for the news.

"What did you do, actually," I asked her, "before you came to New York?"

"Oh," she said without taking her eyes off the set, "I flirted."

"With whom?"

"With everyone."

"How did you do that?"

"By smiling."

"And what else?"

"By looking sly."

"Are you looking sly right now?"

"No," she said, "not at the moment."

She turned off the TV and went into the bathroom. When she came back she was wearing only a T-shirt and panties. She lay down on the other bed.

"Good night," I said.

"Yeah," she said.

In Europe it was now one o'clock in the afternoon.

I pretended to be asleep, and kept that up until I really was asleep.

*

The phone woke me. A cheery voice asked, "Will you be staying with us for another night?"

I tried to see what time it was. There was a clock on top of the TV. It was twelve-thirty in the afternoon.

"Yes," I said, "we'll be staying one more night," and hung up.

Rebecca was sitting straight up in bed, looking at me. She must have been awake for a while.

"Did you sleep well?" I asked.

She nodded. "Aren't you sorry?"

"About what?" I asked.

"About being here with me in a hotel room."

I looked out the window. The rain had stopped, but the clouds were still low. The boardwalk looked pretty forlorn.

"Feeling sorry? No, not that. Why should I?"

"Well, waking up and seeing me."

Less than ten days before this, one of my wife's patients had thrown a chair at a social worker. The social worker had to be taken to the hospital. There'd been a huge ruckus in the day clinic, and four security people had jumped the patient right away.

"Aggression on the part of the patient," my wife had said, "is something you should never take personally, otherwise you might as well quit on the spot. And you have to put up with a fair amount of aggression. One of my patients thinks I'm the devil."

"I think that sometimes too," I said. "If I were you, I'd wear a crash helmet when I went to work."

"You know, it was actually one of those people I never would have expected," my wife said.

Now, in this hotel room at Bally's Park Place Casino Resort, I also suddenly felt the overpowering urge to start throwing chairs and tearing paintings off the walls and breaking them in two. There were two paintings in this room, one of them a landscape, the other one of a bird. It wasn't something to be taken personally. I could tell the hotel that too, later on, that above all they shouldn't take it personally.

"I have twelve dollars and sixty-four cents left," Rebecca said. She was still sitting straight up in bed, acting like we'd been engaged for three years.

"Well," I said, "that ought to tide you over for a while."

I wanted to flee the life I'd been leading for the last five years, the way you flee a holiday spot you've visited too often, but I didn't know how.

I went into the bathroom and peed. Then I hung the do-not-disturb sign on the door.

About two months ago, I bought a new bookcase, a huge thing that cost me hundreds of dollars. The piles of books along the walls had grown so high they'd started falling over. The time had come to put an end to that, the fairytale princess felt.

Rebecca was standing at the window now in a pair of baggy white panties. An extremely old-fashioned pair of panties, it seemed to me. I hadn't noticed them the night before. She was yanking on the window.

"Those things don't open," I said.

"Why not?"

"Because otherwise people would jump out of them. And casinos aren't particularly fond of people jumping out their windows. If you're too warm, we can turn on the air conditioning."

"No, that's okay. You know who my idol is?"

"No, who?"

"Mata Hari."

"Mata Hari."

She was still yanking on the window, so I said, "The hotel would rather you didn't commit suicide."

"I wanted to be like Mata Hari. She's the reason I went to college."

"What do you mean?"

"Before that I worked in a stable, and I read everything about Mata Hari I could get my hands on. After a while, I started studying history, to find out more about her."

"And?"

I sat up in bed and looked at the woman who wanted to be the Mata Hari of our day.

"My professors didn't know anything about Mata Hari. But I entertained the vital parts of many a man, because that's what she did."

"Vital parts," I echoed. I went and stood at the window and I realized there was no way back for her; once you'd decided to become Mata Hari, you had to plow on.

"Mata Hari was a genius," Rebecca said.

"Do you still have a lot of family?" I asked.

"Here and there. What about you?"

"My mother," I said. "My mother's dog died not too long ago. Of cucumber peels."

"That's sad." She sat down on the bed, at precisely the same spot where she'd been sitting yesterday. In front of the television.

My life had started resembling a seaside village, not a particularly unattractive village, but I'd counted every cobblestone and climbed every dune more times than I could remember. I'd created the village myself, of course, but that didn't make the desire to flee it any less relevant.

"What makes you want to stop writing?" my wife had asked.

"Listen," I'd told her, "when someone gives birth to idiots, mongoloids, two-headed girls, Siamese twins, after a certain point they don't go on bringing children into the world anymore, do they?"

"Do you consider your books Siamese twins, two-headed girls, mongoloids?"

"I'd never put it that way myself, of course, but if you ask me point-blank: sometimes, yes."

"Do you have a lover?" Rebecca asked.

The question took me by surprise. It didn't seem like Rebecca. To ask that right now. To use that word right now.

"Platonically," I said.

"Platonically. A platonic lover?"

She started laughing, she roared with laughter, saliva ran out of her mouth. I'd never seen her like this.

"Sort of like alcohol-free beer?"

Rebecca came and stood right in front of me. I smelled her breath, which smelled the way people's breath smells when they smoke, drink, sleep and eat the occasional green-onion chip.

"Maybe I should open a sandwich shop," I'd once told my wife.

She'd tapped her forehead with her finger. "You, a sandwich shop? After two months you wouldn't have sold a single sandwich, and there'd be nothing left of your shop."

"Listen," I'd said, "without language there's nothing left, nothing at all. Everything is made of language, so why shouldn't I start a sandwich shop? Language is a prison—the same prison your patients are in."

The fairytale princess had pinched my cheek. "No," she said, "my lovely. My patients' prison is a very different kind of prison from yours. Make no mistake about that."

Smoking, drinking, sleeping and onion-flavored chips, yes, that's what Rebecca's breath smelled like. Not bad. Human, actually.

"You're completely unreachable, you know that?" Rebecca said.

I stepped back. "Me, unreachable? I've got a telephone, a post-office box. Anyone who needs me can reach me."

But, I thought, the banks are the only ones who need me. And then, right afterwards, but as long as your creditors need you you've got a reason to live.

"She's going to die soon," Rebecca said. She was down looking for something under the bed.

"Who?"

"My mother. But she's got someone who comes in to do the ironing. They come by twice a week."

"That's good. What are you looking for?"

"A box of matches," Rebecca said, crawling out from under the bed.

There was a knock at the door. Someone shouted, "Can I come in and clean the room?"

"Give us half an hour," I shouted back. "There's a sign on the door: it says 'do not disturb.' What do you think it's there for?"

Then Rebecca went into the bathroom. "I'm going to take a shower," she said.

I picked up my notebook and wrote, "Mata Hari. Mother will die soon."

This I could use.

*

Rebecca said, "I need stuff for my lenses."

We were walking along the boardwalk in Atlantic City, looking for a place to eat breakfast. In the end we bought two hot dogs, which the man selling them said were a hundred percent beef. I was willing to believe the part about a hundred percent. But beef? Never. We ate them while we walked. We were cold.

When we got to the bumper cars, we stopped to watch. A man yelled to us that we should try our luck throwing softballs, but we didn't feel like it.

"We also need toothbrushes," I said.

"And toothpaste."

"No," I said, "now you're stretching things."

It was a quarter past three and it was going to start raining again soon. In Europe it was now a quarter past nine in the evening. I needed to call Basel.

*

The day the bookcases arrived, I told my wife, "Maybe we should disappear."

We were sitting in a taxi. The sun was shining.

"What do you mean, disappear?"

"Maybe I should disappear from your life," I said. "Maybe I'm getting in the way of your happiness."

"What kind of a cowardly solution is that?"

"You're the one who told me you're not doing well."

"That's because of the patients, that's because of my work. One of our psychiatrists committed suicide."

"See?" I said. "That's the beginning of the end. Patients jump, we've gotten used to that, but once the psychiatrists start offing themselves it's all over."

"Yes, it's very difficult, especially for the patients."

"It's like an epidemic. I'm trying to remember a meal during the last three months when someone hadn't died, or wasn't wanting to die, or hadn't taken the wrong medicine."

"The wrong medicine, that's a big problem. Today a patient told me he thought the medicine we gave him was meant only to monitor him. So the president could monitor him."

"Which president?"

I paid the cabbie and we climbed out.

"The president of the United States; he thought the intelligence agencies were monitoring his thoughts, through the medicines we prescribed for him."

"Maybe he's right. It doesn't sound that crazy to me."

"So now you're starting. I hear stories like that all day. When I come home, I don't feel like hearing them all over again."

She stopped suddenly.

"You know what the problem is with you men?" my wife said. "If you don't get praised to the skies, you can't even fuck."

*

There was a trickle of mustard coming from the corner of Rebecca's mouth. I took my paper napkin and wiped her lips.

"You look better without makeup."

"Thank you," she said.

"You want to go on a ride?"

She looked around.

"Bumper cars?"

She shook her head.

"Throw some softballs?"

"No thanks."

"Ferris wheel?"

She looked at the Ferris wheel. It was a really little Ferris wheel, a miniature Ferris wheel, and a pretty rusty one at that. She nodded. The Ferris wheel had won her approval.

The man who sold tickets was also the man who tore them in half. We were the only ones on the whole Ferris wheel. When we were all the way up at the top, she asked, "What are you thinking about?"

"About fifty thousand dollars," I said.

"Why fifty thousand?"

"That's what I have to pay American Express next week."

"How did you ever get them to lend you so much money?" She seemed to regard it as an exceptional achievement on my part.

"It's easy," I said. "Once they have the illusion that you're creditworthy, it's hard for them to rid themselves of that illusion. You really have to do your best."

The Ferris wheel started moving again, and Rebecca asked, "Are you actually one of those people who starts kissing right away?"

*

"Happiness," said my wife, that day they'd delivered the bookcases, "is not an extenuating circumstance."

"You're wrong about that," I replied. "Happiness is precisely that, an extenuating circumstance. Or rather, the sum of all extenuating circumstances, that's happiness. If you don't think so, then you have unreasonable expectations for this world, and this life. And besides, what do you mean when you say that men have to be praised to the skies, that otherwise they can't fuck?"

She stopped in front of an antique shop. "I mean that you've made me your lap dog. Because I didn't praise you to the skies. A lap dog, living under extenuating circumstances."

"What do you mean a lap dog? You've got a job, a job you like, in any event the kind of work you've always wanted to do, you've got a comfortable apartment by New York standards, you've got a fireplace, goddamn it, a fireplace! You go out to dinner every night, you can buy all the clothes you want, you can take trips whenever you want."

"Christ, Robert," she interrupted, "don't you get it? Are you really that stupid? Do you really know so little about people? I don't want your money, I want feelings."

Now it was my turn to stop in my tracks.

"Feelings, is that what you want? So read Barbara Cartland, that's feelings."

She pinched my arm. "You know what's too bad, Robert?" she said. "That God gave you all those brains. Because you don't really need them, your dick is the epicenter of the universe."

My arm was bleeding.

"You're a violent person," I said. "For a psychotherapist."

"Around you, everyone becomes violent sooner or later. Your words generate violence. And you know why? Because you've detached yourself from your words, from what you say. People think there's a living creature behind your words, but that's an illusion. Behind your words, the black hole begins. And once a person's finally figured that out, they really do become violent."

*

The Ferris wheel had made one more turn. We were stopped at the top again.

"Rebecca," I said, "do you think that we . . . do you think these are extenuating circumstances?"

We looked at the hotels in the distance, the casinos, the boardwalk below and the rare individual walking along it.

"It could be more extenuating," she said. She took off her right shoe and threw it off the Ferris wheel. Then she took off her left shoe and threw it down too.

"They had holes in them," she said. "I should have thrown them away a long time ago."

The Ferris wheel creaked into motion again. I stared straight ahead and, shy of feelings as I was, I searched for words to say to someone who had just thrown her shoes off the Ferris wheel.

The words didn't come, and we started kissing. Carefully at first, then less carefully, as if we had to kiss away the disappointment. Energetically, the way you clean toilets that haven't been cleaned for a long time. Ones where the brown has baked its way into the porcelain.

We got off the Ferris wheel and walked down the wet boardwalk, Rebecca in her pantyhose.

"How can you walk like that?" I asked.

"I'm used to it," she said.

*

At the sporting goods store where she tried on shoes, Rebecca said, "They're friendly."

"Who?"

"My parents."

"I thought you were talking about the salespeople."

"Yeah, they're friendly too."

"Friendly parents are pretty unique," I noted. "I think it's sweet of your mother to be dying and still send me tablets."

"She heard I was going to look you up. And she said, 'The last time I saw him on TV, he looked so terrible, so pale and unhealthy, take these along for him.' She can be real nice, my mother, but she looks very pale and unhealthy too."

*

In Europe it was now a quarter past eleven at night. It wouldn't be long before my wife would be going to bed in a hotel in Basel. Maybe she would read a little, or try to call New York to see if I was home yet. But maybe she'd gone out with her friends in Basel, and later she'd come walking into her hotel, a little tipsy. Maybe she'd take a bath before going to bed, to relax a little.

A few days after I'd run into my wife-to-be and her mother in the shoe store, she'd called me. It was the first time she'd ever called me.

"The all-night deli isn't what it used to be, not since you don't work there anymore."

She didn't even say her name, but she didn't have to. I didn't get called that often.

"Isn't it? I wouldn't know. I haven't been back."

"Did you have a fight when you left?"

"No, not that. Sometimes I disappear for a while, and other times I disappear forever."

"What are you doing these days?"

I hesitated for a moment. "Oh, this and that."

"And is this and that keeping you occupied?"

"No," I said, "this and that never keeps you occupied."

"Well, I thought maybe we could get together sometime."

"To continue our therapy?"

"I suppose you could call it that."

We agreed to meet at a little grocery shop. We were going to cook a meal together. Cooking, she thought, would do me good. I never cooked, so there was always the possibility that it would do me good.

She arrived late. I'd been walking around the grocery shop for twenty minutes. I was starting to draw some attention, but I figured: I can't stop now, otherwise we'll miss each other. I acted like I was searching for all kinds of things, and when there was absolutely no way around it I actually put something in my shopping basket. When one of the salesgirls tried to offer me assistance, I smiled and said I was finding everything I needed.

I was wearing a fur coat I'd bought from a Yugoslav on the Zeedijk in Amsterdam. The fur coat smelled faintly of dead Yugoslav. I didn't mind that; the smell of dead Yugoslav was the kind of smell that fit me to a tee.

When my wife-to-be finally came in, she looked very strange. She was wearing a raincoat with all kinds of flowers on it. An extremely striking raincoat. Back in those days I wasn't particularly fond of striking clothing.

"What have you been buying?" she asked.

"I wasn't really paying attention," I said. "Every once in a while I just took something off the shelf."

My basket contained a peculiar assortment of commodities, ranging from baking powder through birthday candles to trout eggs.

"You know what?" she said. "I think maybe today we should forget about cooking."

"Oh," I said. "But what about my therapy? I thought cooking was going to be the therapy."

"That's right," she said, "cooking and shopping. First you have to learn to shop."

"I don't shop much."

"That's exactly it."

I was still standing there with my baking powder, the trout eggs and the birthday candles.

"Let's put those things back first."

I had no idea where I'd found it all. I wanted to stuff everything away in some dark corner, but she insisted that we put it all back where it belonged.

"That's a really nice coat you've got on," she said.

"I like yours too."

"Where did you get it?"

"From a dead Yugoslav."

"In a store?"

"No, in a café."

"You buy clothes in cafés?"

"Sometimes. These days people are always trying to sell you things. And I hate to say no."

We left the grocery shop.

"Actually, it's a good idea to wear dead people's clothes. Just because people are put out with the garbage, that doesn't necessarily mean their clothes have to go in the garbage too."

She agreed with me on that. She agreed completely.

I said, "When I die, I'd be content with a pet cemetery, I don't care about lying there with all those other people, and a pet cemetery is bound to be a lot cheaper."

So we went and visited a pet cemetery. It wasn't easy to find one.

The security guard asked whether we had any dead animals buried in the cemetery.

"Oh yes," I said. "Three of them."

There in the pet cemetery, amid the interred dogs, cats and rabbits, we got engaged. I asked my wife-to-be, "Does this fall under therapy, or doesn't it?" But she said there could be no clear-cut answer to that question. Later perhaps, when everything fell into place.

"What is it about psychotherapy that appeals to you?" I asked while we were admiring the cat-and-dog graves.

She stopped. She toyed with her earring.

"It's working with feelings," she said. "That appeals to me. It's the same reason why I studied economics, but that made me sick."

"Feelings? Funny, I never knew they were something you could work with."

"And what appealed to you about the all-night deli?"

I wiped the mud from my shoes. What was I supposed to say?

"I was qualified for it," I said after a long pause. "And the job interview was very pleasant."

"What kinds of questions did they ask?"

"The owner wanted to know whether I was planning to rob him. That was pretty much it."

I heard myself talking, and I heard her asking questions, but I felt a peculiar nausea coming on and the equally peculiar desire to throw myself at the feet of my wife-to-be, there in that pet cemetery.

"So," I said as we were leaving the pet cemetery, "I think you'd better come and live with me now, otherwise this therapy could get out of hand."

She moved in that same day, with two suitcases and a basket. It was the first time since I'd left home that I'd lived in the same house as anyone else.

Happiness became the present tense, and happiness that's become the present tense is a terrifying happiness; happiness in the past tense or future perfect is much easier to bear.

A year later, when she said, "They've asked me to go work in America," I said, "Oh, that's fine, I'll go with you, I'm sure they have all-night delis there too."

Rebecca picked out a pair of tennis shoes that cost forty-five dollars.

"The old ones were shot anyway," she said.

The salesgirl didn't seem surprised to see a woman in stocking feet come walking into the shop. As if that happened fairly often.

"Now we'll go buy some stuff for your lenses," I said, "and we'll be stepping high and handsome."

We were back on the boardwalk. It had started raining again. A lukewarm spring shower.

In Europe it was almost midnight. I had to find a phone. It was getting urgent.

*

Between ten o'clock and noon, it's happy hour at the Bikini Bar. If you wanted to attend happy hour here, you either had to get up early or go to bed late. The name bikini was a reference to far-flown times. There were no bikinis here anymore, only a fat man behind the bar who looked like he'd survived yesterday's happy hour by the skin of his teeth.

Rebecca ordered a glass of wine. I wanted something stronger, but I didn't know what. For the last few months my life had been marred by acid indigestion; there were evenings when I could taste the acid in my mouth. Red port, I thought, might be good against acid indigestion.

*

The day the bookcases arrived at our home, I started hoping my wife would go away. That I would come home one afternoon and find a message on the answering machine: "Robert? This is the fairytale princess. I'm not coming back. Have my things sent over."

But the fairytale princess left no such messages on my answering machine. And nothing on the counter. No letter of farewell, in any case.

She came home from work every afternoon. Sometimes we broke things. I told her she couldn't eat cookies in the living room, because I couldn't concentrate when she smacked her lips like that. She didn't want to sleep in the same bed with me anymore, the stench I gave off at night made her nauseous. But no one left.

I think we were both trying to create the ideal conditions under which it would be very easy for the other to leave. But the other didn't leave. The other stayed. We planned a vacation in Acapulco together, while around us vases were being shattered and the psychological warfare became more cunning with each passing day.

Chimneysweeps were phoned and summoned, while the fairytale princess shouted that I was a virus with which she'd been injected against her will.

"I'm going to pack my bags!" my wife would shout at moments like that. And I'd reply, "Yes, please do that, please pack your bags."

She'd yank a few suitcases out of the cupboard, and I would ask, "Would you like me to help you pack?"

But her things remained unpacked, and my things did not disappear into suitcases either.

We started buying clothes, as though buying clothes was the only way to catch our breath before the next round of bombing began.

In our new-bought clothing we visited nightclubs, where we threw glasses of wine in each other's face.

At a bistro one evening, we ran into a psychiatrist we knew. During the appetizer, I said, "Princess Fairytale, would you please stop picking your nose. Your nose isn't very pretty anyway, and if you drill away at it like that, you'll start looking even more like a potato."

"That's great, coming from you," she said. "Your nose looks more like a genetically manipulated cucumber."

Our psychiatrist friend said, "You're such a great couple, your relationship is still so fresh, like you met yesterday."

We tossed around candles, books and money. Our cold war was a romantic war. But no one left.

Without noticing it, the present tense of happiness had shifted to the past tense, but neither of us knew exactly when that had happened. Every once in a while we met each other in that time that no longer actually existed, but our memories were so much alive that it seemed as though everything kept happening over and over.

*

"Are you worrying?" Rebecca asked.

"About what?"

"About American Express. About those fifty thousand dollars."

"Worrying isn't really the right word. It's more like an inconvenience dangling above me."

"Am I an inconvenience too?"

"You? No, you're not an inconvenience."

"So then why do you act like you don't like it?"

"What?"

She shrugged and rummaged through her purse in search of cigarettes. "What do you think? Kissing me, okay?"

"I always act like I think it's kind of so-so. Even when I'm lying naked next to someone, I still act as though I'm there involuntarily. It seems to me like the way you're supposed to do it."

She looked at the bartender and said, "Olive oil is an incredibly disgusting lubricant. Especially when you have to go down on him halfway through. Have you ever tasted a dick dipped in olive oil?"

I had never tasted a dick like that. But what was not, could always be.

Maybe I should have said right then that I loved her, that we would stay together, if not forever, then at least for the next twenty-four hours—and didn't twenty-four hours seem a bit like forever? But all I could say was that I wanted to write about her, that American Express was waiting for fifty-thousand dollars, that I wanted to search for words for her while she talked about olive oil, and that in the long run even murder seemed a matter of semantics. A matter of the right words, the right rhythm, the right turn of phrase at the right moment. But what words are the right words?

*

Back at the back of the Bikini Bar were the restrooms and a phone. The phone smelled like piss. In my pants pocket I found the number of the hotel in Basel. The smell of piss became even stronger once I got the operator on the line and asked to make a collect call to Basel.

"Will you accept a collect call from Robert Mehlman?" I heard a voice ask. And my wife said, "Yes."

The trouble started with the bookcases. Or rather, the actual outbreak of war came the day the red bookcases arrived.

When they arrived my wife was still at the day clinic, and I had to sign for them myself. She'd left written instructions for me about the things I had to check. She'd hung the list on the refrigerator. Only if the shipment was in order was I allowed to pay for them.

The bookcases were supposed to be delivered between noon and one. But they didn't get there until three thirty. Two Latinos, apparently just arrived in New York. They carried the bookcases upstairs.

My wife had designed them herself; in her spare time she de-
signed bookcases, and mirrors. She'd done a coffee table once too.
I'd told her, "There's already one creative person in this house.
Isn't that enough?" But apparently it wasn't enough.

While the delivery men were putting together the bookcases,
there was a bloodbath. They were busy mounting handles on the
doors, and one of the men drilled a hole in his finger. I didn't know
where the bandages were, because I never drill holes in my fingers. I turned the whole bathroom upside down, everything fell
on the floor: lipstick, dental floss, razor blades, anti-wrinkle cream.
But no bandages. In the living room, an innocent illegal alien was
bleeding to death. That seemed a bit overdone to me. My bookcases were not worth dying for. By the time I'd found the bandages,
there was blood everywhere—on the wall, on the floor, on the
bookcases, on the man's clothes, on the couch. My wife was going
to love that last bit.

"Are you okay?" I asked when I handed him the bandages.

He swore in Spanish. It looked like he was going to lose his finger. All I knew was if that had to happen, I didn't want it to happen in my house.

"Go on," I said. "I'll take care of the rest myself."

I paid them the amount we'd agreed, in cash. They'd told me I
could choose between cash on the line with a hefty discount, or
no cash and no hefty discount.

The delivery man who wasn't injured signed the invoice. "Jun-
ior, pd," he wrote.

I hoped his boss would believe me. They left without even saying goodbye.

When my wife came home, she asked, "What happened here?"

There was a trail of blood and sawdust across the parquet. Here
and there lay tools the men had forgotten in their haste. And door
handles. My wife had designed bookcases with doors, to keep the
dust out.

"A bloodbath," I said. "A bloodbath, but other than that nothing to worry about."

*

The woman who had flirted with everyone was waiting for me at the bar, flirting with no one for the time being. The owner of the Bikini Bar must not have approved of flirting.

"Where were you?"

"Making a call."

She didn't pursue the questioning. She never pursued it, not at first. Which made me think she never would. Acceptance of the world as it is is an important element of happiness, or at least a pre-condition for recognizing the extenuating circumstances *an sich*.

Which was how I came to be walking through the streets of Atlantic City with a woman I'd met less than twenty-four hours earlier in the Museum of Natural History, and about whom I knew little more than that she had monstrous hands, a mother who would die soon and a girlfriend with psoriasis.

That not-knowing was an advantage: if I'd known everything, everything I could have known, I wouldn't have been walking there with her, looking for stuff for her lenses, nor she with me.

We stopped in front of an optician's window.

"There was a time," Rebecca said, "when I thought I was only a body."

"One with a head on it?"

"Yes," she said. "There was a head on it."

I said we should go and eat a decent meal. But Rebecca said winter stamina tablets were enough for her. I bought some plastic plates anyway, to make it all a little more festive. I wanted to say, "I'm here to write about you, Rebecca. That's the truth, I'm here because I have the feeling there's a story in you, and if there's a story in you, there's money in you, and if there's money in you, I'm here to get it out. In exchange, I can offer you my obsessive and unconditional attention, temporarily of course, I can buy you clothes and you may partake of my company, for a bit. I can loose words on you that have proven their effectiveness in the past; the way hunters loose their hounds, that's how I loose words. But what I feel is nothing. Or, to put it more accurately, I feel there's something missing at the spot where I should be feeling something.

"Of course we'll remain strangers to each other, but isn't that the prime condition for infatuation, Rebecca, and for what people—with so much twisted longing—call love? That you remain strangers to each other, that what you do is precisely not get to know each other, that the other remains a black hole of which only the contours are visible, a black hole that needs to be filled with fantasy? Isn't that the unspoken promise of infatuation: I am your fantasy, coming true? What I really am will remain hidden. Given that there is any such thing as really being something."

That's what I wanted to say, and also that she shouldn't be surprised, some Saturday afternoon, to find herself back in a second-hand bookstore. Maybe she'd have a child with her, in a baby carriage, and a husband. She shouldn't be horrified with herself, she shouldn't be angry; after all, she knew what she was doing when she went with me, she knew the conditions attached to my attention, she knew what I was offering and what I wanted, she was smart enough to know that she'd put her life on the auction block. And she could have known that I was the bargain-hunter, searching for lives that were up for sale. The bargain-hunter she might secretly have been waiting for. That's why she'd come to me, with that statue from the psoriasis patient. Maybe she'd been hoping that I'd write about her as queen of the night. But that story didn't interest me; besides, there was more night than there was queen.

I wanted to tell her that my unspoken promises were lies, that even my presence was a lie, just like hers. She was no more present than I was; a person who reflects the desires of another in the hope of being redeemed doesn't exist at all.

We put our arms around each other and held each other tight, as though we were afraid that, in an unguarded moment, we'd turn and walk away inadvertently and never come back.

She said, "You always think you're the exception."

"Who does?"

"I do."

"Everyone thinks that," I said. "That's why people get married, that's why they have children, that's why they go on living, because they think it applies to everyone but them, because they think they're the exception."

*

My wife was furious. And not just about all the blood on the wallpaper and the couch. The bookcases had been delivered all wrong.

"How could you sign for something like this?" she said. "Are you completely blind?"

"I thought it was okay, I'm not an expert."

"Here, look at this, bonehead!" she yelled. "Look at how they've put these things together!"

I couldn't see anything.

"Leave me alone," I said. "I've got better things to do than get all worked up about bookcases. If they're no good, then put them out with the garbage and we'll buy new ones. What do I care? I don't need this."

She swept all my papers off the table. I had huge piles of papers, and I always put them on the table, so it was a good bit that got swept off there.

"Stop it," she said. "Stop thinking that those shit stories you write are the only thing that matters. Stop terrorizing people."

"I'm not terrorizing anyone. I'm the one who's being terrorized, by you—if you hadn't been born, I'd be a happy man. Maybe you should stop and think about that. I paid for those bookcases, that's my contribution to those bookcases, and otherwise I don't want to hear about it."

"But it's your books that are going into them, dickhead. *Your* books."

"Because you're the one who doesn't want them piled up against the wall. I don't care if they're piled up along the wall, I kind of like it. You're the one who wants to make it cozy here, I have no need of coziness. Go get cozy with those loonies of yours."

"If you don't call the manufacturer of these bookcases and complain, I'm leaving," said Princess Fairytale.

"I'm not calling anyone, especially not now."

"Then I'm leaving," she said. "Then you can stick your dick in all the women you want. You don't stick it into me anyway, not anymore. Go on and surround yourself with all kinds of yes-sayers. That's what you like best, isn't it, people who lie at your feet and grovel in adoration? You have no idea how grateful you should be to me for disagreeing with you sometimes. No one else dares to contradict you, do they? Besides, it costs a lot more energy to disagree with someone than it does to nod and say 'hallelujah.' But you don't know that. That's how blinded you've become."

"What I stick my dick into is my business. I'll stick it up the chimney if I feel like it."

"Your dick disgusts me," the fairytale princess said. "God only knows the places you've stuck it in. Maybe you should start washing it first, so other woman don't have to lick the stale piss off your dick before they blow you."

"Does my sperm disgust you?"

"Your sperm is the least of it. I'm talking about your dick that tastes like stale piss and tuna-fish salad that's been out in the sun too long."

"Thanks a lot."

"What do I care? I don't taste it anymore anyway. It's just that it seems like such a terrible thing for the other women."

"I'm deeply touched by your concern for other women, but we weren't talking about my dick, we were talking about the bookcases you ordered. You hear me? The ones *you* ordered. You. You ordered them, you were the one who wanted new bookcases."

"For your books, your books, Mr. Mehlman."

"I don't have time to worry about imperfect bookcases. In fact, I'm not even interested. I have to write a new book, they're waiting for a new book."

My wife started laughing. "A new book. A new book. Who's waiting for a new book? Your Sidney Brochstein cycle is headed for the bargain basement. I've heard people say the whole cycle is depraved. Well, you're depraved. But no one wants to tell you that because they all think: we might need this Mehlman sometime to edit an anthology or take part in some retarded jury."

"Who says the Sidney Brochstein cycle is depraved? Who says that?"

"Who cares? Everyone says it."

"I want the names and addresses of the people who have said that my Sidney Brochstein cycle is depraved, their names and addresses, you hear me? Then I'll pay them a little visit to show them what depraved really means. Have they lost all sense of discernment?"

"Listen, Robert," said the fairytale princess, "move back in with your mother. That would really be the best thing. The two of you are equally disturbed, so I think you could be happy together under one roof. But except for your mother, don't ever live with anyone again, that would be criminally negligent."

I started picking my papers off the floor. "I'll call The Baron of Bookcases," I said. The Baron of Bookcases, that was the name of the company where she'd ordered the bookcases.

The owner insisted on coming by that same day to inspect the damage. Consolation came an hour and a half later in the person of George, a voluble Greek, owner of The Baron of Bookcases. He inspected the damage. The signs of the bloodbath were still visible. "Yeah," he said, "some of my employees are a little mixed up. This guy wasn't allowed to work for a while. Then he came back and told me the doctor had said he could work again, but he's not better at all." He promised that all imperfections would be eliminated within a week or two. He would send a couple of guys over.

*

She couldn't sleep, Rebecca couldn't. At eleven o'clock she woke up and wanted to go downstairs. "I'm restless," she said. "I feel like pounding my head against the wall."

"No," I said, "please don't do that."

I gave her a few winter stamina tablets.

"What about your father?" I asked. "Is he dying too?"

"No," she said, "he's into porn. When I'm at his house I find porn in the strangest places: in the laundry basket, between his bank statements, on his desk under piles of professional journals."

"In the laundry basket, that's pretty creative."

She shrugged.

I laid a comforting hand on her head. "Older men and their hobbies, it keeps death from the door."

We got dressed again and went downstairs.

I asked whether she minded not gambling that evening, or maybe only gambling with quarters we could toss into the machines.

"Let's gamble with quarters then," she said.

*

The Sunday after the bookcases arrived, the weather suddenly turned gorgeous. My wife wanted to go out for a walk.

I'd worked that morning. On a TV series for young people. The only reason I'd agreed to do it was the money. I often agreed to things only for the money. American Express was pounding on the door, VISA was tapping at my windowpane, so I figured: a TV series for young people, why not?

It was a complete mystery to me why they'd asked me to do it. They probably thought I was funny. Once people form an image of you, they'd rather not change it. That's why it's best to remain the way people think you are, at least if you don't want to confuse them.

That Sunday morning I'd written one episode and was greatly looking forward to the impending quarrel with the producer. She'd said the script shouldn't be too absurd. And she hadn't said it once, no, she'd said it three times. Sooner or later people give themselves away with their choice of language, they betray how important they want to seem, how ambitious they are.

Someone once said to me, "Don't impress on people the fact that they have no talent, they can't do anything about it." But I didn't impress on them their lack of talent, I impressed on them how badly they'd prepared themselves for the role they were trying to play.

At twelve-thirty my wife said, "Why don't we go for a walk?"

We took a taxi to an Italian restaurant in SoHo. Before walking, we reasoned, one had to eat. The restaurant had a garden. It was a little too cold for the garden, but we sat in front of the open doors. I ordered a kir royal, my wife wanted only water.

The argument started, as I recall, with a mix-up in appointments. She'd made a date with a fellow psychiatrist to go listen to some jazz that next Wednesday evening, and I'd asked if I could go along. I couldn't remember asking that, but there was a lot I couldn't remember.

What I'd done, in fact, was to make a date with my mistress for that same Wednesday evening, our first rendezvous in weeks. But not to fuck. She'd said there was something she wanted to talk to me about. Upon which I'd suggested that we go catch a bite to eat somewhere that Wednesday evening. As a token of reverence. No, not as a token of reverence, don't let me make myself out to be better than I am. I said yes out of curiosity, out of interest. I thought: who knows, maybe she'll tell me something I can use. Maybe it was pure sentiment. My neighbor's trauma is often my bread and butter.

Which meant I couldn't go listen to jazz. I had a date with Evelyn. When Evelyn and I stopped meeting each other in local hotels, that's when the problems started. Two people who know more about each other than they should, and who now see each other under different circumstances.

When people don't disappear from your life, it had become clear to me, that's when the problems start. The best thing is to disappear from people's lives, and then to appear in the lives of others to whom everything is new, for whom the glitter hasn't faded, who are still resilient enough to see gold in your gold-metallic paint, to hear in your harsh croaking the sound of an opera singer, and to see your cheap presents that arrive each day as the very embodiment of love.

"You said yes," my wife said. "I asked whether you wanted to go, and you said yes."

"I wasn't listening."

"You never listen when I talk, your mind is always somewhere else when I'm talking, it all goes in one ear and out the other. I refuse to be treated like this any longer. Are you listening?"

"You don't have to scream, we're not at home."

"Why do you foul up our appointments? Why does everyone else always come first?"

I took a sip of my kir. A waiter asked whether we'd made a choice, and I said, "Give us a few more minutes."

"I'm not some dog you can drag along when you don't have anything better to do."

"I don't drag you along like a dog, you follow me around like a dog. When you're in town and you're not with your loonies, I don't have a second to myself, not a second."

"Everyone is supposed to drool at the thought of having your dick in their mouth, including the men, but I refuse."

"Fine," I said. "So what are we going to order?"

"You know what's too bad? What's too bad is that your ego is bigger than Russia and China put together, maybe you could do something about that sometime. And while you're at it, maybe you could stop thinking that every second of your life is a competition. You don't have to compete with everyone, you don't have to win from everyone."

I closed the menu. "The rest of the world competes with me, not the other way around. And as far as my ego goes, if it's too big for you, then leave. Actually do it, leave. Give me a chance at some happiness too for once."

That got me a glass of mineral water in the face. It was bubblier than I'd thought. It had been a long time since I'd had mineral water thrown in my face. Wine, champagne, iced tea, yes, but not mineral water.

I paid for the water and the kir and we left the premises. It was busy out on the street. People were walking around in the sun. We walked in the sun too, not saying a word, until we got to the Hudson. We sat down on a bench and looked at New Jersey. And at the people who came by. Bicyclists, semi-nude young people on roller skates, couples with children, old men sweating and running their way to total fitness, romantic young couples, women in wheelchairs.

So the Sunday slowly passed, but we weren't hungry.

"What a beautiful day," I said.

And the fairytale princess said, "Yeah, what a beautiful day."

"We can't go on like this," I said.

The fairytale princess said, "No, we can't go on like this."

"What a beautiful day," I went on. "Spring sure came early this year." And I thought about the television series for young people that wasn't supposed to be too absurd.

"A little absurdity is fine," the producer had said, "but not too much, it has to stay recognizable." She'd underlined that sentence in red.

I felt like going to some other country, I felt like never answering the phone or letters again. They'd wait forever for the TV series for young people that wasn't supposed to be too absurd, and they could all wait ten thousand years for my next novel, too, because this was where it all stopped. I would disappear and then pop up again somewhere else as a beautician, for example.

"This can't go on," the fairytale princess said, "this is hell."

If I were to portray myself, I'd mutilate myself beyond recognition. I'd mutilate everyone beyond recognition, the whole world would be mutilated beyond recognition, I'd go to work with hammer and shears, there would be a lot of things torn apart, with my bare teeth.

"Aw hell," I said, "it's not that bad."

We walked home. I said, "This evening I'm going to write another episode of that series that isn't supposed to be too absurd because it has to stay recognizable."

"That's important for those TV series," the fairytale princess said. "Recognizability, I mean."

"It all boils down to recognizability," I agreed. "They need to see the things they've always known about, but in a way that makes it seem like they're hearing it for the very first time. Then everyone's satisfied."

My courage had limits. My courage could fit in an airmail envelope. That's what I put it in, and then I mailed it.

*

"I won," Rebecca said. "I think something like a hundred dollars." The sound of coins tinkling out of the machine reminded me of a death march.

"Congratulations," I said, and hugged her. "At long last, luck is hanging over us."

*

That next Wednesday evening, I didn't go listen to jazz with my wife and her fellow psychiatrist. I said I had an appointment with a foreign publisher. At a hotel. Foreign publishers do have a way of staying at hotels.

"Where's this publisher from?" my wife wanted to know.

"France," I said.

"France?"

She frowned. "Have you ever been published in France?"

"Amazingly enough, yes."

"And haven't they sent you to the French bargain basement yet?"

"No, not that I know of."

"What do you think's wrong with the French?"

"I have no idea."

I brushed some dust and dandruff off my dark-blue sports coat.

"And now this publisher is taking you out to dinner?"

"Yup. He's got big plans for me."

"Big plans?"

"He says I'm an important writer."

My wife started laughing, and opened the window.

"So when you're finished, are you going to come to the jazz club?"

"Sure," I said. "When I'm finished, I'll come."

I put on my shoes. I'd polished them, just to be sure. You never know.

"You're looking pretty natty," my wife said.

"You know," I said, "how the French are."

"Well, I hope he has something great to offer you. What did you say his name was?"

"Mastroianni." It was out before I knew it.

"Mastroianni," my wife said, "that's funny. Like the actor?"

"Yes, just like the actor. Distant relatives, I believe. His father is Italian, his mother French. He grew up in Paris."

"Wasn't your French publisher's name Nabokov?"

Of course his name was Nabokov, how could I say Mastroianni when I meant Nabokov?

"Nabokov is the managing editor. But Mastroianni is the editor I work with most. Mastroianni does the foreign fiction."

"How peculiar," my wife said. "Nabokov and Mastroianni, both working for the same publisher."

"I guess they like famous names there. But listen, I have to get going, otherwise the poor guy will be sitting there waiting for me."

She walked me to the vestibule. "Have fun, sugar pumpkin."

"You too, Princess Fairytale," I said, "have fun at the jazz club. I'll come as soon as I'm finished."

"Take something with you for luck," the fairytale princess said. She looked around. "Here, a hairpin." She handed me a hairpin that looked like a butterfly.

"It's only a meeting with a French publisher."

"You never know," she said. "Just take it."

I glanced at my wife, then put the hairpin in my inside pocket.

*

Josef Capano had arranged the evening's program for me. I didn't like organizing things. Cars, restaurant reservations, little presents. We weren't planning to go and fuck, but I took five condoms with me, just in case. You never know what people expect from you.

Capano always sent me his secret arrangements by messenger service, in a manila envelope with PRINTED MATTER on it. Before he sent it, he would call up for safety's sake. "Are you going to be at home?" he'd ask. "Something confidential's on its way."

"Hello, Robert," Capano wrote. "The Goddess will arrive at The Kitano at 5:15. I'll be waiting there at the door, in the limousine. (Eight-person vehicle, seventy dollars an hour plus tip.)

"From there I'll take her to the Waldorf-Astoria, where you'll be waiting in the bar from 5:20 on. Don't arrive too late, and don't forget that it's almost impossible to get a cab at that time of day.

"I'll tell her where you'll be seated, but I won't go inside with her. Come too late, in other words, and you'll look like a prime ASSHOLE. *I'll have myself driven home and then send the car back to the Waldorf-Astoria. If, because of traffic, police, etc., the driver can't wait at the door, he'll come back every fifteen minutes from 6:30 on. Don't forget your watch!*

"After that, dinner. The Terrace. 400 W 119th St, tel. 666-9490. Between Amsterdam and Morningside Drive. Table for two at seven. Should you want to change this, for example because things get awfully cozy at the Waldorf, call them from the hotel.

"I figure it takes about half an hour to get from the hotel to The Terrace.

"Does this sound like a plan?

"Fond regards,

"Josef Capano

"P.S. Learn this by heart, then swallow it."

I was a producer of delusions. Anyone who wanted to see me had to come looking for me in a delusion of my own design. The drinks were on the house, the food was excellent and the sheets were of Egyptian cotton.

"Rebecca," I said, "when no one ever gets in your way, that's loneliness, isn't it?"

She put the quarters she'd won in big plastic cups.

"Who's getting in your way?"

"No one," I said, "no one at all. You have sexy eyes, you know that?"

That made me think of Evelyn, because she'd said that to me one morning in the restroom, and I hadn't believed her. Not that morning in the restroom, and not on the mornings that followed. And now that I'd repeated her words myself, I still didn't believe them.

"Evelyn," I said.

"Rebecca," she said, "the name's Rebecca."

I usually went to the coffeehouse in the morning, at eight-thirty. Sometimes by myself, sometimes with my wife. Some days she didn't go along. Whenever she had a day off, for example, the fairytale princess liked to sleep in.

This was one of those mornings when she didn't go along. We'd come home late from a vodka bar, where we'd been drinking vodka from heart-shaped vases. Along with one of the fairytale princess's girlfriends, another fellow psychiatrist, albeit one who worked in a regular institution. That morning I took my newspaper and walked to the coffeehouse alone. It felt like this time the alcohol had actually got the best of me. I sat down at my regular table. Evelyn brought me my coffee and orange juice. There was no one else in the place.

"Croissant?" she asked.

"No," I said, "not today." After a night like that it's not wise to start bolting down greasy croissants, it will all come right back up again.

I started reading my paper.

Evelyn went into the restroom and came back out a few minutes later. "Could you give me a hand?" she asked. "I need to change the light bulb, but there's no ladder. If you hold onto me, I can climb up on the toilet."

"Are you afraid of heights?"

"A little."

Of course I could have offered to change the light bulb myself, but that idea didn't occur to me. I guess I'm not much of a light-bulb changer. I said, "I'll hold on to you."

She climbed up on the toilet; I held the door open with my left leg so some light came into the toilet, and I held her calves with both hands. She changed the bulb. It was sort of difficult, because the old bulb was screwed in tightly. At a certain point she looked down and said, "You have sexy eyes."

That made me laugh. It made her laugh too.

"Thank you," I said. "No one's ever said that to me before."

"Still, it's true," she said, and handed me the old bulb. She was working on the new one.

I looked at myself in the mirror. I didn't find myself really sexy.

Then Evelyn said, "Stop torturing me, I haven't had a man in two months." She climbed down off the toilet. The light was working again. But I was still holding the door open with my foot.

"But you've got a husband, right?"

"We don't do it. The last time we did anything was on Valentine's Day, and it lasted two minutes."

"Oh," I said, "but don't you masturbate?"

"No," she said, "that only makes it worse. All it is is a hand, down there."

Maybe I should have let the door fall shut right then, but I just stood there, waiting until she'd tidied up the restroom, then I went back to my table.

While I was paying for my breakfast, she said, "Am I going to see you later on?"

"Maybe," I said. "Maybe at lunchtime."

The day Evelyn said I had sexy eyes was the day she had to change a light bulb in the restroom. The day The Empty Vessel walked into my life was the day the chimneysweeps had made a fruitless attempt to sweep my chimney. Between those two days lay a trail of other days, meetings and requests for payment, but there in the casino, with all those quarters she'd won rattling in those plastic cups, it seemed to me that the two days were inextricably linked. As though the one encounter had automatically followed from the other.

I went back home with two cappuccinos for my wife.

That morning I couldn't get any work done. On a scrap of paper I wrote, "Don't torture me like this, I haven't had a man for two months."

*

It took a few weeks, but one morning I was once again the only one in the coffeehouse.

"What kind of food do you like?" I asked.

"Something simple," Evelyn said. She was counting the change.

"What do you usually eat?"

"I only eat when I have time. What kind of food do you like?"

"French, Italian, Spanish."

"I shouldn't actually tell you this," she said, "but I watch you: how you come in the door, how you drink your coffee, how you tear open your bag of sugar, how you talk to your wife, how you put on your coat, I see everything. I see things I should never see at all."

"What do you mean?"

But just then some customers came in and she said, "I'll talk to you later."

That morning I wrote a story entitled "Don't Torture Me Like This, I Haven't Had a Man in Two Months." The magazine I wrote it for later informed me that they liked it, but the title was too long.

Princess Fairytale had lunch from noon to one. I often went to where she worked, so we could have lunch together. Our whole lives, after all, were a sort of runaway lunch break. When the weather was nice we'd buy sandwiches and eat them outside. We looked at people and talked about the passers-by. I liked looking at people and talking about them with the fairytale princess.

That particular day there was no one to discuss. The fairytale princess said, "What did you do this morning?"

"Worked," I said.

We ate in silence.

"Are you going back to the house?"

"I'm going to do some more work."

But what I was planning to do was to go to the shop and buy a little present. A little make-up bag, a vase, a little basket to keep earrings in. Candles that lit themselves again after you blew them out.

A producer of delusions. Back-to-back delusions. In order to feel without really feeling, to feel just enough, but not so much that it would become painful. I should actually have placed ads in the paper: "Call Mehlman and turn your life into a delusion. Custom-built to fit every need."

After all, isn't that what everyone wants? To dream, and to think that all you have to do is wake up in order for it to be over, that all you have to do is open your eyes in order to see things the way they really are?

*

We cashed in the coins and got banknotes in return. Rebecca had won a hundred and twenty dollars. After that we went back out onto the boardwalk. It had stopped raining at last, now it was only cold. We sat down on a bench. All the liquor stores were closed. So we drank water and iced tea.

"What do you think about when you write?" Rebecca asked suddenly. The question took me by surprise.

"What do you think about when you flirt?" I asked. Then I moved up behind her and put my arms around her.

"Am I your first lover?" she asked.

I said, "Yes."

"You're not lying?"

I looked at the hotels, I looked at her tennis shoes, I looked at the half-empty bottle of water.

"No. I'm incapable of lying."

"What about all those stories you write?"

"I don't lie about those," I said, "they're true. Stories can be true in so many different ways."

Some people are surprised when you say that all human contact could be explained in terms of a transaction in which something is bought and something sold. If the laws of economics apply to anything at all, they certainly apply to emotions.

I bought some knickknacks for Evelyn, from a Russian who smelled like an old horse. His entire shop smelled of old horse. Outside it was spring and the sun was shining, but in the Russian's shop it was still winter and it smelled of old horse.

The knickknacks were cheap, but they looked nice. I wrapped them up nicely. Then I went to the coffeehouse. My wife came home from her loonies between three and four. It depended a bit; sometimes the loonies hung around for a while. And sometimes they refused to get into the bus, or one of them would turn violent, and then my wife would have to wait for the police to take the patient to the hospital. Sometimes six policemen were needed for one loony.

I sat down at my usual table in the coffeehouse and read a magazine. After half an hour and half a bottle of mineral water, I got up, walked to the cash register and said, "There's a bag under my table. You can take it home with you, or you can throw it away. It's up to you."

She smiled. I noticed a little scar, just under her chin on the right. "I'll see," she said. Then she looked around to see whether anyone was watching and said, "You're my first cappuccino."

"What do you mean?"

"In the morning," she said. "Marvin comes in before you do, but he drinks straight coffee. Gertrude drinks tea, and then you come in, at eight-thirty. You're my first cappuccino. And whatever happens, you'll always be my first cappuccino."

I slowly rolled my magazine into a tube. The paper stuck to my hands. "Your first cappuccino," I said. "That's nice."

"Are they good?"

"Your cappuccinos? Nothing to write home about."

She walked me to the door. "Other customers ask for me specifically when they order a cappuccino, did you know that?"

"The other customers are nuts."

"Okay, I'll ask Sonya to make your cappuccinos from now on."

Sonya worked at the coffeehouse too. She was a homeless person from Algeria who claimed she was from Paris, where she'd worked as a fashion designer. The owner liked to hire homeless people, because they were cheap and never in a hurry to get home.

"Why don't we go to Atlantic City sometime?" I said to Evelyn. "Why?"

"So you can learn how to make cappuccinos."

"All right," she said, "and I'll teach you how to dance the salsa."

Back then no one was talking about sending my Sidney Brochstein cycle to the bargain basement. The debts on my credit cards were not yet mountains, only friendly little hills full of rich meadows. People still thought I was somebody. At least some of them did. But I already knew better. The wheat was about to be separated from the chaff. I sometimes received threatening letters from people who were unwise enough to take the written word personally. "That your books sell so well," one gentleman wrote, "causes me to doubt the intelligence of mankind."

I wrote back: "That you have only started doubting the intelligence of mankind on the basis of the sales of my books makes me doubt your own intelligence. Nevertheless, I wish you all the best. And by the way: my books haven't been selling well for a long time. You're running slow."

I'd signed a contract to write a cookbook. The advance was fairly generous. The contract, in order to soften the blow, spoke of "a literary cookbook." But there's no such thing as a literary cookbook. Cookbooks are cookbooks. Not that I knew anything about cooking, but that didn't seem particularly important to me.

A few weeks later, the two of us actually ended up in Atlantic City, Evelyn and I.

"Forget the gambling," she'd said in the car on the way down. "Let's concentrate on the love part."

"As you wish," I replied. So we concentrated on the love part. And it's true, love requires more concentration than gambling. All the delusions look alike, only the actors are different.

I wanted to make of language a whip with which to put people through their paces. A human-trainer, that's what I actually was, but my circus was being threatened by an unreliable bookkeeper and a tent that had blown away.

The coffeehouse closed at eleven. At ten-thirty I told the fairytale princess, "I'm going out for a drink."

That was the same evening I'd bought the candles that relit themselves after you blew them out, and the little basket for earrings. My first presents for Evelyn.

"You want me to go with you?" she'd asked.

"No," I said, "you go on to bed, you have to get up early again tomorrow to go to your loonies."

"You're right," said the fairytale princess. "That's a better idea. Have fun."

Two nights a week, Evelyn closed up the coffeehouse.

"I thought you were never going to show up," she said.

There were still a few customers, four tourists applying themselves to huge slices of apple pie. I sat down at the table close to the restroom, where I always sat. The tourists paid and left. She turned off the big lights, locked the door, put the chairs up on the tables. Then she came and sat beside me and said, "So."

*

According to the newspaper, nihilism led to violence. If that was true, then pornography led to love.

Rebecca was lying on the bed, watching television. I was sitting in my underpants in a chair by the window, on which the previous guests had left nondescript spots, but that didn't bother me.

In Europe my wife was waking up. She would take a shower and pack her suitcase and then begin getting ready for the flight back. When she got home, I wouldn't be there. No one would be there. In the refrigerator there would be only the smoked breast of duck that I had neither eaten nor thrown away.

I was too big a coward to sit down across from the fairytale princess and tell her that a person who wanted to escape from himself
had first and foremost to disappear from the lives of those who
knew him best. Whom he loved most. Instead, I would send her a
letter, special delivery.

I dropped the newspaper on the floor.

"Does pornography lead to love?" I asked Rebecca.

There was no reply. She was wearing headphones. She couldn't
hear me. She was happy because she'd won something, because I'd
said that luck was looming over her and would continue looming
there for a while.

I took some hotel stationery and wrote as neatly as I could:

"Dear Princess Fairytale,

*"Hopefully you had a good flight, hopefully the conference on
dreams wasn't too exhausting. Sorry about the problem with the
credit card, I'll find out how that happened and fix it. I just read
in the paper that nihilism leads to violence. The theories get wilder
all the time. Do you still hold truck with theories, or is every treatment custom-tailored to the patient? I've noticed that some people,
especially women, think that the route that leads to love goes by way
of sex. We haven't thought that for a long time, fortunately—if
we ever did. What route does lead there is unclear to me.*

*"Sorry about neither eating the breast of duck nor throwing it
away. I was busy with a new book. Working title:* Letters to My
Chimneysweep. *Although* Letters to the Weatherman *seems
like a good alternative to me.*

*"The route I've taken went by way of deadlines. Or better said,
the route was an escape route, and deadlines were the lifesavers,
the structure in my life, the answer to almost every question.*

*"What am I doing here in Atlantic City? I have a deadline,
there's a story to be written. In fact, deadlines are the solution
to my life. Other people have ideals, families, children—my
God, maybe even something you could reasonably call a vision*

of the future. I have deadlines. But they're starting to bore me, these deadlines.

"By the way, The Baron of Bookcases called. The extra shelves you ordered will be in next week. Sorry about jumping around like this. It's late, and my head is full.

"I won't be coming back for a while. You're free to disappear from my life. I don't have the courage to disappear from yours, that's why I won't be coming back for a while. I'm going to write a cookbook. I signed a contract a while back, for a cookbook, a literary cookbook—do you know what that is? Neither do I, but I'll find out. Motel rooms are apparently dirt cheap in the Midwest. I've used part of the advance, which was fairly generous, to pay a few months' rent. Once again, that was a while back. There seems to be a market for literary cookbooks.

"Money is unimportant, but that truth cannot disguise the fact that only a bestseller can save us from financial ruin. Being homeless saves a lot of money too, but that won't help us pay our debts.

"How do you come up with a bestseller fast? They don't seem to fall from trees like overripe fruit. You and I know all about that. A rich psychiatric patient who included you in his will would help a good deal, at least if the patient died soon afterwards.

"I'm here with a woman, but we haven't done anything yet. We kissed. With other women, however, I have done all kinds of things. You may have suspected that for a long time. I don't know what you suspect and what you don't. You don't have to blurt out everything you know.

"The deadlines from the newspapers, magazines and publishing houses bored me, or did I say that already? So I began inventing my own deadlines. I'm not complaining. I was in full possession of my senses when I undertook to prove the applied effectiveness of words. My words were charming and my money was too; which of the two was more charming is up to others to decide.

"Sorry that my dick tasted like stale piss, I'll wash it better from now on.

"Be careful. I'll call or write soon.

"Kisses,

"Robert, writer of literary cookbooks

"P.S. Do you think it was justified of them to relegate me to the bargain basement? Do you know what art is, or whether nihilism leads to violence? Pornography that leads to love, that's art. Now I'm going to sleep."

But the letter I finally sent went as follows:

"Dear Princess Fairytale,

"How was the flight? How was Basle? How was the conference?

"Sorry about the problems with the credit card.

"I am, as you see, still in Atlantic City, doing research for a new book. Will tell you all about it later.

"I forgot to throw away the breast of duck, and I didn't eat it. Maybe that's a good thing. I don't know how long breast of duck stays good.

"Many little & tender kisses,

"Robert, cookbook author, professional hedonist"

I tore up the first letter and tossed the scraps into the trash can in the lobby. I took the second letter to the desk. The woman who'd been there the previous night was at the desk again. I handed her the letter and said, "This needs to go special delivery."

She smiled politely.

If I had the ability to invent a story, if I had the ability to make her laugh, everything would be all right.

"No problem, Mr. Mehlman," the receptionist said.

"Do you like cookbooks?" I asked. "Do you do a lot of cooking?"

She didn't answer, she just looked at me.

Rebecca had fallen asleep with the headphones on, still dressed. I turned off the TV and carefully took off her headphones. She didn't wake up. I also took off her shoes. The rest I left on. Just to be sure, I covered her with a bedspread.

I went down to the bar where we'd sat the first night, where Rebecca had consumed coffee with a skin on it. There was no one at the bar. The same barkeep was on duty.

"Peter," I said.

He looked up in surprise.

"You remember my name?"

"I have a good memory."

I asked him for a double espresso with a little bit of steamed milk.

I had walked through this same casino with Evelyn, not so very long ago, and now there was a woman sleeping in my room whom I knew nothing about, not even her address, and who herself probably didn't exactly know what she was doing in that room. Maybe she thought I could make something special of her life. I couldn't be held accountable for the misunderstandings people called down upon themselves—all right, I helped the misunderstanding along a little, but was that the same as accountability? Was it my fault if other people were blind?

*

My wife and I once went to Florida for a week, because that's where we got married. She needed a break from the loonies. A series of suicides, some successful and others not, had left her completely exhausted.

We checked into a hip and expensive hotel. My wife saw famous people everywhere. Not that she's impressed by famous people, but she liked seeing them. And she saw them everywhere.

"There goes another one," she said. I would look up from my paper. But I'm not very good at recognizing famous people.

This was not long after the morning I'd helped Evelyn change the light bulb in the restroom. The morning she said I had sexy eyes.

Before I left town I'd asked Josef Capano to have a suitcase full of roses delivered to the coffeehouse every morning during my absence. For Evelyn. I'd never had suitcases full of roses delivered before, but it seemed that it might be a welcome change from bunches.

"Don't put my name on it," I'd told Capano. "If she's smart, she'll know who's sending her suitcases full of roses."

Buying six suitcases and knowing they were going to be filled with lovely, long-stemmed roses made me cheerful. All added up, it came to three hundred and fifty roses, packed and well. How was Evelyn going to react?

In Florida, I sat with my wife at the poolside. I'd bought her a little buckskin bag with the hairs still on it. The fairytale princess liked bags.

We didn't go to bed together once, we were too busy doing other things. We fought. Fighting was our daily dose of tranquillizers; as long as we were still fighting we knew that everything was okay. The negative form of love, love turned inside out, was our form of intimacy. We listened to a lot of Madonna too, and in the afternoon we slept, while outside on the beach young people not so much younger than us, some of them maybe even older, amused themselves with various types of ball sports. We rented bikes and analyzed the world and ourselves. Analyses that were by no means hopeful. We came to the conclusion that there were no hopeful analyses.

One evening, during dinner, the fairytale princess said, "Remember back when you worked in the all-night deli?"

"The pet cemetery," I said.

But shared memories proved too painful to talk about. And you couldn't really call them shared. Both of us remembered things differently, and the differences were yet another reason to fight.

I'd call Capano while my wife was on the toilet, or lying in the bathtub with a book.

"Did the roses arrive all right?" I asked.

"One suitcase a day," he said. "Everything's running smoothly."

"And has she said anything?"

"She calls me about every hour to find out how she can reach you," Capano said. "It's driving me crazy."

On two separate afternoons, while my wife was down at the pool, I locked myself in the hotel room, closed the curtains to keep out the heat, and worked on my stories. Because the deadlines didn't stop. The deadlines were meant to give my life the semblance of structure, and to comfort me with the absurd proposition that this all served some purpose.

On our last day in Florida, my wife said, "You have systematically reduced my happiness."

The word "systematic" has stuck with me. It reminded me of my father. He always said, "If it's worth doing, it's worth doing systematically."

"Systematically," I said. "What else is there to do with happiness but reduce it systematically? That's the only logical solution to happiness."

We rented bikes for our last few hours in Florida. Then we flew back to New York, where it was almost as hot as it had been in Florida.

"I hope your patients will restrain themselves from now on, when it comes to suicide," I said in the taxi home from the airport.

The next day we walked to the coffeehouse together, as usual.

"What happened here?" the fairytale princess asked.

The coffeehouse looked like a florist's. There were roses everywhere. On the tables, on the counter, on top of the fridge, there were even roses on top of the espresso machine.

"Must have been someone's birthday," I said, burying my nose in the paper.

The fairytale princess ordered two cappuccinos from Evelyn, then took her taxi to work. Five minutes later, Evelyn came over and stood at my table.

"Thanks for the presents," she said. That morning she was wearing her hair down. She usually wore it up. They say that's more hygienic for the customers.

"My pleasure," I said.

"Is my cappuccino as terrible as always?" she asked.

"Perhaps even more terrible," I said. "Your cappuccino has never been as terrible as it is today."

But now it was three-thirty in the morning, and I was sitting at the bar in Bally's Casino. I was drinking double espressos with badly steamed milk, Rebecca was asleep upstairs. My wife was on her way to the airport in Zurich, and where Evelyn was, who knows?

Peter came over to me. "Like another one?" he asked. "What's your name, anyway?"

"Robert," I said. "Yes, I'd like another espresso, and could you please steam the milk a little better this time?"

"I'll give it my best shot."

"Just give it enough steam. There's no one else here anyway, so take your time."

He came back with an espresso and some reasonably steamed milk.

"You work in computers?"

I looked at him. He had a slight tan. I wondered whether he was a good-looking man, and where his ancestors had come from.

"Computers? No, I write cookbooks."

I stirred a little cane sugar into my coffee. My mother always said you'd live longer if you used cane sugar.

Peter didn't seem too impressed by writers of cookbooks.

"Cookbooks," he said. "Nice."

"It pays the rent. At least, it paid the rent. With cookbooks you never know what tomorrow will bring."

"The rent," Peter said. "I lived in a trailer for a while. But that's no solution either. You here on vacation?"

"Vacation? Not really," I said. "I'm working on leaving my wife."

"You're working on it?"

"Yeah, it's pretty time-consuming."

"And does she know you're working on it?"

"Not yet. She's still on the plane."

Peter added a little more steamed milk to my espresso. He didn't understand at all. The principle of steaming milk hadn't registered with him.

"This is what they call a macchiato," I said.

"I've considered suicide before, too," Peter said.

Jesus Christ, this was all I needed.

"I didn't say I was considering suicide, I said I was working on leaving my wife. That's something very different."

"All I said was I'd thought about it."

I looked at him. "People say," I said, "that suicide is a final solution to temporary problems. That's not my kind of thing. I don't like final solutions."

"And what if your problems aren't temporary?"

This wasn't a barkeep, this was more like a case for the fairytale princess. "Listen," I said, "I don't know much about it. But my wife, she does, she knows everything about it."

"About what?"

"About suicide."

"And you're working on leaving her."

"That's right."

"Because she knows everything about suicide?"

"Maybe, yeah."

"I couldn't live with a woman who knows everything about suicide either. Another espresso?"

"No thanks, I'm already about to go through the roof."

"Cola?"

"No, nothing, really."

He leaned across the bar. "Everyone has to go through some phase," he whispered.

"What do you mean?"

"What I said. Everyone has to go through some phase. I lived on the street for a while. That was a phase I had to go through."

"Are you suggesting that I should live on the street?"

"I'm not suggesting anything. I see you sitting here alone, and I sense that you're not feeling well, you sense things like that when you've been through phases."

"I say I'm working on leaving my wife and you start talking about suicide. Don't ask me why. How should I know? Maybe because you know nothing about steaming milk?"

I was talking too much. Normally I never talk much to strangers. It was the fatigue, the badly steamed milk, the espresso. The idea that it wouldn't be long before I defeated myself. A position had arisen on the board that I couldn't win anymore.

Peter picked up a rag and wiped the bar.

"What do you mean with this steamed milk business?"

"I'm saying you know nothing about steamed milk. That's a phase you have to go through. The steamed milk phase."

"And you think you know so much about steamed milk? Just because you happen to write cookbooks?"

I had to laugh. He was getting pretty familiar. That's what happens when you're the only one at the bar.

"I once knew a woman who knew a lot about steamed milk. And when I say a lot, I mean a lot."

"Was she the same one who knew everything about suicide?"

"No, that's someone else."

He stuck out his hand and counted off. "So you know a woman who knows a lot about suicide, and a woman who knows a lot about steamed milk."

I nodded.

"You're in a bad way," the barkeep said. "So who's the woman you were in here with yesterday?"

"Oh," I said, "that's someone else again. I met her at a museum. She's got ugly hands. She's asleep up in my room right now."

Peter put a cookie on my saucer. "Eat," he said. "You're not leaving here until you've had something decent to eat."

I ate the cookie. His voice suddenly sounded so imperative. First I felt nauseous, then I started crying. It came up in waves. This night nausea came with tears.

"Some phases you have to go through," Peter said, like he was on the radio. He laid his hand on my arm, but then I got aggressive.

"Listen, you prick," I said. "I don't want to go through any phase whatsoever. I want you to learn to steam milk, that's all I want right now."

But he said, "You don't impress me. I've seen worse than this."

*

After my wife left the coffeehouse with her two cappuccinos, and a croissant if she happened to be feeling hungry, Evelyn would sit down beside me and smoke a cigarette. I didn't get to read the paper much after that.

Her hair hung looser every day, and her nails changed color every other.

My wife said, "What's she done with her hair?"

"Oh," I said, "maybe she's got a new lover. As long as it doesn't affect her cappuccinos."

"Yeah," said the fairytale princess, "that's what counts."

Evelyn's oldest son was named José, but she called him J. The youngest one she just called "baby." She had a jeep too, and she called that her baby as well.

She said, "I read the papers you leave on the table, to find out what you're thinking about." She started leaving messages on the backs of the bills, in childlike handwriting with big circles over the *i.* About pieces of her heart I took with me when I left the coffee-house. Maybe she meant it. Maybe she didn't. These were questions I preferred not to think about.

I started lingering at the coffeehouse. For half an hour at first, then an hour, finally an hour and a half, sometimes two. My work suffered, but I didn't care. Let it suffer, I thought, that builds character.

On the days my wife didn't have to go to her loonies, when we sat together at the coffeehouse and read our papers, Evelyn would act as though nothing was going on. She was good at playacting.

One time she asked, "You're not ready to leave your wife yet, are you?"

"No," I said, "I'm not ready for that yet."

She knew she couldn't replace my wife, and she didn't hanker after what she couldn't do.

The fairytale princess didn't seem to suspect a thing. But why should she? Why should I be interested in a slightly overweight cappuccino-maker from Puerto Rico? One who, before applying herself to the making of cappuccinos, had worked at a dry cleaner's? Who had told me, "My life is real simple; I have no life."

One morning I woke up with a cold. It was the air-conditioning that had made me sick, the fairytale princess said. There were a lot of customers at the coffeehouse. To perk myself up a bit, I ordered a tea grog. Every time Evelyn was about to sit down with me, a customer would come in.

"What's going on this morning?" she wailed.

The newspaper served as my excuse. I just sat there at my usual table. As soon as she got up, I'd pick up my paper, as soon as she sat down, I laid it aside.

Things quieted down around eleven. Sonya, the semi- or completely homeless waitress, was changing her clothes in the kitchen. The toilet was too confined for her.

Evelyn smoked one of her menthol cigarettes and asked, "What is it? Why do you look like that?" It was a question she always asked.

"It's nothing," I said. "Shall we change another bulb in the restroom? I think it needs a new bulb pretty badly."

"Okay," she said.

The cigarette still in her mouth, she went into the restroom. I followed her.

There are lots of little restrooms in the world, but seldom have I seen one as tiny as the one in that coffeehouse.

"What are we doing here?" she asked, and giggled. Then she showed me her breasts. And she squeezed me to a pulp. But maybe that had to do with the size of the restroom.

"Careful of my glasses," I said. "I don't have spare frames."

"So take them off," she said.

I took off my glasses.

"I've neglected my body," she said. She showed me a few rolls of fat.

Some people neglect their bodies, others their minds. Then there are people who neglect body and mind. What I liked most was a neglected mind in a reasonably well tended body. But actually, neglected bodies attracted me too. I felt at home around all things neglected.

"My husband's a bus driver," she said. "If he discovers us, he'll kill me first, then you."

"Something to look forward to," I said. "What kind of bus does he drive?"

"The M1, he comes past here twenty times a day. I want you," she said.

"And what if we get killed?"

"I don't care, as long as I can take my children with me."

It was a tiny little restroom, but when you really want to, there's nothing that can stop you. Certainly not the size of a restroom. So the restroom in the coffeehouse became the spot where we praised the Lord, the first few weeks of our romance.

*

When it came to frying hamburgers, Peter was about as hopeless as he was at steaming milk. I ate the hamburger anyway. I'm a polite individual.

I hoped that by the time I got back Rebecca would have disappeared. I'd left some cash on the writing table. I hoped she'd taken it. It was more than enough to pay for a car to drive her back to New York. I didn't want her to have to go by bus.

When you're working on leaving your wife and the life that goes along with her, you have to do it on your own. And not with delivery girls who bring you statuettes made by psoriasis patients. But I was afraid she'd still be lying on the bed, just the way I'd left her. Some people are persistent. They hook up their lives to yours, and uncoupling becomes a difficult process.

"How was the hamburger?"

I nodded.

"I told you you needed to eat something."

I nodded. "Do you have any mineral water that doesn't bubble?"

"Tap water?"

"Mineral water that doesn't bubble," I repeated.

"I'll take the bubbles out," Peter said.

*

On workdays we fucked in the restroom at the coffeehouse. Not every workday, of course, because sometimes there were too many customers. Then all we did was kiss. Those were nice days.

We giggled a lot. Not because we were doing something forbidden, but because we were sometimes in such a hurry—after all, a customer could come in any moment, and they had a right to a cappuccino too. Haste leads to misunderstandings, which in turn lead to giggling.

Maybe fucking isn't the right word, maybe I should stick to "praising the Lord." Especially because Evelyn always succeeded somehow in establishing a connection between sex and God. The flights only left three times a week, but they were always non-stop. Straight from Evelyn's body to God. And she'd always add, "I'm no angel, not in bed."

Who wanted an angel in bed? Our intimacy was anonymous. Not that we didn't know each other's names, we knew those, and Evelyn even knew where I lived.

Anonymous were the burns on her arms, anonymous were her plasticized fingernails, anonymous was her uniform. Always black and white, because that's the way the owner of the coffeehouse wanted it. What ultimately makes anonymity anonymous is that you don't have to keep asking yourself, "Where do those burns come from?" That you're not always being reminded of where those burns come from. The burns on her arms were there, and I saw them, but they didn't count.

Anonymity is no past, no dead people, no births, no warning notices, no sales figures, no waiting rooms, no hospitals, no family members, only the present tense of a restroom in a coffeehouse. A continually expanding present tense, until it blows apart. The soap bubble as bunker.

Our intimacy was futureless. We made no claims on each other's futures. I've met people who feel that anonymous, futureless intimacy is loveless. What madness. What's loveless about giving someone the illusion that he's wanted and desirable?

She knew I was a writer, but to her that was like being an astronaut. One time she asked whether my books could actually be bought in bookstores.

"In some bookstores," I said.

She didn't pursue it any further. She had no time to read. She barely had time to live.

We once took her children out picking blackberries. I carried the baby. The baby was fat. It was a real chore to carry that baby. I didn't pick many berries, because I was carrying the baby, the fat baby. Besides, I'm not much of a blackberry-picker.

After that, we ate all the blackberries, in that jeep of hers, which she'd parked fairly close to the beach. I still had the baby on my lap.

When the blackberries were finished, Evelyn said, for the first and last time, "I'm your wife."

"No, Evelyn," I replied, "you're not my wife. You're the bus driver's wife."

Much later, when our romance was already a few months old, I went to her house. It smelled of cleaning fluid. She did a lot of cleaning, Evelyn.

We ended up in bed; where else were we going to end up? Every human has the right to relatively anonymous, futureless intimacy. Intimacy that doesn't ask, "Do you really love me?" because that little word "really" points to nothing within that constellation. Intimacy that doesn't say, "I want to be able to lie on the beach for a change," or complain about the cleaning lady who doesn't scrub hard enough.

My love was portable. Luggage that couldn't get lost, not even when you changed flights often. Try to beat that, portable love in a world where, after three days, people want to change their love into an apartment building sixty stories high.

POLISH-JEWISH CUISINE IN 69 RECIPES

The car rental agency only had a white one, a convertible. "Okay, I guess that will have to do," I told them.

Rebecca said, "I love snow." Which is why we drove up north. Maybe there was some snow up there.

I'd suggested bringing her back to New York, to the Museum of Natural History, so she could continue her research.

"Maybe we should break off the trip right here," I'd said early that morning, when I walked into the hotel room.

"Don't send me away," she said.

"I'm not sending you away," I said. "I just thought it might be better."

"That what might be better?"

"That you go back to the museum, that you continue your research."

"I don't want to go back," she said.

I'm not much good at sending people away.

We spent a few more hours in Atlantic City. Finally we decided to go north.

"What about your wife?" Rebecca asked. "Won't she be worried if you stay away so long?"

"She spends all day with her patients, she barely notices whether I'm there or not."

Rebecca nodded. My answer seemed to please her.

"Have you ever taken a romantic journey with your wife?"

A romantic journey with your wife . . . a strange question coming from someone who identified with Mata Hari. I had to think about that one.

"We went to Lisbon once."

"What was that like?"

"Lovely city, lovely streetcars, beautiful streetcars, the most beautiful streetcars I've ever seen. Only we never got around to fucking."

I started cleaning up the room, I wanted it to be a bit neat when we left.

"Didn't you have time for it?"

"It was too quaint and cozy: fucking isn't cozy, it's actually pretty uncozy."

"That's true," Rebecca said, "you can't really call it cozy."

"What about you, did you ever take a trip with your men?"

She shook her head. "We never got any further than the beach."

After that we rented a car. We turned on the car radio and tried fruitlessly to find some music Rebecca liked. There was no music she liked.

After we'd driven for two hours, she got tired. "Why don't you drive?" she asked.

"I can't. I never learned how."

We stopped at a Burger King. "Good food is different," I said. "But at least you know what you're going to get." I thought about Peter and his steamed milk.

At Albany we decided to look for a room. There was still no snow in sight, but she was too tired to drive on.

"This is like some city in the Eastern Bloc," Rebecca said.

The streets were empty. The only people out were two Negroes at a bus stop. We had to drive through downtown three times before we found a hotel. From the outside, the hotel looked like a model penitentiary.

"I'll go in and ask," I said. I put on my coat and went inside to the desk. There was a huge Easter bunny in the lobby, with a fence around it. A man in a cowboy hat was standing at the desk, complaining about his room.

"How can I help you?" asked a girl with glasses.

"I need a room for one night for my wife and me."

Outside the window I could see the white car. Still a bit too gaudy for my taste, but Rebecca said she liked white cars. She liked snow too, so it seemed plausible.

"I have one room with two single beds."

"I'd rather have one big bed."

"Then it will have to be a suite."

I didn't have to ponder that one too long. "That will be fine," I said. The longer you think about the money you spend, the more painful it becomes. That goes for more things than just spending money. My teacher at grade school used to say, "Think first, then act." But if you actually did that, you'd run the risk of never doing anything again.

"Your name is?"

I handed her my credit card, my American Express. There was still some leeway on that one.

"Where can I park?"

"If you leave the keys with us, we'll take care of it."

"It's the white one," I said, pointing at the car. I saw that Rebecca had climbed out. She was smoking a cigarette and wearing the fur hat I'd bought for her from an old Greek lady in Atlantic City. From a distance like that, with the hat on, she had something Russian about her.

"What's the license number? It's for the parking attendant."

"I don't know," I said. "We just rented it."

It had been less than three days since I'd accepted a statuette from a woman, a psoriasis patient who made statues of people she saw on television. And now I was in a hotel in Albany that looked a lot like a model penitentiary.

"Do you need any help with your bags?"

"Yes," I said, but then corrected myself. "No, no, we don't have much luggage, we won't be staying long."

I waited for the keys; they were those plastic cards.

*

Back when the money had just started to take on the form of nice little mounds, I still thought about my retirement. Those were in the days when I was still living off of *268th in the World*. A spending pattern that wasn't exaggeratedly stingy, more like what some people would call "sensible."

My wife and I got married in Miami. There wasn't a lot of family there: only my mother, an aunt, my wife's parents and my dentist, but that was only because I'd run into my dentist by accident in Miami. He was staying at the same hotel. When he'd asked, "What are you doing here?" I'd told him. "I'm here to get married," I said. To which he replied, "Then I'd be glad to come to the wedding." By then, of course, there was no getting out of it. My dentist had a way of inviting himself to things. I think that was sort of his philosophy of life. If others fail to invite you, you just have to do it yourself. It's strange, but whenever I think about my wedding, I see my dentist. In a white suit, talking a mile a minute. But he always does that. I think he's the only American who's ever read my books. He says he loves European literature. In his case, it's probably more snobbism than a love of anything. But I'd be the last person to worry about the distinction between snobbism and loving things. In my book, anything that presents itself as love is welcomed with open arms.

*

"They're still authorizing your credit card," said the girl with glasses.

I blush easily. I hoped I wasn't blushing.

"That's okay, I've got another one," I said.

*

Getting married happened on impulse. A lot of things have happened on impulse. My mother was ill, I thought: it would be nice for her if we got married. But looking back on it, she didn't think my getting married was nice at all, it only made her feel worse.

The whole thing cost me a fortune. I'd never do it again.

My wedding day ended in a fight with the photographer. He wouldn't stop, even though I'd hired him myself. He drove my mother crazy. He was a strange man. He did a lot of animal photography, but also the occasional wedding. There was food left on the table, and he started eating it. My mother thought that was impolite, I thought it was a bit peculiar too, but nothing to get upset about. My mother doesn't like it when other people eat her food, she can get very aggressive about that. In fact, I don't remember much of it anymore, I was pretty drunk that evening, but later my dentist gave me a blow-by-blow account. He said, "That's a wedding I'll never forget."

"Well," I said, "that was the idea."

*

"Here you are," said the receptionist, "room 429. Have an enjoyable stay."

I went outside. Rebecca was still leaning against the car, smoking. I wondered whether she had any idea at all where she was and, if so, whether she even cared.

"I took a suite," I said.

She crushed out her cigarette with her shoe. "That's good, I have really smelly feet."

"Oh yeah?"

She nodded. "Normally I use this cream for smelly feet, but I forgot it. Of course I don't use it every day, only when I think people might be able to smell my feet."

"I have no objection to smelly feet."

I took a plastic bag out of the car. That was all the baggage we had. The doorman watched us walk past.

I'm not sure whether I was ever in love with Rebecca. People are too quick to see their hormonal eruptions as falling in love. I've learned to mistrust my own feelings, which has caused some people to conclude that I have no feelings. But if I was ever in love with Rebecca, then it began with that cream for smelly feet. And if I had to find a metaphor for being in love—which fortunately I don't—then I would choose cream for smelly feet.

The suite was the sorriest set of rooms I'd ever seen. The bedroom window looked out onto a blind wall, and otherwise there were no windows at all. The furniture in the living room was vaguely reminiscent of the fifties. A conference table, a dry bar, two barstools, a refrigerator, a coffee machine.

Rebecca plopped down on the bed. She turned on the television. "We need to buy underpants," she said.

"Again?"

I went into the bathroom and held my head under the tap. Rebecca came and stood behind me. "These towels have seen better days." She rubbed a towel between her hands, like she was doing a test for a consumer guide.

"Another year and they'll be saying that about me."

"They already say that about you."

I'd won four prizes. The latest one was three years ago. When my mother had people over to visit, she'd read them the jury reports out loud. To my mother, the jury reports were lovelier than anything I'd ever written. Sometimes the neighbor lady would say, "But I've already heard all those jury reports."

"Sure," my mother said, "but you can't remember it all after only hearing it one time."

I thought of myself as an important writer, but that was starting to become a little awkward. Being the only one. In my wife's clinic there was a patient who also thought of himself as an important writer, and as an important philosopher. My wife told me that the patient had once said, "If I'd had the time, I would have been an important politician too."

"Okay," my wife had told him. "I understand that, you just didn't have enough time." Because it's no use getting into senseless discussion with patients.

When you're the only one who thinks of you as an important writer, that's awkward, but when ten thousand other people also think of you as an important writer, you're a success.

"Listen, Rebecca," I said, "my first book, *268th in the World*, changed the face of Dutch literature, and my Sidney Brochstein cycle changed the face of Western European literature."

"Oh," said Rebecca.

"Oh, what's 'oh' supposed to mean?"

"'Oh' means oh," Rebecca said tersely. "'Oh' means that I've heard differently about that Brochstein cycle of yours."

"That's because everyone's against me, darling. The publishers, the professors of literature, the sociologists, the literary journals, the opinion weeklies, the TV guides, the women's magazines, my best friend David, my own publisher, who earned millions off me—my own publisher doesn't even want me to come to his New Year's reception anymore. Can you imagine that, your own publisher sending you an invitation in March for a New Year's reception that was held on January 8th, simply because he's scared to death that you'll actually hop a plane and show up?"

"It could have been an oversight."

"An oversight. Reliable sources have told me it was no oversight. Reliable sources have told me that my publisher told the girl in the mailroom, 'Post this invitation to Mehlman in March, so we'll be sure he won't come.' The only thing I want anymore is to write my own obituary, so some third-rate journalist doesn't ruin it. And get it buried somewhere back on page ten."

"You mean you're dying?"

"No, not that, but an obituary isn't something to put off till the last moment."

*

When the publishing house informed me that they were obliged to rid themselves of the spare copies of my books, I didn't bother to reply. I had decided that, whatever happened, I wasn't going to start acting like one of the patients from the fairytale princess's clinic.

And now that I was about to write a cookbook, they were bound to say that I'd actually been a writer of cookbooks all my life.

The fairytale princess said that sooner or later anyone who counts on being understood has to go crazy. The wisest thing was to assume being misunderstood. To count on one big misunderstanding, that was the healthiest thing you could do.

When she wasn't reading jury reports to the neighbors, my mother did the dishes. Nothing made her happier than doing the dishes. Sometimes she'd wash a glass four times, because it still had little spots on it. She would have loved to wash the dishes at the neighbors' too, but the neighbor lady had bought a dishwasher two years before her husband died. And even my mother couldn't compete with that machine. We all have our ways not to have to feel pain. My mother did the dishes.

I turned to Rebecca. She was standing right in front of me.

"Your pimples have started their Ardennes Offensive," I said.

"The Ardennes Offensive, that was a last-ditch offensive, wasn't it?"

"That's right," I said, "a last-ditch offensive, not much more than that. Let's get something to eat."

*

We went to the first restaurant we could find in Albany that was still open. An older gentleman welcomed us as though he was truly thrilled to see us.

"Are they always that friendly here, or is he insane?" Rebecca asked.

The man seated us at a table beside an extremely fat woman who was celebrating her birthday. "Where are you two from?" the birthday lady asked. Apparently she'd run out of things to talk about with the other guests.

"New York City," I said, before Rebecca could say anything.

"And what are you doing around here?"

"We're looking for snow."

"Sometimes there's still a whole pile of it here this time of year, you never know."

Then the other guests sang happy-birthday-to-you and she had to stop talking to us.

Rebecca ordered a fish, which she didn't eat.

"It's staring at me and talking back."

I took a good look at the fish. "It's not staring at you, and it's not saying anything either."

Later, in the hotel bar, we played darts. "Pretty quiet tonight," the barman said. A dwarf from South America came over and started hanging around us. He was visiting family in Albany.

"In Paris," he said in broken English, "in Paris, there the people know how it is to live. Have you two once been to Paris?"

When the dwarf went to the men's room, Rebecca said, "Your first book was good, but after that it kind of petered out."

"Why?"

"Why what?"

"Oh," I said, "forget it."

She turned her back on me again.

I put my hand on her shoulder. "Now tell me why you really put that piece of cardboard in front of my door."

She shrugged. "I thought we could go out and have fun together. I told you that already."

Have fun together. Those words seemed to mean something very different from "have fun together." From the very start, from our meeting in the café at the Museum of Natural History, her words had meant something very different. A psoriasis patient who made statues of people she saw on TV, what could that mean?

The dwarf came back. He started talking again, but I couldn't focus on what he was saying. Until he tapped my hand. It felt like a little bird. His forefinger felt like a bird's beak.

"Sir," he said, "your wife has left you."

She was standing across the bar, next to the man in the cowboy hat who I'd seen at the desk earlier.

"That's not my wife."

"Who is it then?"

"My sister."

"Your sister." He made sounds like he was driving a mule. Then he pulled a photo out of his wallet. "My wife," he said. "From Paris."

I couldn't tell by looking at the picture whether his wife was a dwarf too. She looked a bit like a French teacher. Maybe she really was from Paris.

From across the bar, Rebecca shouted, "I'm buying this man a drink, all right?"

"All right," I shouted back. "Have them bill it to the room."

When you've got debts that run in the hundreds of thousands, twenty dollars is nothing to worry about. To worry about that would be petty. I had no idea exactly how much had been billed to the room this evening. All I knew was, it was a lot.

Again the dwarf tapped his sharp little forefinger against my hand. "You're in trouble."

"What do you mean?" I must have looked at him with a shocked expression, because he started laughing.

"Don't take me serious," he said. "I say that kind of things all the time. When you tell people they are in trouble, they always believe. Funny, right?"

"Very funny. Please excuse me." I got up and walked to the exit.

"Is there a payphone here?" I asked the clerk.

He pointed to the men's room.

I put in a collect call to New York.

"The name?"

"Mehlman, Robert Mehlman."

"Will you accept a collect call from a Mr. Robert Mehlman?" I heard a man ask, and then my wife's voice nervously saying yes. Before I had a chance to say anything, she shouted, "Where the hell are you? What's going on?"

"Nothing's going on. I'm doing research."

"Research? What do you mean research? What kind of research?" She seemed on the verge of hysteria. Which wasn't like her.

"I'll explain it all later. I've been talking to a dwarf."

"A dwarf? What kind of dwarf?"

"A dwarf, with a very interesting background. I went with him to Albany, because he has family here."

"So now you're going to write about dwarves? Have you gone completely off your rocker? You're starting to sound like my patients. Who goes traipsing off after a dwarf?" She wasn't talking anymore, she was screaming.

When I heard footsteps I held my hand over the mouthpiece, but it wasn't Rebecca or the dwarf. It was a young man.

"Didn't you get my letter?"

"Of course I got your letter, but it didn't say anything. As usual. Everything you say and write to me is empty."

"I was in Atlantic City."

"And there you met a dwarf?"

"This isn't just any dwarf, I'll explain it all soon."

"But why the hell did you go traipsing off after him? Am I allowed to know that?"

"To hear his story. He said, 'Come with me to Albany, I've got family there.' It was rash of me, but believe me, this dwarf's story is going to be our ace in the hole."

"You're out of your mind. You and your aces in the hole. Do you know that my credit card is blocked? Everything is blocked."

"Not everything."

"Almost everything."

"I need some peace and quiet. I have to get writing and quick, otherwise everything really will be blocked."

That seemed to calm her down a bit. The perfect lie consists of ninety-five percent truth. All you have to do is alter or leave out the important details, and otherwise tell the truth as much as possible. The more truth in a lie, the better it is.

"Listen," I said, "use the MasterCard from Ireland, that still has to work. In Ireland there's no problem."

It's always been my policy to have as many bank accounts as possible, in as many countries as possible. Now that was starting to pay off.

"And some man from the bank has already called twice."

"Don't answer. Just don't answer it."

"What do you mean don't answer? How am I supposed to talk to you if I don't pick up the phone?"

"Okay, but just tell them that everything will be paid off next week. That I'm expecting a big advance any moment."

"Are you expecting a big advance?"

"Of course not, but I'll work something out. Just believe me. I have to write that cookbook, then everything will be all right. Fifty percent when I sign, fifty when I turn it in. As long as I turn in something, there's still hope."

The young man was washing his hands. He looked at me as though there was something interesting to see.

"Next week everything will be fine," I said as calmly as I could.

"You've been saying that for years."

"Not to the bank."

"No, but to me, and that's a lot worse."

The young man was still washing his hands. Every once in a while he glanced over at me. I looked at myself in the mirror, but I couldn't see anything strange.

"We'll talk about it quietly when I get back. How was the conference? How was your presentation?"

"Good. Very good. Only I couldn't pay my hotel bill because my credit card was blocked."

I sighed. "You already said that."

"It was very embarrassing. Fortunately that nice psychiatrist from Rome loaned me the money."

The young man finally left the men's room. Something suddenly reminded me of *Letters to My Chimneysweep*.

"Thank God there are nice psychiatrists in Rome, let's get down on our knees and thank God for all the nice Roman psychiatrists."

"Stop the joking, I can't stand it anymore."

"That's not a joke, that's the way I am."

"I cried."

"When?"

"When my credit card was refused."

"Don't cry over credit cards. Believe me, within a week that credit card will be working like a charm. Oh, before I forget, the chimneysweeps came. I'll tell you about it when I get back."

"Will you be back soon?"

"Real soon, but first I have to finish this. This dwarf, this isn't your run-of-the-mill dwarf. I'll call tomorrow and tell you all about it."

"What's wrong, Robert?"

"Little kisses."

"I ask what's wrong with you and you say 'little kisses.' Do you know what it's like to be ignored?"

"I don't have any answers at this moment. You have all kinds of questions and I have no answers. I have to think about how to formulate those answers."

"When you're talking to me, you're not writing a book, Robert."

"Lots of little kisses. And don't cry over that credit card. It doesn't matter. Never cry over credit cards."

"Kisses."

Then I hung up and held my head under the tap. Maybe it really wasn't such a bad idea, a dwarf, along with the chimneysweeps. From my inside pocket I pulled out the notepad Capano had given me. The first page said: "Lady + weatherman. Mata Hari. Mother will die soon." And beneath that I now wrote: "Dwarf and chimneysweep." Then I went back to the bar.

*

The dwarf was the only one still there. He was shuffling a deck of cards. My half-full glass of calvados was on the bar, and my blue jacket was still draped over the stool. Rebecca's raincoat was gone.

The dwarf kept shuffling the cards. Imperturbably, like some machine.

"Where did she go?" I asked, pointing to where Rebecca had last been seated.

"She'll come back," the dwarf said, but the thought that she wouldn't be coming back suddenly seemed entirely plausible to me. The kind of person who comes moseying into your life with a statuette from a psoriasis patient also disappears discreetly from a bar in Albany. That was to be expected. And that thought made me so sad that I slowly became angry. Less than six hours ago I'd been hoping that she would disappear from my life for all time, but that was six hours ago.

The dwarf had stopped shuffling and was looking sadly at the deck of cards. Maybe he'd been hoping that I'd play a game with him, but I didn't like cards.

Then I saw Rebecca coming through the revolving doors. She walked up to me and shivered.

"Where were you?" I asked.

"Outside," she said. "I went for a little walk. You never came back from the toilet."

"Who goes outside in this kind of weather wearing a coat like that?"

Rebecca's coat was covered with ill-defined stains.

"Candle wax," she said, following my gaze. "I'm kind of careless with my clothes."

"Careless with raincoats and with the pill?"

"Yes," she said.

"Your brother is a worried gentleman," the dwarf said.

"That's what brothers are for," Rebecca said.

"I have only sisters," said the dwarf, and he raised his little hands to heaven, as if that one statement explained all his suffering.

We said goodbye to the dwarf, but the dwarf said, "Till tomorrow, at breakfast." And he winked, as if he knew more. As if he knew everything.

In the elevator I asked, "That man with the cowboy hat, he wasn't outside with you, was he?"

"Oh no," she said. "He went up to his room, he was really boring."

I looked in her eyes. The eyes of a woman who was careless with raincoats and with the pill.

Some people suffer because they don't have to live. They have everything. Their food, their drink, a roof over their heads. But they don't have to live, because they have everything. If they were a book, some critic would be sure to write: "All well and good, but was anyone waiting for this?" And that they don't have to live, that gnaws, apparently that gnaws something terrible.

That was the kind of person Rebecca was, it seemed to me. That she suffered, there could be no doubt about that. You don't go along with me to Atlantic City of your own free will, and then on to Albany, not if you don't suffer. Her life was volunteer service, and she wasn't the volunteering kind.

There were also people who suffered so they wouldn't have to live. Who saw suffering as a daily routine that allowed you to avoid living.

"Do you think I'm flat?" she asked.

"Flat?"

"I mean, upstairs?"

"No, I don't."

Flat wasn't what you'd call her.

The suite seemed even more dismal than it had earlier in the evening. I hung my clothes over one of the office chairs lined up around the conference table.

Rebecca was already in bed. She was a fast undresser.

"You don't have any regrets about lying here next to me?" she asked.

"No," I said, "you already asked me that. I have no regrets, I'm not a regretter."

It was a big bed. I lay on the side with the telephone and an old-fashioned clock-radio. She pushed her feet up against my leg. To warm them up, I guess.

"Jesus Christ," I said, "those aren't feet, those are icebergs. Haven't you ever heard of a circulatory system?"

"Would you do me a favor?"

"Yes," I said.

"Do something that shocks me."

Her request took me by surprise. I couldn't remember anyone ever asking me that before.

"If I went and slept in the bathroom, would that shock you?"

"Yes," she said.

"Then that's what I'll do."

I spread out a blanket in the tub, but after fifteen minutes I decided it was too uncomfortable for a whole night. I got back in bed beside her. She was asleep. I thought about my cookbook. I kissed her and said, "Dream something beautiful." She couldn't hear me anymore.

Despite the state of affairs in which I found myself, strangely enough I felt happy for a moment there.

Tomorrow was Wednesday. On Wednesday my wife made marionettes with deaf-and-dumb loonies.

*

Next morning it still hadn't started snowing. We were too late for snow. I suggested to Rebecca that we drive further north, and she said that sounded like a good idea, she didn't want to spend another day in that miserable room.

After she went into the bathroom, I dressed quickly and hurried downstairs. There were a lot of people in the lobby, two tour buses had come in.

I used the same telephone I had the night before. It took a while before I got my German publisher on the line. I was put through a few times, and had to keep repeating that it was urgent.

"Stephan," I said, "Robert Mehlman here."

"So, we haven't heard from you for a while."

"I've been busy, doing lots of traveling. Listen, I have an idea for a book, and I thought maybe you'd like the world rights."

"Yet another idea?"

I detected an ironic, perhaps even sarcastic, tone.

"A very good idea."

"Listen, Robert, we're still waiting for your cookbook. You were supposed to turn it in two years ago, and you got a contract and an advance."

I was being hounded by a cookbook, that was all I needed.

"Are you still there? I was talking about the cookbook."

"Yes," I said, "I'm still here."

There were so many books I still had to write, books I'd promised to write and for which I'd received contracts and advances. I'd had a dream that all my publishers came to visit me at home and took turns figuring out how much they'd paid me for books that had never appeared. And now they were demanding their money back, plus compound interest. It wasn't pleasant dreaming about compound interest, it was actually exceedingly unpleasant. But still there was no denying that recently I dreamed a great deal about compound interest, at least three times a week.

"Yeah, that cookbook," I said, "I know, but that kind of thing takes research, lots of research. Give me six months."

"Six months," he growled, "six months. I've already given you two years. I want it now."

"Now?"

It felt like I was standing in court, negotiating for a reduced sentence.

Some time back, probably around the time that I consented to write a cookbook, I woke up in the middle of the night. It's not like me to have trouble sleeping, I've driven out insomnia with drink. I looked at my wife, I saw her childlike face, her pajamas, her hair sticking out every which way. Because she was always cold, she slept ten months of every year in thick pajamas. They were taken off only in July and August.

I went and sat on the toilet: I'd taken my books from the kitchen cupboard in there with me. I began to read. In the margins I noted the things I wanted to have changed in the next edition. But there were so many things I wanted to have changed that it was no longer any use, I had to stop after a few pages. I looked at myself in the mirror. Then I flipped through a few of my other books.

My wife came into the bathroom. She was still woozy with sleep.

"What are you doing in here?"

"I'm reading my books."

"In the middle of the night?"

She shooed me aside, sat down on the toilet and peed, staring pensively into space.

"What would you think if I started a florist's shop?" I asked.

"A florist's shop? But flowers don't even interest you."

"Exactly. Which means I wouldn't be carried away by all kinds of sentimental considerations. Could you see me as a florist?"

She glanced up at me. "No, Robert," she said, "you as a florist, I can't see that, no one could see that. All you'd have to do is wrap paper around a flower and it would already be dead."

I looked at myself, at the books lying beside the toilet, at the hair on my toes.

"If you ask me, it's a kind of general allergic reaction," I said, "something like prose allergy. I need to get into flowers, otherwise I'm in real trouble. Another year of this and I'll be walking around with a flute in my pocket and a beret on my head, telling everyone who'll listen that I'm Rasputin."

"I wouldn't do that if I were you," my wife said.

I stayed in the bathroom, and when it got light outside I decided that "Rasputin Flowers and Plants" was a good name for a flower shop that specialized in toxic plants. Within four days after that, so many bills had come in that I decided to accept the offer to write a cookbook. All I had to do at that point was sign the contract.

*

"Just finish the cookbook first, then we'll talk about your new idea."

"Stephan," I said.

"Listen to me, I've been in this business for years. First the cookbook. Do that first and finish it. And quickly."

I mumbled something, but my German publisher said, "I want to see it within four weeks, otherwise don't bother. I'll have the contract annulled."

"Everything will be fine," I said, and hung up.

Then I placed a collect call to Chicago. David had gone to Chicago at the same time I went to New York.

"Why are you waking me up?" he asked. "And why are you calling collect?"

"I'll pay you back, David," I said. "Don't talk so loudly, I'm in Albany."

"What are you doing there?"

"I ended up here. Listen, how are you doing? Aren't you done writing that thesis yet?"

"Writing a thesis takes years, Robert," David said. "I've told you that before. It's sort of like writing a novel. Writing a thesis demands real research."

"Okay, but that's not what I called about. I'm in Albany and I think it might be a good idea for me to leave my wife, temporarily at least, and so I figured: would you call her for me?"

"What? Who do you want me to call?"

"My wife, the fairytale princess."

"Why should I call her? What am I supposed to say?"

"Well, that I'm leaving her temporarily."

"Why should I be the one to do that?"

"Because you're my friend. Listen, if she starts crying I'll go all wobbly, I'll collapse, you know me, I'll do whatever she wants. If she murders me, all right, but if she starts crying, I'll fall apart."

"You need a psychiatrist, Robert."

"The fairytale princess *is* a psychiatrist, that's exactly the problem."

"Do you want me to call a doctor? I've got family in Albany, I bet they know some doctors. I haven't spoken to them for a long time, but if it's really an emergency I'm sure they'd be willing to help you."

"You always got along well with the fairytale princess," I said. "Maybe you two could get married. That would be ideal, then I could be a close friend of the family."

"Are you working on a book?"

"I'm working on reality here. I can't call her, you have to call her, tell her I'm in Japan if need be, for research."

"What kind of research? Cancer research?"

"I'll pay you for it, I'll give you all my first editions, but please call the fairytale princess! And why don't you want to marry her? It's in your own best interests too, you don't want to spend your whole life alone with your dog, do you?"

"I don't want your first editions, Robert, and I've already told you to leave my dog out of your fantasies. All I want is to go back to sleep now, I don't want your second or third editions, either, and I don't want to call your wife to tell her you're leaving her. I'll give you the telephone number of my relatives in Albany; call them and tell them you know me, and that you need to see a doctor very badly. That's all I can do for you right now."

"Rebecca's waiting for me upstairs, I can't stay on the phone that long."

"Who's Rebecca? Are you running around with whores again?"

"No, no, definitely not a whore. What am I supposed to say, she's just someone who left something in my stairwell. She looks like Mata Hari. She thinks."

I heard David sigh and groan.

"Okay, Robert, have you got a pen? I'm going to send you to the doctor."

"I don't have time for a doctor!" I shouted. "I have a cookbook to write, you idiot! And I want to write my own obituary, I'm not going to leave that to some third-rate journalist. And I'm not going to let you do it either, David, because you're worse than a third-rate journalist! You're a third-rate philosopher!"

I hung up and blew my nose.

When I got back to the room, Rebecca was standing at the window.

"I've been wearing the same underpants for two days, and for a woman that's a lot more unhygienic than it is for a man."

"Is that so?"

"Yes," she said, "that's so. If you'd paid a little more attention in biology class, you'd know that yourself."

"Rebecca," I said, and sat down, "I have something to confess. I'm actually a writer of cookbooks."

She looked at me and she began to laugh, to laugh so hard, almost hysterically, that it frightened me.

"So what kind of cookbooks do you write?"

"About Polish-Jewish cuisine. At least, that was the agreement. That it should be about Polish-Jewish cuisine."

"Do you know anything about that?"

"Not really."

And she started laughing again, so hard it frightened me.

*

That same morning I placed an ad in *The New York Times*. "Reliable writer of cookbooks seeks expert in Polish-Jewish cuisine. For cookbook. Excellent rates." I paid for the ad with my Irish MasterCard. They said it would appear in the paper the next day.

So began my life as a writer of cookbooks, and I thought of
Evelyn, who would have cooked for me if I'd lived in her neighborhood. And who, whenever we went out to dinner, would hand
me the menu and say, "You choose, I don't know what's good
anyway."

*

We had a breakfast of muffins in a shadowy coffeehouse not far
from the hotel. Snow was nowhere to be found, but there was an
icy wind blowing.

"Not only do we have to buy underpants, but you also need a
coat."

"I've used this one for the last two winters."

"Well," I said, "two winters don't make a spring."

If I could have rid myself of my nagging sense of shame by buying twenty winter coats for her, I would have done so without
hesitation. But I was afraid that even winter coats couldn't help
that.

She looked at me with those expectant eyes of hers and took another bite of her blackberry muffin.

"Listen," I said, "I really have to get started on that cookbook."

"Am I a hindrance to you?"

A hindrance? If anything was hindering me, it was probably
myself.

"No," I said, "you're no hindrance to me."

"But why is it so urgent all of a sudden?"

"What?"

"That cookbook."

"The publisher's waiting for it. That's how publishers are. First
you don't hear from them forever, then suddenly they're in a
hurry."

I conjured up a charming smile. Maybe that was also a form of
salvation, to no longer have to smile charmingly. Never to smile

charmingly again. I'd sold myself to people with great willingness, to increasingly fewer people lately, but still with a great deal of willingness. The shop that bore my name was empty now. The liquidation sale had been going for some time, and it had, undeniably, been a roaring success.

I knew that the most important thing was that I pay off, within the next ten days and at least in part, the debt on my American Express card. When your life is reduced to paying off the debts on your credit cards, you've done something wrong. I just didn't know what.

A few weeks earlier my wife had said, "Wouldn't it be a good idea if we went out for dinner less often? Are sales still going well?"

"What do you mean, go out less often?" I'd shouted. "I'd rather hang myself than go out less often. Sales are fine. In some countries, they're even excellent."

"Which countries are those?" she wanted to know.

"Korea," I said. "The Koreans understand me."

I don't know whether she believed me, maybe she only pretended to. When they believe you it can be painful, but when they act like they believe you, that's a fairly terminal form of loneliness.

*

"Can't I help you with that cookbook?"

I looked at Rebecca. "No," I said, "you really can't."

Then the dwarf from the night before came in. He'd already spotted us and came over to stand at our table.

"Good morning," he said. He'd smeared oil in his hair. His haircut looked like a motorcycle helmet.

"Brother and sister, traveling together, this is wonderful," the dwarf said. He smiled the way he had the evening before, as if he knew everything.

The first story I ever had published was called "Green Tea." It appeared in a magazine that no longer exists, and which, to tell the truth, barely ever existed at all. When it came out, I bought three copies. One of them I took with me everywhere. I showed the magazine to everyone. Even to a few unsuspecting customers at the all-night deli.

The story wasn't so much a boost to my status as it was the very proof of my existence. Later, at David's expense, I actually had it reprinted and distributed in a limited edition.

Two critics in other magazines dedicated a clause to "Green Tea." The clippings of those parts of sentences I also carried around in my inside pocket.

I called up everyone I knew, and there weren't too many of those, to ask if they'd read the paper. "Have you seen it?" I asked. "There's something in the paper about 'Green Tea.'"

The acquaintance at whose house I had once eaten pasta casserole with blue cheese called me back. "I can't find it," she said. "I've been through the whole paper three times. Where is it?"

I gave her the page number. When she called back, she sounded disappointed. "It's only part of a sentence, and they spelled your name wrong."

Maybe that's the cycle you have to go through. You start off as part of a sentence with your name misspelled, and you end up that way too. And all that lies between those points is barely worth mentioning. A party with vague acquaintances where you've stayed too long, half against your will. One of those parties where you wake up in the morning in a living room not your own.

"Will you be continuing your journey today?" the dwarf asked.

"Perhaps," I said, "perhaps."

I looked at Rebecca, who was plucking crumbs out of her muffin. At this very moment, my wife was making marionettes with the deaf and dumb. She was one of the few psychotherapists at the clinic who knew sign language.

"And where will you be going?" the dwarf asked.

"In the direction of Canada," I said.

"Canada is a big country," the dwarf said. "I have been to it. Big and empty." He looked at me triumphantly.

The liar is the one who isn't there. I hadn't been there for a long time. I'd disappeared from the lives of others long ago; my lies were there, and they happened to have the same physical appearance I did, but that was all you could say. All I had to do now was disappear from my own life. A final vanishing act, it had to be a piece of cake after all the vanishing acts I'd pulled off thus far.

The dwarf sold me a lucky coin on a string. It would protect me, although it remained unclear against exactly what.

For Rebecca I bought a coat for two hundred dollars, which—if anything like an impartial jury exists—was an entirely defensible expenditure.

*

Twelve people had reacted the very same morning the ad appeared, all experts in Polish-Jewish cuisine, reported Princess Fairytale, who I'd called from a pay phone.

"What's going on?" the fairytale princess had asked. "There are all kinds of people on the answering machine who say they're responding to some ad."

I explained to her in a few sentences that I was working on a cookbook, and that I needed the help of experts.

"Why don't you ever tell me anything?"

"What do you mean?" I asked.

Rebecca was sitting in the convertible. The roof was up. She was reading the paper.

"You never say anything. I have to drag it all out of you. I'm your wife, for Christ's sake, I have a right to know what's going on!"

"How can I tell you what's going on if I don't know either? How did it go with the loonies?"

"None of your business. Why didn't you tell me you had to write a cookbook? Why don't you ever tell me what's happening?"

"It's a literary cookbook. With stories sandwiched in between the recipes. I still have to find a form for it: something sentimental about the *shtetl*, followed by yet another recipe. I don't know what's going on, I don't have the slightest idea what's going on."

"So what are you doing in Albany when you're supposed to be writing a cookbook about Polish-Jewish cuisine? Can you explain that to me?"

Rebecca waved. I waved back.

"What I'm doing in Albany? I'm working on leaving you."

"What do you mean? Working on leaving me?"

"That's what I said. I'm working on leaving you. There's no better way to put it."

"And why, if I may ask? You jerk."

"Because . . . because we drive each other crazy. The way two dogs in a single kennel drive each other crazy, until they're put in separate kennels."

"So you think we're two dogs?"

"Sometimes."

"Stop these games. What are you doing, Robert?"

"I'm working on leaving."

"That's no news. You've been doing that for the last century. David called."

"What did he say?"

"He asked whether you were all right, he asked whether you needed help."

"He's frustrated. I write the books, and he has to write about them. I'd be frustrated too if I were him. What does he have in his life? A dog and a couple of students. And he has lousy table manners. Have you ever watched him eat? He eats like a pig."

"He's worried."

"Actually, getting divorced is just a negative form of love. You love someone for one second, or at least you think you love someone, and the rest of the time you're busy saying goodbye to that person, busy getting free, and the longer the goodbye takes, the greater the love was, I guess. Living is really nothing more than saying goodbye to life. That's the core of living, and love is saying goodbye to love—it's all one big farewell party. It was a great farewell party, but now I have to get on home, catch some sleep, do last week's dishes. You understand?"

I was cruising now. I had to remember this.

"Robert, you're not right in the head, you should have yourself committed."

"You're the professional, I'm not going to argue with you about your policy with regard to having people committed, but your advice does come a bit late. One year ago, two years ago, I would have had myself committed, but not anymore. Not now. Now I'm a part-time genius."

"Try to become a full-time genius, Robert. That would make things a lot easier for everyone. And I want you to come home right now."

"I can't. I've rented a car."

"I don't care what you've rented. I don't even want to know all the things you've rented, or what whorehouses you've been frequenting, I only know that you don't let anyone into your life, absolutely no one, and that you've been busy for years removing yourself from my life. And I promise you: before too long, you're going to succeed."

"I haven't been to any whorehouses. It's been years since I went to a whorehouse. Otherwise, I'm calling from a pay phone, I don't have much time, I have to go."

"Whenever you call me, you always have to go. Why do you call if you have to go?"

"Because I'm working on leaving you. So I could tell you that. Give me the time to finish it off."

"To finish what off, what are you talking about?"

"Leaving you. And you're right about what you just said, about not letting anyone into your life. That's my theory."

"I'm sick of your theories."

"Could you give me the numbers of the people who called?"

"Robert, you can't treat me this way."

"What way am I treating you?"

"Like your mother."

"You're worse than my mother. Even in Albany, you won't leave me in peace."

"What do you mean, not leave you in peace? You're the one who called me."

"To talk. Not to listen to a barrage of accusations. Actually, what you're accusing me of is being alive."

"That's all in your mind, Robert."

"When the bookcases are delivered wrong, it's my fault."

"It was your fault, because you should have kept your eyes open. But again you were too busy with those shit books of yours."

"Cookbooks, not shit books, the shit books are behind me now."

"Doesn't matter: you weren't paying attention when the bookcases were delivered, that's what this is about."

"Exactly, that's what I mean. A long, incessant flow of accusations. When I want to hear something negative about myself, I don't even have to read a review, all I have to do is listen to my wife. Now give me those phone numbers."

"Robert, I don't know what you're up to, but you'll come home when you get hungry."

"My father always said that too."

"Stop comparing me with those psychotic parents of yours."

Rebecca honked. I waved again. She waved back again.

"You're a lot more psychotic than my parents, believe me. That's why your patients are so fond of you. When they look at you, they recognize their own madness."

"Let's not talk about it anymore. I'm leaving, Robert. I'm leaving you."

"I've heard that so many times before."

She gave me the phone numbers of the people who had called and claimed to be experts on Polish-Jewish cuisine. I jotted them down on a newspaper.

"I'll call again soon," I said once I'd written down all the numbers.

She said nothing.

"Does the Irish credit card work?" I asked.

"Yes," she said, "that one works, but Citibank sent you another letter today."

"I'll fix it," I said, "I'll fix that one."

"Be careful."

"Yes," I said, "I'll be careful."

I hung up. Then I called my mother to see how she was doing.

Once I had that out of the way, I called the numbers the fairytale princess had given me. Most of them weren't home, or else they were home but turned out to know nothing about Polish-Jewish cuisine, only Peruvian cuisine. Or they started griping about money right away. Until I got Mrs. Fischer on the line. She lived in Yonkers. She'd grown up in Poland, in Breslau, spoke English with a heavy accent. She said the world was still as much a riddle to her as it had been when she was four, but that there was nothing she didn't know about Polish-Jewish cuisine. I could come by right away.

"Anyone who wants to know more about Polish-Jewish cuisine is always welcome," she said.

We made an appointment for that evening. Then I went to the car and climbed in beside Rebecca.

"That took a long time," she said.

"Do you think," I said, "that happiness is something you can skip?"

"What do you mean?"

"The way, for example, after dinner you can skip dessert, because you've already had too much soup and meat. You're too full for dessert. Do you think you can skip happiness that way?"

"Happiness isn't a kind of dessert."

She'd bought new lipstick. This one was pink.

"How's your marriage, anyway?" Rebecca asked.

My marriage, how was it?

"Good," I said. "Standing room only."

She nodded.

"You're not laughing?"

"I'm laughing inside."

"Listen," I said, "how do you think a clown feels when afterwards people say: 'We were laughing inside'? Do you think he likes that?"

*

We went back south, to Mrs. Fischer. Along the way we had to get something to eat. Rebecca wanted a cheeseburger. She ate well when she was with me, even though she'd said that sometimes weeks went by during which she ate nothing but a few leaves of lettuce and some dry rice.

We had a table by the window, with a view of the parking lot. Rebecca was picking the onions off her cheeseburger and laying them carefully on the plastic tabletop.

I was the lifeboat drifting by that she'd jumped onto, not knowing that the lifeboat had sprung a leak as well.

"I think," I said, wiping her onions into the cheeseburger box, "that I should say it one last time. The person you're looking for no longer exists. The person your mother saw on television and thought looked so unhealthy does not exist. I write cookbooks, I'm on the verge of writing cookbooks. I have debts, not romantic debts you can muffle away by stealing from your parents, but real debts, grownup debts. What's grownup about me are my debts. Do you understand?"

She nodded, and I had the feeling she was more involved with her cheeseburger than with me.

"Six-digit debts. So if you're looking for adventure, you've come to the wrong place."

"I'm not looking for adventure," she said. "Have you still got those tablets my mother gave you? I could use a couple of them."

I looked at Rebecca. She smelled so wonderfully of old meat, she'd been walking around in the same dress for days, but at least she had a new coat and new lipstick.

The future, which had always kept its distance so discreetly, was about to come down on me. My future was Mrs. Fischer. My future was Polish-Jewish cuisine, my future felt horribly definitive.

My hand was on Rebecca's leg, not because I was feeling so lustful, but because I didn't want to be alone there in that Burger King halfway between Albany and Yonkers. I thought about a drawing of a dachshund. Memory must be some kind of illness, a fever that won't be extinguished, not even by a hundred cold washcloths.

"Of course, we could always go to bed together," I said, "but I don't know if that would help much."

Rebecca said, "I think it would help."

*

It was a warm evening, one of those evenings when the town steams. I like steaming towns, I like garbage that lies there decomposing in the heat beside an outdoor café where they don't believe in closing times.

Evelyn got dressed, slowly. Then she gave me a drawing of a dachshund.

"Here," she said, "my son drew this for you."

The drawing was rolled up and had a rubber band around it. The kind of rubber band postmen use.

I looked at the drawing. "A dachshund," I said, "that's sweet."

I rolled the drawing back up, slipped the rubber band around it, and when I got home I put it in my desk drawer.

A few weeks later the fairytale princess said, "I found a drawing of a dachshund in your desk."

"Yeah," I said. "Someone gave me that."

"Cute," she said.

*

The town was still steaming, but a few leaves had already turned yellow and brown and the fairytale princess had pointed out several red ones. We went roller skating, the fairytale princess and I. Or rather: she went roller skating and I sat on a bench and waved whenever she rolled past.

After three laps she came and sat beside me.

"Finished already?" I asked.

"If I had an affair," she said, "I'd never tell you. What good would it do?"

"You're right," I said, "what good would it do?"

She took off her skates.

Faithfulness and unfaithfulness are concepts that, at a given moment, lose their relevance. Or, to put it more precisely, they're concepts that change their meaning. What binds you to another person is no longer anything as nebulous as faithfulness. What ultimately binds you is the negative form of love, the fact that you've had enough of each other, that the other one has to go, get lost, drop dead, and that the other one just won't go, won't get lost and won't drop dead. A penalty shot you keep taking and keep missing—and that you can laugh about, about missing, because that's a prerequisite for enjoying the negative form of love. Being sick and tired of each other is something you can keep up for years, for a whole lifetime if need be.

"That's enough roller skating for one day," said the fairytale princess.

Maybe, in order to really live, you need to surrender control. But I couldn't surrender control. That's the whole point of the game, to make sure that it's not you but the other person who surrenders control. That the other person suddenly notices that the ground they stand on has become quicksand.

In the same way you can use a lens to blur the background, you also can make another person's reality slowly grow fuzzy, grainier, increasingly grainy, until the grains turn into promises. Follow me and we'll walk together into the promised land. Sure, you'll get sand in your shoes, but I'll polish those shoes and lick your feet clean.

Only somewhere along the line I had made a crucial mistake, overlooked something I shouldn't have overlooked. And so control had sneaked away from me. A position had arisen that I could no longer win.

"You can't see everything as a game," the fairytale princess had said, "that's sick."

Maybe she was right, but I couldn't rule out the possibility that I'd simply examined reality much more acutely. A wee bit undercooled, perhaps, but all the more acute for that.

You can always outsmart people, but it's a mistake to want to rub that in. You have to give them the feeling that *they're* smarter, that they have everything under control, and once they're feeling sure of themselves, then you must strike, like a tiger pouncing from the undergrowth.

*

My hand was still resting on Rebecca's bare leg.

"I don't think it would help," I said. "Fucking is a deplorable business."

Her mouth fell open, then she almost spit in indignation. "Half the books you've written are about fucking, and now you're telling me that fucking is a deplorable business?"

She squeezed her cheeseburger. Juice ran out of it. "Too much cheese," she said. "One slice, that's nice, but not a whole pound."

And I replied, "I like to write about deplorable businesses. And now I'm on my way to Mrs. Fischer."

"Have you ever even thought about what I'm here for?" she asked. "Have you ever actually thought about why I let you drag me to Atlantic City and then to Albany and then on to Yonkers? Have you ever actually stopped to think about me for a moment?"

"You were the one who begged me to let you go along. You said, 'Don't send me away'."

"Don't go twisting my words," she said, "you brainwasher."

"I'm not a brainwasher, Rebecca. I'm a writer of cookbooks."

She stood up and tossed the remains of her cheeseburger into the trash can. Then she came back.

"You're a writer, I understand that," she said. "You need inspiration, I understand that too, and that you draw that inspiration from little lambs who you then jump like some ram, I have no trouble featuring that either."

"Wait a minute," I shouted, "I haven't jumped anyone. And I'm not a ram and you're not a little lamb. May I remind you that you are the one who contacted me, ostensibly to deliver a statuette from a psoriasis patient. I had no idea you existed. I didn't ask for you at all."

"You didn't know I existed," she shouted mockingly. "You didn't know I existed, but you were all too pleased to take me with you to Atlantic City."

"Sit down, Rebecca," I said, "everyone's looking."

"I'm no fool. Within a few day's time you've milked inspiration out of me like I was the chicken and you were the egg farmer. But that's not the way it works, I have needs too. And before long it will all be in the papers. I can even live with that, I almost never see my parents anyway. But what's in it for me?"

The people in the roadside restaurant looked at her. And then at me.

"No one's saying you don't have any needs. We're not talking about an egg farm here, and the last thing I wrote for a newspaper was a piece about Svevo. Sit down and tell me more about your needs."

I pulled out my little notebook and a pen. "So what are your needs?"

"I'm not telling you anything!" she screamed. Then she got up and ran out the door, and a man at the counter applauded.

At first I felt like just sitting there, but then I decided I'd better run after her.

She must have been in pretty good shape, because by the time I got out the door she'd run right across the parking lot and was heading for the freeway. It made me think of my wife's client who had run naked through the Holland Tunnel one night. Close to the shoulder of the freeway, I caught up with her.

"What do you think you're doing?" I shouted. "Were you planning to throw yourself in front of a car, you bimbo, were you going to run across the freeway? What were you planning on doing?"

"Leave me alone," she said, "I'm going home, this was a mistake."

"We have to stay calm," I said. "We have to pull ourselves together. The two of us are locked into this cookbook."

"I'm not locked into any cookbook."

"I'm locked into the cookbook and you're locked in with me, which is why we have to stay calm. And now that we're on the subject, I haven't milked anything out of you, especially not inspiration. When it comes to inspiration you're a bony cow, a very bony one, a cow the butcher wouldn't buy for half an ounce of bologna. Okay, don't start crying. We can talk about everything. What did you really do in Amsterdam?"

She looked at me.

"Officially, I was studying."

"And unofficially?"

"I'd buy a raisin bun with cheese and eat it, then spend the rest of the day in the house."

"And what did you do in the house?"

"I thought."

"About what?"

"I wanted to do something special."

"And that's what you thought about while you were eating your raisin bun with cheese?"

"Yeah," she said. "And I also worked as a cashier at one of those discount supermarkets, for a week."

"Okay," I said, "now we're going to walk back quietly to the car, and we're going to think. We're locked into that cookbook now, and we have to go on with that cookbook. But we'll make it, as long as we don't make any mistakes, as long as we stay calm."

"Do you really think fucking is a deplorable business?" she asked.

I nodded. We stopped beside the car.

"We have to go to Mrs. Fischer's now. She's waiting for us."

"Is she a deplorable business, too?"

"No, not that, she's the beginning of new life. You can go along, but maybe you have something you'd rather do?"

"What do you mean, are you trying to get rid of me?"

"No, but maybe Mrs. Fischer isn't all that exciting. For you."

The person who constantly tries to outwit others ends up in no-man's land. The person who assumes that the other will always betray him, betrays everything and everyone in order to beat them all to the punch.

"I think I'll find Mrs. Fischer very exciting," she said.

I ate the leftover pieces of meat out of her mouth, and pieces of cheese, a few stray onions, our tongues found each other in no-man's land.

"I'm not wearing any underpants," Rebecca said.

"Why not?"

"That's more hygienic."

*

Mrs. Fischer lived in a villa at the edge of Yonkers, not on the seventh floor of some simple apartment building the way I'd expected. Mrs. Fischer had two dogs that started barking when we got out of the car. She was already waiting for us.

She led us through the garden, through the kitchen and into the living room. We sat down, I sat on the sofa, Rebecca in an easy chair. Mrs. Fischer remained standing.

"Do the two of you work together?"

"She's my secretary," I said, and I glanced over at Rebecca. She nodded, she didn't seem to mind playing my secretary.

Mrs. Fischer spoke English with the heavy accent of a person who has continued to think, dream, count and curse in their own language.

"So," Mrs. Fischer said, "here's something to nibble on," and she set a bowl of peppermints on the little table.

I had never considered it a particularly good omen when women offered you peppermints, but this had stopped being about good omens long ago. This was about a cookbook, a deadline, the second half of an advance: all extremely practical, almost comforting matters.

On the sideboard were photographs of Mrs. Fischer in her younger days, with a husband, with children, with even more children, with dogs, Mrs. Fischer on her wedding day. A whole life stood there on display on the sideboard; Mrs. Fischer had seen to her own mausoleum.

"And you're a journalist?"

Mrs. Fischer was seated now too, her skirt pulled down over her knees. Time had left no mark on Mrs. Fischer's coquetry.

"Not a journalist," I said, crossing my legs. My beige trousers were in bad need of laundering. "I'm working on a book about Polish-Jewish cuisine." I leaned forward and took a peppermint.

"Then you two have arrived exactly in the nick of time," said Mrs. Fischer. It felt good to be on time for once.

"I was just about to get rid of my collection," Mrs. Fischer said. "It was taking up too much room." She leaned back in her chair.

Rebecca and I listened attentively, outside the dogs barked and there in Mrs. Fischer's living room I became the writer of cookbooks I always should have been. If one believed in providence. If not, I was slowly transforming into the writer of cookbooks that I had made of myself.

"I'm not going to move yet, but in three or four years I'm going to find a smaller place," Mrs. Fischer said. "When the dogs have passed away."

"Ah yes," I said. "What's this about a collection?"

"The archives," Mrs. Fischer said. "My mother knew everything about Polish-Jewish cuisine, and she kept archives, huge archives. It would be a pity if it should all be lost."

"Mrs. Fischer," I said, "you're exactly the woman I've been looking for."

She blushed. "Is that really true?"

"That's really true, isn't it, Rebecca? Mrs. Fischer is the woman we've been looking for."

Rebecca's leg swung back and forth. She nodded.

"I've always known it."

"What have you known, Mrs. Fischer?"

"That someone like you would come along."

"And how did you know that?" I asked smiling. I leaned forward charmingly and took another peppermint. I had reinvented myself once again. A shy but charming Robert G. Mehlman, traveling through the world with his personal secretary, in search of recipes from the almost extinct Polish-Jewish kitchen.

"Because I have a guide," Mrs. Fischer said.

"What kind of a guide?"

Every love, even the most minor, begins with attention. Attention is the battery of desire.

"A guide," Mrs. Fischer said, "who leads me."

"And where does this guide live?"

"This guide doesn't live, this guide speaks."

I looked Mrs. Fischer right in the eye. "Over the telephone, on the radio, on the TV?"

"No," Mrs. Fischer said, "the guide is in my head. He protects me."

I looked at Rebecca, but she didn't look back at me. I rubbed my leg, all the words I'd weighed and never spoken came back, dozens of declarations of love, unwritten letters, tears I'd held back, insults I'd swallowed. I hadn't lived my life, I'd looked for ways to formulate it, formulations meant to leave no one untouched, to change reality for all time, but which I had finally decided not to speak out loud, or only there where no one else could hear.

"That's fine," I said. "And useful. A guide who leads you."

At that moment it occurred to me that Mrs. Fischer might very well have a great deal of money.

"Mrs. Fischer," I said, "what we should really do is set up a foundation to preserve your mother's archives, and to make them accessible to a broad public. The torch must be passed along."

Mrs. Fischer looked at me questioningly. For a moment there, I was afraid I'd started in too soon about that foundation, afraid I'd been too eager, that I'd made another wrong move.

"You put that so beautifully, that about the torch being passed along. Yes, I've often thought of it that way myself."

She thought I'd put it beautifully. That was a good sign. Sweat was dripping down my forehead, but there was no going back now: a big fish had swum into my nets and I couldn't let it escape. God was having pity on me.

"I'm going to give it some thought," I said. "About how we can let your mother live on in her recipes."

"That would be wonderful," Mrs. Fischer said. "But who on earth is still interested in Polish-Jewish cuisine?"

I looked innocent. That's my strong point, that I look so innocent, so needy, lost with eyes that plead "have mercy on me."

"I think she would be very pleased to live on in recipes," Mrs. Fischer continued. "She spent so much of her life in the kitchen."

"Maybe," I fantasized, "maybe we could even name a dish after your mother. What was her specialty?"

"Gee," Mrs. Fischer said, "she had so many specialties."

I wiped my forehead. Rebecca was staring into space, or else she was thinking about the strange situation she'd landed in, or about her life and how she had been careless with men.

"But there must have been some dish she cooked best, something she put the most love into. Something you liked most."

Mrs. Fischer was deep in thought. Her brow was furrowed and her lips moved as though she was praying silently. "Carp," she murmured.

"Carp," I repeated, "as in the fish?"

"Jellied carp."

I pulled the little notebook out of my inside pocket and wrote: "Jellied carp."

"You're a real journalist," Mrs. Fischer said.

"I'm not a journalist," I said once again. "I'm more a cookbook expert."

"How long have you been doing this?"

"About ten years." I nodded earnestly a few times, as though ten years of writing cookbooks was passing before me. "The secret of a good cookbook writer is in his alertness, his readiness to make notes at any moment, because you never know where a recipe will come from."

"That's right," Mrs. Fischer said. "My mother did the same thing. When would you have time to look at her archives? I'm a little tired now."

"Tomorrow morning?" I suggested.

"Tomorrow morning at eleven then," she said. "The pedicurist comes at ten."

We got up. In the kitchen she shook Rebecca's hand and gave me a little peck on the cheek.

"You remind me so much of my mother," I said.

"Oh," she said, "now I'm flattered. Is she still alive?"

I shook my head, almost imperceptibly. Mrs. Fischer pressed my head against her shoulder and murmured a few unintelligible words. Then she said, "As soon as you came in the door, I knew you were an orphan. My guide never lets me down."

"Apparently not," I said. "Until tomorrow morning, Mrs. Fischer."

In the car, Rebecca said, "But you're not an orphan?"

"No," I said, "I'm not an orphan, I'm a half-orphan. Is someone keeping count?"

At the edge of Yonkers we found a motel where, after some fussing, they finally gave us a room.

There, in that motel, Rebecca and I went to bed together for the first time. Mrs. Fischer sat on my shoulder the whole time, murmuring, "Jellied carp, jellied carp."

Sooner or later, anonymous love leads to sex. To keep the anonymity going, you need flesh, not words. You need fingernails, not theories; you need teeth, not sarcastic comments.

With Evelyn the anonymity had gradually disappeared: our anonymous love had slowly taken on a past, accumulated bric-a-brac. Drawings of dachshunds, wristwatches with Mickey Mouse on them, bills with little notes on the back, that kind of bric-a-brac. In that way our anonymous love took on a future as well, and so became no longer anonymous. It even had a room number of its own, Evelyn's and my love did. Anonymous love can just barely tolerate a room number, but not much more than that. Love that's no longer anonymous can become a menace.

One time I saw the bus driver. That was enough. He came into the coffeehouse and said, "Quick, give me some coffee."

When he was gone, Evelyn said, "That was the bus driver."

*

I held Rebecca's head, her warm head, and I prayed, asking that she wouldn't say she loved me. Years ago I would have prayed that she'd say she loved me, now I asked for the complete opposite: irony wasn't even the right word for it.

I held Rebecca's head: wallpaper with all kinds of dachshunds on it went sliding past, the fairytale princess taking off her skates, Mrs. Fischer standing at her side table, and I myself in the all-night deli, busy warming up a slice of vegetable quiche. And I kept hold of the head of the woman beside me, as though she could put an end to my runaway memory. As though her body, her stories, her sweaty skin, her cigarettes were doors I had only to open to find myself standing barefoot in the grass.

"What are you thinking about?" she asked.

"About you," I said, "and about those seven men. Did you have them in the palm of your hand, did you toy with them, the way a puppet master toys with his marionettes?"

"Sometimes. But I wasn't out for power, I wanted love."

Perhaps later we would say, "We were careless with each other, but we were relatively young and our carelessness was merely symptomatic."

"I feel happy traveling with you," she said at last.

"Me too."

I put on some clothes and went downstairs to call the fairytale princess. Mrs. Fischer was still sitting on my shoulder. I had the feeling I'd already laid the noose around my neck, that the worst was behind me now. All I had to do was jump. From here on out, the rest was pussy stuff.

"Hello, fairytale princess," I said.

"Are you still working on leaving me?"

"Yes," I said, "and I'm also working on solving our financial problems."

She didn't ask about anything else. She talked about the marionette theater she was working on with the deaf and dumb patients.

"It's going pretty well," she said. "They're enthusiastic. All the deaf and dumb patients used to do was watch the plays the other ones put on, but now the other patients finally have to watch the deaf and dumb ones."

"So justice really does exist," I said. Then I let the receiver slip from my hand and imagined that I was a deaf and dumb patient playing with marionettes, under the expert supervision of the fairytale princess.

*

At precisely eleven o'clock, Rebecca parked the car in front of Mrs. Fischer's villa.

Mrs. Fischer was already in the front yard with her dogs. The green dress with black patterns she was wearing left her knees uncovered. It was a nice day, but a bit too cool for bare knees.

Mrs. Fischer led us to the kitchen, where she gave us coffee and freshly baked cookies.

"Did you sleep well?" she asked.

"Wonderfully," I said.

"Where are you two staying?" She took a new load of cookies out of the oven. While I was in the shower this morning, thinking about how to set up the Jellied Carp Foundation, Mrs. Fischer had been baking cookies.

"At Motel Silver Lake."

"Oh, that's where I send my family whenever they come from out of town. It's clean and not too expensive."

I looked at Rebecca. "May I smoke?" she asked.

"I'd rather you didn't," Mrs. Fischer said.

"Then I'll go out in the yard."

She stood up and went out to the yard.

"What a sweet girl," Mrs. Fischer said. "But she doesn't eat my cookies."

"She had a big plate of fried eggs for breakfast."

"Oh, that's so unhealthy, fried eggs."

"I know."

"Is she Jewish?"

Was she Jewish? I'd never asked. You couldn't go by appearances anymore. Racial purity was a rare item these days.

"She has a Jewish soul," Mrs. Fischer answered her own question.

"How can you tell?" I asked, glancing just to be sure at the Jewish soul out smoking in the yard.

"My guide told me."

I nodded. Show no amazement, that was the most important thing. "What kind of guide do you have, exactly?"

Rebecca came back into the kitchen.

"Have a cookie," Mrs. Fischer said. "It's so much healthier than fried eggs." She took some more cookies out of the oven, even though the plate on the table was already overflowing.

"The guide chooses us, we don't choose the guide. And my guide is an Indian."

"An Indian? How come?"

Rebecca was nibbling on a cookie, and I was suddenly reminded of how I would stand barefoot in the grass, early in the morning.

"I used to be an Indian."

"As a child?"

"In a former lifetime," Mrs. Fischer said.

"But your parents were born in Poland, weren't they?"

"And my grandparents on my father's side came from Russia," Mrs. Fischer corrected me. "But long, long ago, I was an Indian. I healed people. That's why I'm so at home here in Yonkers. The place I lived wasn't far from here. I was a medicine woman."

"Unbelievable," I said. "Absolutely unbelievable."

"I can also transfer energy," Mrs. Fischer said.

I weighed my words. "That's fantastic," I said after a brief silence.

The woman who could transfer energy looked at me gratefully. "I talk to a lot of people," Mrs. Fischer said, "but I can tell that you are very special."

I bowed my head humbly to receive the compliment. It was only a matter of minutes before I could bring up the Jellied Carp Foundation.

"Shall we take a look at your archives?"

She led us up, up the stairs, to the top floor. On her legs I saw blue veins that branched like rivers into increasingly smaller tributaries. Mrs. Fischer stopped in front of a door.

"This," she said, "is the shrine, the shrine of Polish-Jewish cuisine."

"Maybe you'd like to go in alone?" I said. "We can wait outside."

I looked at Rebecca, she nodded, and I remembered how one day the fairytale princess had come home and started vacuuming like a madwoman. She knew I hated vacuuming—a very well paid cleaning lady came in for five hours once a week, and I'd always leave the house when she did. Outside those five hours, I didn't want any vacuuming or mopping in my vicinity. The world might not abide by my laws, but I at least demanded compliance from the little world I lived in.

Whenever she started vacuuming like that, it usually meant something bad had happened at work.

"Did they jump in front of the subway again?" I asked. They preferred jumping in front of the subway to jumping out the window. There was something like the theater of love, but there was definitely also something like the theater of suicide.

The fairytale princess let the handle of the vacuum cleaner drop to the floor and began weeping. I said, "If the job's too much for you, look for another job. What's wrong?"

But she didn't want to tell me.

"Did the deaf and dumb patients break their marionettes?"

"No," she said, "the marionettes live in a bag, they're not broken."

"So what is it?"

"Why is it that the patients who commit suicide are always the ones who are doing so well?"

I sat down on the floor. "Because they're not on their toes, because they're doing so well," I said. "You have to approach life like a war in the trenches, you have to stay alert, you never know where the shooting will come from. And if it takes too long for the shooting to start, you start the shooting yourself, because the silence is so unnerving."

"Life isn't a trench."

"You bet life is a trench, you better believe it. Just look at me."

She shook her head.

"Maybe it's better this way."

She shook her head again. "They're pumping his stomach right now."

It was a patient who had once drunk beer, a great deal of beer, so much beer that his little daughter had drowned right before his eyes. That was more than ten years ago, but since then the man had tried at least once a year to force his way into the world where his daughter was staying. There were apparently malignant tumors of guilt as well, tumors that couldn't be made to remit, not even with heavy medication.

"It's not our problem," I said. "Don't take the suicides home from work with you. Leave them there. Or in the taxi, or the subway, I don't want them around the house."

"Why do you have to react like this?"

"Because emotions get in the way of survival. Emotions make you weak, vulnerable, a prey for the hounds."

Then we put on some Moroccan music and started dancing. All through the house. To celebrate the triumph. Our house was a house of the postponed-and-nevertheless-botched suicide, but we went on. Other people jumped in front of the subway or out the window or ate sleeping pills till they burst. But not us, we went on. That was what you called a triumph.

"No," Mrs. Fischer said, "I'd like you to come in along with me."

She opened the door, and the first thing I saw was dust. Then I saw a table covered in books and scrap paper.

"I almost never come in here anymore, not since my husband died," Mrs. Fischer said. "My daughters live in Texas, and they're not interested in recipes like these."

I looked at the stuff lying on the table. Cookbooks with notes in the margins, and things scratched out, lots of things scratched out.

"Oh yes," Mrs. Fischer said, "my mother corrected cookbooks."

"Mrs. Fischer," I said, "all this should really be saved for generations to come. A foundation should be set up to manage your mother's estate. Do you understand what I mean?"

"Yes, certainly, that's what you said yesterday, isn't it? That my mother should live on in her recipes?"

"Exactly," I said, "exactly."

"But she *does* live on in her recipes," Mrs. Fischer said hesitantly, wiping some dust off a book whose pages were almost falling out.

"But no one knows about it," I said. "People should know about it. They should know that your mother lives on in her recipes. You could even turn your house into a museum."

"Oh God, no, not a museum."

The museum was out.

"I'm only thinking out loud," I said, "but how about if you were to set up the Jellied Carp Foundation?"

"Me?" Mrs. Fischer said. "You want me to set up something? But isn't there already a Jellied Carp Foundation?"

"No, no such foundation exists," I said.

"And what would this foundation do?"

"Guard your mother's heritage," I said. "See to it that your mother's work becomes accessible to the many people interested in Polish-Jewish cuisine. Promoting Polish-Jewish cuisine through your mother's recipes."

Mrs. Fischer sighed deeply.

"Yes," she said, "that would be lovely."

"All right, but let's talk about this some other time," I said. "First we have to get to work."

From my leather portfolio I pulled pens, scratchpads, erasers, pencil sharpeners—I'd done a lot of shopping at the stationer's that morning. Mrs. Fischer should at least have the impression that I was an old hand at writing cookbooks.

Mrs. Fischer started talking and I started writing. Maybe I'd started in too quickly about the Jellied Carp Foundation.

That afternoon I bought a typewriter, and started typing out my notes every evening. That's how I began working on what would later become *Polish-Jewish Cuisine in 69 Recipes*. Never have I written a book that quickly. It took me three weeks and two days.

Two weeks later, Mrs. Fischer was dough that had leavened and was ready for the oven. She wrote a check for ten thousand dollars, so I could set up the Jellied Carp Foundation.

I immediately transferred the ten thousand dollars to my own account, and paid off part of my debt to American Express. VISA would just have to wait.

At a cheap print shop, I had stationery made with a Jellied Carp Foundation letterhead and "Robert G. Mehlman, Chairman" printed on it. Mrs. Fischer was ecstatic about the stationery, and the foundation: in me she saw the grandson she'd always wanted. She introduced me to her neighbors and bridge partners, and one evening I even had to accompany her to the movies. Rebecca understood. She had seen the check for ten thousand dollars in my hand, and she was wise enough to realize that jealousy would have to be put aside temporarily for the sake of ten thousand dollars, and for who knows what would follow once the Jellied Carp Foundation had truly taken root in Mrs. Fischer's mind.

Mrs. Fischer told me everything, about her boat trip to America as a child, about her father's travel agency, about her husband's cement factory, about her miscarriages, her daughters.

Sometimes she insisted on cooking something so I could experience how certain dishes were supposed to taste, but I tried to avoid that whenever possible. There was no time for tasting; there was a cookbook to be written.

I seasoned her recipes with her spiciest anecdotes, and after spending an hour or two each evening typing out that day's notes, I would drop onto the bed a satisfied man.

Late in the evening I would call the fairytale princess and bring her up to date on the progress I was making, particularly in a financial sense. The fact that said progress was directly connected to the Jellied Carp Foundation was something I nimbly avoided mentioning. It didn't seem to me that the fairytale princess's ability to get a good night's sleep would be aided much by the Jellied Carp Foundation.

*

Mrs. Fischer had told me, "If you stay at Motel Silver Lake for longer than a week, be sure to negotiate a discount."

I negotiated a discount.

The days kept getting warmer. Rebecca used my deodorant. The fairytale princess had always used my deodorant too. And so it happened that Rebecca and the fairytale princess began smelling like each other.

Rebecca believed that she loved me, at least that's what she said, sometimes she even whispered it in my ear. And I had gradually come to believe that I loved Rebecca, without directly attaching to that any consequences for the future. A fire fueled by what may be remains a roaring fire.

The days grew longer, Rebecca's skirts got shorter, the sex kept getting better, and the cookbook kept getting fatter.

*

Now the time has come for me to talk about happiness. It's not something I like doing, because there's so little to say about happiness. During those three weeks at Motel Silver Lake, I was happy. At least, that's what I think now. Maybe happiness is the blocking out of certain brain cells; when certain brain cells have been silenced, you're happy.

We ate a lot of mashed potatoes. Mashed potatoes and happiness, therefore, are not mutually exclusive.

Actually, what we were doing was impossible, but we had removed reality to a safe distance.

It seemed to me that I had finally succeeded in leaving the fairytale princess. All right, I still called her once a day, sometimes twice, and Rebecca would say, "Why do you call your wife all the time?" but it seemed normal to me to call one's wife on a regular basis, even if it was all over between you. I had, after all, responsibilities of a financial nature.

The phone calls with the fairytale princess were marked by the occasional difficulty.

"What are you doing with that woman in that motel in Yonkers?" she might ask suddenly, for example, while we'd just been talking about Citibank and the term "deferred payment" had barely crossed my lips. Deferred payment, the mantra for the sceptical man with a taste for meditation nonetheless.

"I'm writing a cookbook."

"But you don't need that woman around to do that, she knows as little about cooking as you do, right?"

"Okay, but she's good at shorthand."

"Do you plan to spend the rest of your life with her?"

The rest of my life, a thorny question. I didn't think so, who would I want to spend the rest of my life with? What I especially wanted was not to think about the rest of my life, and to strike the term "deferred payment" from my vocabulary.

About the Jellied Carp Foundation I had as yet told the fairytale princess nothing. I was afraid tears might come to her eyes, and that she might even go running to Mrs. Fischer to protect her from any further skulduggery, from the brute I had made of myself.

But of course there had always been difficult moments, even long before I had begun my retreat from the life of the fairytale princess. So in fact nothing had changed, and some of the phone calls were actually quite jovial. The suicide epidemic wasn't over yet, but then it probably never would be. It went with a certain brand of employment, and as long as it didn't involve patients with whom the fairytale princess had a special bond, it was something she could live with.

Every once in a while I called my German publisher to let him know that the cookbook was progressing at a remarkable rate.

One evening, after Mrs. Fischer had made *tschulent* for us and afterwards produced a bottle of slivovitz from behind the bookcase, I was able to convince her that the Jellied Carp Foundation needed more money to continue her salutary work and to preserve the memory of her mother, the late Mrs. Fischer (née Feinstein).

I had won Mrs. Fischer's confidence, and after we had knocked back a third of the slivovitz she wrote out another check for ten thousand dollars.

This, therefore, was the form my happiness took: Motel Silver Lake, a typewriter, Rebecca, a bed, Mrs. Fischer, the Jellied Carp Foundation, and mashed potatoes. Rebecca truly believed that we loved each other, if not for all time, then at least in the present tense of Motel Silver Lake.

One evening I asked Rebecca, "I bought a pair of pants, but they're too long. Could you sew up the hems for me?"

She looked at me in amazement.

"I don't have the money to pay a tailor," I said.

"Okay," she said, "give them here."

I typed out a few recipes and wrote about Mrs. Fischer's wondrous life's journey. About her youth in Breslau, her trip to America, about her father who had begun a travel agency without speaking a word of English. About her husband, who had owned a cement factory. And about how, after her husband had died, she discovered that in a former life she had been an Indian. And of course about her mother, who could never get used to America and who lived in the kitchen amid recipes she'd typed out herself, amid disintegrating cookbooks and slowly rising dough.

There was nothing that harkened to the style of my other works, I exceeded my own bounds. There was no aggression, no hauteur, only a cookbook in which the good powers—Mrs. Feinstein's recipes—won out, and the evil and dark forces slowly ebbed away. This cookbook, as the publisher would later write in the blurb, was a song of praise to life, without the author ever closing his eyes to the horrors of this world.

It was written in a way that made even intelligent and sceptical readers wonder whether perhaps, in Mrs. Fischer's head, there wasn't actually an Indian standing by her.

*

I called the fairytale princess, who told me that all the checks she'd written had bounced. All the accounts were overwritten.

"Don't write any more checks," I said. "Pay everything in cash. I'll send you a money order."

In turn, the fairytale princess sent to the motel in Yonkers all the mail she thought might be urgent.

A few vague acquaintances who knew what I was up to said I was crazy. But I simply stopped calling or writing them, so they could no longer disturb me with their good advice.

David, who had received my number from the fairytale princess, called up and, before I could say anything, shouted, "Did you get in contact with my family in Albany?"

"No, of course not," I said.

"We're worried. What are you doing, Robert, if I may ask?"

"Who's 'we,' David? Have you been in contact with Van der Kamp?"

"Who's Van der Kamp?"

"My editor, in Amsterdam. Have you been in contact with him? Have I told you that they didn't even want me to show up at their New Year's reception? They sent me an invitation in March for a reception that was held on January 8, you know what I mean?"

"The only person I've talked to is your mother."

"She's against me, too. She always wanted me to become a tennis player."

Rebecca was sitting on the bed, taking up my trousers. She'd been working on them for three days. The trousers seemed to be ruined.

"David, you're the one who told me I was past my prime. I didn't want to believe that then, but now I do. So all I'm doing now is drawing my consequences from the truth."

"What truth? What are you doing?"

"Just leave it," I said to Rebecca. "Those pants are shot anyway."

It was hot, I had to wipe the sweat from my forehead. With one hand I tried to open the window a bit further, but it wouldn't go.

"I'm working on a cookbook, and to tell you the truth, it's almost finished."

"You're squandering your talent, Robert."

I heard David's dog. He liked dogs, when he let his dog out he made contact with other people. He'd met almost all his girlfriends through that dog.

"If I've squandered it, then that happened a long time ago."

"I've always had faith in you, Robert, but I can see that was a mistake."

A remarkable sense of calm came over me. David was a rhetorician, and I was a cookbook writer; there was no longer any reason for us to compete. The competition was finally over.

"What did you write to me once?" I said. "That, in your humble opinion, I had no idea how to live, but that I had succeeded in giving sublime expression to that approach to life?"

"You need to see a doctor."

I heard his dog bark again, and I suddenly remembered that I'd once sent him some presents for the dog.

I had a deep longing to lie down beside Rebecca and hold her tight. And I wanted to believe that I loved her and that the cookbook would work out and that I would become monogamous and happy. Maybe at that moment I didn't have any choice. If I didn't love her at that moment, who did I love? And if I didn't believe that I loved her, in who or what could I believe?

I hung up.

"Are you really past your prime?" Rebecca asked. She was sitting on the bed with trousers, needle and thread.

"Oh yeah," I said, "and how. Those trousers are ruined, aren't they?"

She nodded.

I lay down on the bed beside her. Mrs. Fischer was expecting us for dinner in thirty minutes. Thirty minutes, that was an eternity.

We'd fallen into a hole in the world, Rebecca and I. That the hole was located in drab Yonkers, less than half an hour from Manhattan, did nothing to change that fact. It was a hole in the world.

*

We sat by the open windows in Mrs. Fischer's living room and drank sparkling wine to celebrate the cookbook's completion.

Of Mrs. Fischer's hundreds of recipes, I selected the most important. A few times I'd asked Mrs. Fischer, "These two recipes look a bit alike, which one do you think is the most important?" She always had to think about that for a long time.

Mrs. Fischer received a word of thanks in the foreword and in the acknowledgments, and her mother's maiden name was mentioned twice. She squeezed my hand when she saw her mother's maiden name in the acknowledgments. Sentiment is such a superb lubricant.

Mrs. Fischer was so touched that she baked cookies for us, then wrote out another ten thousand dollar check for the Jellied Carp Foundation.

My debt at American Express slowly dwindled, and I kept the fairytale princess well informed of the weekly recompense I paid our creditors.

Sometimes she would ask, "Where's all this money coming from all of a sudden?" And I would reply, "I'm a creative person, re-member? You're married to a creative person, and those are diffi-cult people, but they're also people who can bring about miracles. I've made money out of air, I turn white paper into cookbooks, reality into illusion, and my own life into a vale of tears—that's what creating is all about."

"You're a mad old fool," she said.

"I'm not that old, middle age is still sneaking up on me."

"You're a mad old fool," she said, "take that from me. Is that woman still there?"

"Yes," I said, "she's still here. How's it going with the marionette theater for the deaf and dumb?"

*

Mrs. Fischer's dress was even more girlish than the day we'd met. On her way to the grave, Mrs. Fischer had suddenly been touched by a gust of life and youthfulness. That the gust originated from my mouth was an unfortunate coincidence, but it remained a gust of life and youthfulness.

"Your breath is like a flower shop," Josef Capano had said to me once. "Blow in my face again."

One evening Capano had said to me, "Sorry, don't move, you've got something there."

With his fingernail he removed a piece of food from between my front teeth, then put it in his own mouth. I boxed his ears.

"Capano," I said, "that was the first time, and the last, that you ever take things out of my mouth and put them in your own. There are limits, okay? Especially when there are other people around."

But Capano knew no limits. Capano was beyond every limit.

"Robert Mehlman," Mrs. Fischer said, "you've done something wonderful for me. I'm so happy I responded to your ad."

"Oh, it's nothing," I said. "I'm happy, the Jellied Carp Foundation is happy, and that's sort of our offspring."

"He's such a wonderful man," she told Rebecca, and Rebecca blushed.

The next day I called my German publisher.

"The cookbook is coming," I said. "It's on its way, special delivery. So I'd appreciate it if you'd deposit the second half of the advance in one of my accounts."

"I knew you could do it," Stephan said. "No better medicine than a rigorous deadline."

The rigorous deadline as medicine, that sounded awfully familiar, but maybe you had to be German to formulate it that way.

"Yes, that's true," I agreed. "Working really does help."

I suddenly thought of my father. He had worked too. His work had finally resulted in his crossing the tennis court on a sunny day in June and, before the eyes of a few hundred people, biting his opponent in the calf. That's working too, of course, but probably not the kind that helps.

"Congratulations," Stephan said, "congratulations. I'm sure it's going to be a very fine book indeed."

"Me too," I said, without being sure of anything.

Then I called the fairytale princess.

"The cookbook is finished," I said.

She wished me luck. I inquired, as always, about her financial situation, and she replied, as always, that money was the least of her worries.

"I can do without money," she said.

"No one can do without money," I replied. "No one."

"Are you coming home now? Or are you staying with that Empty Vessel?"

"What makes you think she's an empty vessel?"

"That's what I think. Everything you've told me about that woman points to the fact that she's an Empty Vessel."

"She's not an empty vessel at all. She's a young woman who seems not to function, but she's not an empty vessel."

"Are you coming home?"

"Not yet."

"And what about me? How am I supposed to have a child?"

"What do you mean?"

"How am I supposed to have a child? Before long, it will be too late."

"How should I know how you're supposed to have a child? By making one."

"With whom?"

"How should I know with whom? Do I look like the foreman at the baby factory? Am I in charge of child distribution? It's up to you with whom."

"So you're not coming home?"

"I don't know," I said, "I don't know."

I hate you, because I miss you, that's what I wanted to say. And I didn't even know who I was missing. Did I miss the fairytale princess, did I miss Rebecca, did I miss Evelyn? I didn't know. I only knew that I missed. That was what I did, that was the activity in which I was engaged, missing, and at that moment it seemed like there was no way to get around that missing. Not now, not in the past, and definitely not in the future. There would only be more of it, until it hung around me like a kind of mist, an impenetrable mist. When I walked down the street in that mist to the cigar store, children would say to their parents, "I just saw a cloud walking by. That's impossible, isn't it?" And parents would say, "Oh, that's just Robert G. Mehlman, the cookbook writer."

When you miss someone, you start hating that person, to make the missing stop. When you miss someone, they have to be rubbed out, vanquished, destroyed. Hate is the sea into which all missing comes flowing down. It was the sea in which I swam, but the current had taken me out a bit far.

"Are you still there?" the fairytale princess asked.

A pudgy man walked by, looking for his room. He was carrying a cooler.

I was losing control. I had to concentrate on my breathing, on how I formulated things, on my choice of words, on rhythm. When you're busy finding the right formulation you've got everything under control, and I wanted to have everything, or at least myself, under control. I was afraid I was going to start crying and not be able to stop.

"I'll call you soon," I said to the fairytale princess. "Do you still have enough money?"

"You already asked that," she said.

In the room upstairs at Motel Silver Lake, Rebecca was waiting, but I longed for a brothel. Any brothel would do. It didn't have to be attractive, or even particularly clean. The brothel was the temple of missing, the prostitute the high priestess of missing, and sex the burnt offering sacrificed to our god: the eternal, the omnipotent, the always-silent god of missing. The brothel was the only temple where a respectable person could still show his face, the prostitute the only high priestess I acknowledged, and sex the only offering the god of missing could desire from us.

"I'll call you," I told the fairytale princess. Then I hung up, but I didn't go upstairs, I went to the men's room at Motel Silver Lake and locked myself in. I sat down on the floor. For a moment there I cried, but it didn't last long. Then I looked for a way to formulate what had just happened. I searched for words to help me regain control over my shaking body, to become human again, someone who could show his face among humans.

If I could have swallowed sixty sleeping pills at that moment, I would have been all too pleased to do so, then drink a bottle of champagne and take another sixty sleeping pills, because I despise failures. It was an exam I wanted to pass the first time around. But there were no sleeping pills. And once I'd found words for those sleeping pills, I didn't need to take them.

The survival strategy I had designed, executed and perfected was a success, such a success that I'd made myself redundant. The misstep on the twentieth floor of the high-rise apartment building was optional. I could take it, but I could also leave it, I could leave it up to chance, it was all the same.

I had contracted out everything: the doing of the dishes, the cooking, cleaning windows, shopping, answering phone calls, making hotel reservations—now I'd reached the point where I was about to contract out my own life. I had propagated the interchangeability of people, and I had acted in line with that interchangeability as well, in order to trick the god of missing, and now I'd become interchangeable for myself. Operation Survival had been a success, life a candied praline alongside the coffee. You could simply skip it, if you no longer had the appetite.

I went upstairs. There was a note from Rebecca: "Your mother called. It's urgent. I've gone to buy cigarettes."

I called my mother in Amsterdam.

"Mama," I said.

"I've been looking all over for you. I was so worried. David called me. He told me everything. So you finally left your wife. It was about time, she was no good for you. She never appreciated you, she was too old for you and she had a face like a dog. What's more, if you ask me, she's infertile. I have an eye for that, I can pick an infertile woman out of a crowd. That wife of yours was infertile. It doesn't matter to me who you bring home, as long as she's young and fertile."

"Mama," I butted in, "I've just left temporarily, no one knows what's going to happen. I'm working on a cookbook."

"You can bring home anyone you like, even twenty of them at a time. As long as they're young and fertile."

"I'll talk to you later, Mama," I said, "I have to go now."

"Don't hang up," she said, "don't hang up. If you don't give me a grandchild before I die, I'll disinherit you. Do you hear me?"

I sat down on the bed and waited. I don't know how long I sat there before Rebecca finally came back.

"Where were you?" she asked.

"Making phone calls," I said. "And you, where have you been all this time?"

She threw a pack of cigarettes down on the bed.

We talked about the weather, about dinner, about this and that. Suddenly Rebecca said, "I want to saw my head off."

"Why would you want to do that?"

"Everything in my head drives me crazy, all these thoughts."

"Wait awhile before you start sawing," I said. "It's not something Mata Hari would do."

She grabbed my head in both hands and asked, "I'm your woman, aren't I?"

It was as though my memory had been given a swift, well-aimed punch in the stomach. The punch was so well aimed that my memory doubled over and could do nothing but puke. The last bits of gall came out.

*

It was that evening that I'd said I had an appointment with my French editor, Mastroianni. The evening that I actually had another date with Evelyn, after our romance had experienced a brief intermission. The evening I should actually have been in a jazz club with the fairytale princess.

Evelyn and I had agreed to meet in the bar of a big hotel, a bar where I never went with the fairytale princess, a bar where I never would have taken her. A bar where we could talk quietly and have a few drinks.

Josef Capano had arranged a limo and a good, romantic restaurant. There was nothing to get in the way of an enjoyable evening. Maybe even, if the alcohol, the chitchat and the god of missing did their best, an extremely enjoyable evening. A bit wistful, but not so badly that it had to hurt.

She'd had her hair done, and her nails, the toenails too, because she was wearing sandals. I saw her every day except Sunday, so I could tell exactly when she'd had her hair done. She looked very pretty that evening. Too pretty. I should have been on my guard.

"How's your wife?" she asked. She always asked that. Before fucking, before getting dressed, before getting undressed. And I would always reply, "Good, very good, thanks."

A few days earlier she'd written me a note in her childlike hand and slid it across the counter. It said there was something she wanted to talk to me about. When she saw that I'd read it, she took it back and tore it into tiny pieces.

My wife was reading the newspaper and didn't notice a thing.

Now, with Evelyn sitting across from me in that hotel bar full of men in suits, we didn't talk about that note, or about the pause in our romance; we talked about her work, the quality of the cappuccinos, the boss's problems. Friendly little bits of gossip that cheered us both and put us in the mood to drink even more. It always took a while before I could make Evelyn laugh, but when we hadn't seen each other outside the four walls of the coffeehouse for a while, it always took a lot longer.

Around seven o'clock I said, "It's about time we went to the restaurant."

We walked to the exit, through a crowd of men who all had the same haberdasher. She was carrying a purse, a new purse I saw. From the purse she took a pack of chewing gum. "Like one?" she asked.

My kisses taste like apple chewing gum, which is the secret of my success.

"Take my arm," she said.

I took her arm.

Outside, the car was waiting. The driver was a woman. I gave her the name of the restaurant, and then Evelyn and I started kissing as though our romance had never been on hold, as if she hadn't made dozens of cappuccinos for my wife and me in the meantime. As if a couple of drinks, a bit of gossip, a few jokes, a few sly glances, a leg tossed over another leg, a hand that stayed resting on a shoulder for a moment, were all enough to put us back in the mood we'd started in once, long ago.

We went to a restaurant with a nice view, not far from Columbia University. I'd never been there with the fairytale princess, and would never go there with the fairytale princess. It's important to keep things separate.

They showed us to a table by the window, and Evelyn said, "I don't feel like eating."

"Yes you do," I said, "just eat something."

"But then you order, something simple, something with chicken."

I ordered something simple with chicken. And to the waiter I added, "And I'll have the same."

I asked about her children. We kept moving closer to each other, and we kept eating less chicken.

The dessert consisted of watery fruit salad, and I ate a few grapes from her mouth. Red grapes with seeds I swallowed. Not lust, not love, but hunger is blind.

"So how's the bus driver?" I asked.

"Oh," she said, and pushed another grape into my mouth with her tongue, "I left him."

"What do you mean, left him?"

"I walked out on him."

The grape seeds in my throat popped up into my mouth. I tongued them back into the corner of one cheek.

It was a lovely evening, clear as a bell, a perfect evening for a good view.

"Jesus," I said, "that's a surprise," and now she pushed a piece of banana into my mouth.

Hunger was blind and insatiable, but blindness and insatiability may be prime conditions for survival.

"Why so sudden?" I asked.

She stopped transferring fruit from her mouth to mine.

"I didn't exist for him," she said. "I cooked for him, I paid the rent, half the payments on the jeep, I ironed, I cleaned the house, I took care of his children, but that wasn't enough, I didn't exist for him. Don't get me wrong, he's the father of my children and I'll respect him for as long as I live. And I hope nothing bad ever happens to him, but I didn't exist for him."

She pushed half a strawberry into my mouth with her tongue.

Did she exist for me? Did I want her to exist for me? Who actually *did* exist for me? I felt a pressing need to change the subject, to stop talking about the bus driver, about existing for someone or not. But what subject was left?

"Where are you living now?"

"I'm staying with my sister, temporarily."

"Oh." I thought about money; behind all the pomp and circumstance, presents, tenderness and wedding parties, piles of banknotes rose up before my eyes. I walked past walls of banknotes, in search of a justice of the peace, largely worthless banknotes from countries that no longer existed.

We kissed; when you're a bit tipsy, blouses are no longer an obstacle to hands.

Insatiable and furious was my hunger, out of impotence, out of desperation, the shame, the fear, the disgust.

I remembered how, back when we'd first met, she had once said, "Why are you interested in me? Why are you interested in someone who makes cappuccino in a coffeehouse?"

"Why not?"

She'd hesitated. "According to the owner," she said, "you don't even see me. According to him you're a different kind of person. You can come and go whenever you please, you do whatever you want, you live on Park Avenue. He thinks I don't even exist for you."

"And what did you tell him?"

"That I thought that was ridiculous. He's obsessed with money, see? I told him, 'Frankie, there's more than money; there's love, happiness, friendship, family, children.' But he says, 'I've had all that, I don't need that any more.'"

That was a long time ago, back before we discovered the restroom at the coffeehouse and made it our temple, before we'd gone picking blackberries, before she'd given me little names, when everything was still in front of us.

Now we were sitting in a restaurant high above the city and fruit was passing from mouth to mouth, the way banknotes pass from hand to hand.

"Excuse me," I said, "I have to go to the toilet."

In front of the mirror I wiped the lipstick off my teeth.

One time, just after we'd finished picking blackberries, she'd hit her oldest son right in the mouth. His lip had bled. He'd been talking back to his mother.

"Don't do that," I said, "not when I'm around." The hypocrite, the protector of children.

"He has to show me respect," she'd said, "when you're around."

It occurred to me that I could take the fire escape now, that she'd never see me, she'd never know where to find me, but my escape routes didn't follow fire escapes, my escape routes followed words and what inevitably comes of those words.

Besides, there was the hunger, the hunger to forget, the hunger for narcosis, which in the long run is all the same hunger. Hunger to finally live in the present, no longer with one foot in the steaming wistfulness of a past that never existed, the other in some fanciful construct of a future that never will exist.

I went back.

"And what about your kids?" I asked.

"The oldest one already misses his father," she said. "'Where's Daddy?' he asks me. It breaks my heart, but I don't exist for him anymore."

"I'm going to Europe soon," I said. "A long trip, to promote my books."

That clarified a lot. Don't count on me, that sentence said. Never count on me. And I heard her say again, "He has to show me respect, when you're around."

"I'm going to miss you," she said. "I would have had more time now that I'm not with the bus driver anymore, but that's the way things go."

"Yeah," I said, "that's how it goes."

We kissed again, and it felt like she was biting my lips till they bled, but this seemed to me a suitable evening to have my lips bitten till they bled.

"I have to go to the toilet," I said, "excuse me."

In the men's room I had a sneezing attack. They never seem to be able to adjust the air-conditioning in those places. I felt dizzy, so I freshened up a bit. That was important, freshening yourself up.

Our bill was already on the table. Maybe this restaurant didn't like customers who gave vent to furious hunger, even if they were well-paying customers.

"I'll give you a ride home," I said.

"I live with my sister now," she said, "but it's not so far from my old place."

In the elevator on the way down we tore off half each other's clothes.

*

The chauffeuse was waiting by the car, smoking a cigarette. When she saw us, she put out the cigarette, held the door open and said, "Did you enjoy the restaurant?"

Evelyn gave her directions.

Right before we got to the Brooklyn Bridge, traffic ground to a halt. An accident.

"Shall we just fuck and get it over with?" I asked.

"Yeah," Evelyn said, "let's do that and get it over with."

I closed the black window, so the chauffeuse couldn't see us anymore.

It was a major accident, there were a lot of cars involved.

"I don't have a life," Evelyn said, "but I've got you."

The string of her underpants was pulled up between her ass-cheeks.

We heard a few ambulances going by, fire engines too.

She sat on top of me. The car wasn't moving, so that made it more comfortable.

"You like my hair?" she asked.

"Yeah," I said, "I like it a lot."

"I had it done especially for tonight."

We heard even more sirens.

"There must have been some casualties," I said. I yanked a couple of buttons off her blouse, but she said that was okay.

"Be careful of my glasses," I said. "I don't have spare frames."

A helicopter came over, flying low. The badly wounded on their way to the hospital.

"You know what I want?" she asked.

"Wait a minute," I said. I got up, tripped over something, looked around for a safe place for my glasses, then finally put them in the refrigerator, on top of the ice cubes. A good place for glasses. Then I stumbled back to the seat. My hand slid over her sweaty back, I thought about her children, about the drunkenness that seemed to be gradually taking over my whole body. More helicopters came over low.

"I want to take off your shoes," she said.

"Don't you miss the bus driver?" I asked. "Now that you're living with your sister?"

She didn't bother to untie the laces. She yanked them off, I could hear leather cracking. She pulled off my pants, I heard cotton ripping. She pulled off my underpants, elastic snapped.

The drunkenness had now reached my knees and was slowly descending. It made the hunger worse, the way wind makes the freezing cold worse.

I ran my hands, sticky with sweat, through her new hairdo.

"Don't do anything," she said. "I want to do everything."

She had long nails, very long nails, that she'd had manicured especially for this evening.

I heard more sirens and Evelyn's voice saying, "Don't be afraid, I won't leave marks." But I wasn't afraid of marks. What did I care about marks? My whole life had left no marks, no real ones, it only existed in my head.

Leave marks, I felt like saying, leave lots of marks, make of my body a minefield. But my thing was already in her mouth and heli-copters kept buzzing over and far, far away someone screamed for water.

I remembered how she'd once told me that she was so tight the bus driver sometimes couldn't penetrate her. But she'd also said the bus driver didn't like foreplay, because he spent the whole day in that bus.

"I want to ride you," she whispered.

Of course, the human-trainer had now become a horse himself.

The sirens moved away, the helicopters moved away too. Only Evelyn was there and me and her fat thighs and the sweat between her buttocks and my hands and that she was so tight that sometimes the bus driver couldn't penetrate her and then gave it up and went off to drink beer with his friends.

She climbed off me.

"Now you take me," she said.

I pushed her to the floor. Or else she fell to the floor. Maybe we both fell to the floor. The filthy floor of the limousine where people had puked, where liquor had been spilled, where it was sticky with unidentified substances.

I turned her over. You're so pretty, I wanted to say, why the hell do you have to be so pretty tonight, of all nights, but instead I said, "Your cappuccinos are getting worse all the time, did you know that? I think before long I'm going to start asking Sonya to make them for me."

"How can anyone not love you?" she said.

I saw two mosquito bites on her buns, I pulled her hair and then I held her buns tight. Her buns which she'd said were too fat, but she'd given up the fight. I pushed them apart, saw minuscule pieces of toilet paper no bigger than cookie crumbs, no more than tiny white dots on a canvas of flesh.

Why did she scream like that? Or were those the badly wounded outside who were still screaming? Do you scream before you die? And if you don't scream, how must you then die? Maybe Josef Capano knew, he thought a lot about death, he saw death everywhere, in every cookie, every cocktail, on every street corner. Noises flowed into each other like memories.

"You come so pretty," Evelyn said.

"What do you mean?"

"Your face is so pretty when you come."

"Thank you," I said, "thank you. But you mustn't keep an eye on me like that."

Outside I heard someone shouting, "Keep moving! Keep moving! Keep moving!"

We were crawling along. I opened the window. A truck driver in the lane next to us leaned out his window and held up five fingers.

"Five!" he yelled.

"What?" I yelled back.

"Five dead," the truck driver shouted.

I closed the window.

Evelyn was sitting on the other seat. She was looking in a little mirror. She was tidying up.

"You sure fucked me hard," she said.

I said, "I'm sorry, was it nice?"

"Yeah," she said, "real nice."

"And dinner, you liked that too, didn't you?"

She nodded.

She'd been married twice and then she'd met me. She hadn't had any other men, she said, because she respected the man she loved and there were a lot of diseases out there. When she said that, she pointed out at the street, as if the people walking around were diseases.

We started getting dressed again. As well as you can in a moving limousine.

Evelyn pinned her blouse closed with two safety pins. "I come prepared," she said.

We lay in each other's arms, half undressed.

When we got close to her sister's house, I opened the window so the chauffeuse could see us again.

"Quite some accident, wasn't it?" I said.

"Yeah," the chauffeuse said.

And Evelyn said, "Here, have some chewing gum."

Seduction was the foreplay to missing. The person who got no further than seduction was like the writer who writes ten pages of a book, ten brilliant pages, and then starts on another book and writes ten pages of that. The writer writes the beginning of dozens, maybe even hundreds of books, but never more than the beginning, because after that it could become too painful. Maybe I was a writer who didn't want to know how his own books turned out.

"Right here," Evelyn said to the chauffeuse.

I pulled on my pants.

"This is where I live now," Evelyn said, "and that's my car, see it?"

"Yes," I said, "I see it."

I climbed out first. I hadn't put my shoes back on, I was standing barefoot on asphalt that was still warm and moist from the day.

"Thanks for a lovely evening," I said and kissed her once, quickly, on her lips, which tasted of apple chewing gum, just like mine.

When I got home, the fairytale princess still wasn't there. There was a letter on the fridge saying she might be back late. She hoped I'd had a fruitful evening with my French editor, Mastroianni.

I sat down at my desk. I would tell the fairytale princess that Mr. Mastroianni was a tall, funny man with brown hair slicked back, that he'd been born in Marseilles but had lived in Paris for the last five or six years. He had a wife and two cats, his wife did something in fashion.

I thought I should write a story about Evelyn. The best way to forget people is to write about them.

I poured myself a drink and decided to go to bed. When the fairytale princess was having fun, she forgot all about the time. Then the telephone rang. I didn't pick it up. I never pick it up. On the answering machine, I heard Evelyn leave a message, I turned off the sound, stood beside the telephone and drank a glass of calvados.

In a complete breach of custom, she was calling me at home. She'd always had my number, but she said she'd never call me at home. Until now, she had always abided by agreements like that, by the rules of the theater of false hope. It had to be something serious.

She called six more times, I stood beside the phone and didn't answer. I drank calvados, I heard the phone ring, I saw Evelyn walking through a room with a phone held to her ear, a woman who didn't exist for the bus driver and now no longer existed for me, and I didn't have to turn on the sound on the answering machine to hear her say, "Pick it up, if you're home, pick it up, come on, pick it up if you're home." This was what life looked like as it slipped through your fingers.

If everything that took place between people was a set of negotiations over an empty suitcase, negotiations that went on and on in order to keep loneliness at bay, then this was the final card you could play: "Let's negotiate how we no longer exist for each other, let's negotiate our own mutual liquidation."

When she finally stopped calling, I erased all the messages without listening to them, drank two more glasses of calvados and went to bed.

At three o'clock the fairytale princess came home. She was tipsy and cheerful.

"It's hot," I said, "don't touch me. I'm suffocating. Don't you feel the heat?"

"How was Mastroianni?" she asked.

"A very funny man," I said. "I'll tell you about it in the morning."

The next day Evelyn wasn't at the coffeehouse. Not the day after that either. A few days later, when I was in there alone, I asked the owner, "What happened to Evelyn?"

"Oh," he said, "she's gone, she's not coming back."

A few weeks later the fairytale princess asked, "Where's that girl who always made such good cappuccinos?"

"Girl?" I said. "That was no girl, that was a woman. She has two children."

"Anyway, she made really good cappuccinos."

"She probably found something better. That's how it goes."

"You didn't do anything with her, did you?"

"What do you mean?" I snapped.

"Just kidding. Jesus, man! You make jokes like that all the time. Where's your sense of humor?"

I worked on a story about Evelyn, but I couldn't find the right tone. And because I couldn't find the right tone and because the story was never finished, I couldn't forget Evelyn either.

Weeks went by. Occasionally one of the patients attempted suicide, occasionally an attempt was successful. One patient pushed someone in front of the subway. According to the fairytale princess, some patients committed crimes because they actually wanted to harm themselves, but didn't dare.

There was a conference in Boston, I went along. The fairytale princess attended the conference, I walked through the city.

During dinner that evening, I told Princess Fairytale that I was working on a story about the woman who had always made such good cappuccinos.

"Oh," she said, "that girl."

"Yes," I said, "that woman."

"I talked to her a couple of times, there was something strange about her."

"Why do you think that?" I asked.

She pulled a bone out of her mouth, she was having lamb. "I don't know," she said. "Intuition. That's not a story, that's a patient."

"Oh, will you cut it out!" I shouted. "Just cut it out. You see patients behind every tree, to hear you tell it the whole world is a patient. Why don't you stop healing people? They can't be helped anyway. Go do something useful, raise asparagus or save red ants from extinction or something."

"Don't get so aggressive," the fairytale princess said. "Did you ever talk to that girl?"

"Not very often," I said. "A few times, fleeting conversations."

"Didn't you ever notice anything about her?"

"No," I said, "never."

"But she did make great cappuccinos," said the fairytale princess.

"That's true," I said, "she made wonderful cappuccinos. Wait a minute, I have to pee, I'll be right back."

I held my wrists under the cold tap. It wasn't the first time I'd found myself in a hotel where the walls were all papered with drawings of dachshunds, but it was the first time I'd heard a voice along with it that said, "That's not a story, that's a patient."

The fairytale princess was nibbling happily on her lamb when I sat down beside her again.

"Let's go back to the room," I said. "I'm tired."

The seasons followed each other rapidly, the credit card companies extended me more and more credit, and the story about Evelyn was never finished.

*

When I had finally succeeded in hushing up my memory, at least for the time being, Rebecca was still sitting beside me, there in the room at Motel Silver Lake. I said, "Yes, you're my woman."

In the stories I'd been writing in my mind for days, Rebecca was the one who ultimately lost her grip and went crazy, in order to have at least one thing to grip, that which is diagnosed as one's illness. But I was the one.

"That's good," Rebecca said. And I replied, "We have to go to Mrs. Fischer pretty soon, she's expecting us for dinner."

This then was our happiness: a brief adventure. Of which, looking back on it, the brevity seems more persistently real than the adventure itself, as though the brevity is the thing that sinks its claws into you.

*

What remains is the afterplay.

We spent one more week in Yonkers. I wheedled another fifteen thousand dollars out of Mrs. Fischer for the Jellied Carp Foundation, then Rebecca went back to Amsterdam and I returned to Manhattan, to the fairytale princess.

I worked on a new book that wasn't going anywhere, Rebecca and I met three times in the Bahamas. The fairytale princess knew about it but she didn't leave me, and I didn't leave either—the negotiations about how to disappear from each other's lives had apparently not yet come to a close.

Six months later, in Germany, my cookbook came out: *Polish-Jewish Cuisine in 69 Recipes*, with a word of thanks to Mrs. Fischer.

As subtitle, the publisher had come up with: *Cooking After Auschwitz*.

*

Apparently, after Auschwitz the time was finally ripe to get in there and truly enjoy cooking, because the first edition in a run of ten thousand was sold out within two weeks. Favorable reviews appeared in a number of papers, and a leading German magazine even opened its cultural supplement with a piece on *Polish-Jewish Cuisine in 69 Recipes*. Under the heading "Keep the Home Fires Burning," my book was praised to the skies in a way that none of my other books ever had been.

"This Robert G. Mehlman," the critic wrote, "has succeeded at what no one before him has ever been able to do. He has brought about something we have been waiting for desperately for decades: reconciliation. It is to the credit of Mehlman's genius that he has seen that reconciliation cannot take place in the literary salon, or on the work floor, or in parliament, or in the theater, or in front of a monument—true reconciliation can only take place in the kitchen. With his extensive knowledge of Polish-Jewish cuisine, with an eye for detail, in a heartrending style generously peppered with that inimitable Jewish humor, Mehlman takes us on an odyssey that is unparalleled. [. . .] This book rises above the genre of the cookbook: as far as I am concerned, it is the most important book of the year, perhaps of the decade.

"We needed a Mehlman to show us that Jews and Germans can truly meet in the Polish-Jewish kitchen, where, despite the atrocities of the past, the home fires are still burning."

Within five days after the publication of this review, and another wildly favorable one on TV, one hundred thousand copies had been sold. The chancellor's wife stated that she was going to prepare meals using my cookbook. The German publisher called me every other day to say that he had never witnessed such a success. The money came pouring in. The letters of warning from the credit card companies ceased. I was invited to go to Germany. The chairman of the board of the German central bank offered me twenty-thousand marks if I would speak to him and his fellow top managers for an hour. I flew to Germany and read in packed theaters. Nowhere was any mention made of my literary work. Every once in a while, during an interview, I would try to talk about my novels, my short stories, my books of poetry, but the interviewer would quickly say, "No need to talk about that, Mr. Mehlman, that's all behind you now!"

After a while I stopped trying. I was Mehlman, the writer of cookbooks, the great reconciler, the healer, the redeemer. And the money poured in.

Rebecca traveled with me from Hamburg to Munich, from Munich to Cologne, from Cologne to Frankfurt, from Frankfurt to Berlin. Although there wasn't a drop of Jewish blood in her veins, the press, probably due to her appearance, referred to her constantly as "Mehlman's Jewish bride." And a few times journalists had approached me in the following way: "Mr. Mehlman, could I ask you, as a prominent Jew, the following question?"

I was still calling the fairytale princess three times a day, but the negotiations were still in progress.

The president of Austria invited me to cook one of the recipes from my book for him. An embarrassing situation, but one which I wriggled out of by having an Austrian chef do the cooking. During the dinner at his palace, the Austrian president said, "You are the first Jew I have ever seen who laughs." By the time dessert came around he was so drunk that he said, "Because you are the first Jew I have ever seen who laughs, I would like to give you a medal." Which is how I received an official Austrian decoration.

I sent a telegram to Mrs. Fischer to tell her about the book's success. By that time we had hit 250,000 copies, and the book was being translated worldwide.

I received an enthusiastic call from Frederik van der Kamp: "We're going to push your cookbook in a big way here in the

Netherlands." But I said, "It's not yours to push, van der Kamp. You're not getting it, it's going to the competition. You people didn't even want me to come to your New Year's reception."

The hostess of a major American talk show made *Polish-Jewish Cuisine in 69 Recipes* her book of the month. In front of twelve million viewers she said, "If Auschwitz was the event of the twentieth century, this book may then be the book of the century." *Cooking After Auschwitz* made the bestseller lists in America as well.

In Tokyo a man committed suicide after reading my cookbook.

The German publisher urged me to write a sequel, but there was no sequel. I had stopped writing, writing could do nothing more than awaken the ghosts of the past, and they were just napping so nicely.

When I was on the road I was with Rebecca, but when I was catching my breath in New York, I lived with the fairytale princess again.

Sex was something we'd stopped having long ago, and she'd also stopped asking what I was up to. I in turn didn't pester her by asking whether she had a lover these days and who she was seeing when I wasn't there. Sometimes men called for her, I jotted down their names and telephone numbers and passed the messages along to the fairytale princess without further comment.

We kept on going to dinner at St. Ambroeus as though nothing had happened. Once an old lady came up to me there and asked, "Aren't you the man from the cookbook?"

Sometimes we talked about Rebecca. The fairytale princess said, "I must be crazy, I'm sitting here giving you advice about how to deal with The Empty Vessel. I'm not your relations counselor. I've had it up to here." But she never acted on that.

It was, of course, an abnormal situation, but the money was pouring in, and money makes the abnormal normal.

There were days when the fairytale princess and I talked about divorce, but we never got around to it, it was one of many things we didn't get around to. And the fairytale princess, too, lived well and in comfort.

Life went so quickly that, to my great joy, I didn't have to think much. I played the seer and conciliator as though I'd started believing in the role myself. The aggression and hate that had peopled my first books had made way for a mild humanism. I had become a moral authority. Many were those who wanted my opinion on hotbeds of discontent all over the world, and whatever hotbed it was, on each hotbed I cast my mild humanist light.

A small publishing house came up with *Cooking After Dachau*, but it caused barely a ripple in the press. My cookbook had no real competition.

My mother was proud of me. Although she was still waiting for a grandchild.

*

Rebecca continued to travel with me, from Tokyo to Seoul to Melbourne. What remained of our short-lived happiness was sex, expensive hotels and official receptions. And, on occasion, swimming pools on the twenty-first floor.

That I traveled with a woman not my wife, of course, placed a little taint on my moral authority. But on the other hand, it also gave the cookbook writer and conciliator some added cachet. It made me human. Thanks to my elfin innocence and, cookbook in hand, the quotable humanism I spread around the world, people were prepared to forgive me a great deal.

Occasionally the fire between Rebecca and me would flare up, making it seem as though our days at Motel Silver Lake were about to return. But my quotable and mild humanism banked every fire. I did, however, buy a house in the Bahamas and an apartment in Malta.

There were signs that cracks were about to appear in the clay, that my mask was beginning to break and crumble. But I ignored them.

In Athens I punched a photographer. The incident was muffled away beneath a blanket of money and goodwill. More serious was an incident two weeks later, during a live broadcast for the ZDF, when I suddenly called the extremely amiable hostess a slut and, right in the middle of a successful and moving interview, snapped at her, "Read *268th in the World*. You should be reading that instead of this fucking cookbook!"

My publisher's spokeswoman issued a statement saying I was suffering from a minor depression due to fatigue, and that my comments had been misunderstood.

The mask of conciliator and mild humanist, which had been glued to my face with such professional skill, was now definitely rotting away. No one saw it, and I ignored the process of decomposition, just as I had ignored all processes of decomposition in my life thus far.

*

All this was ultimately followed by a tour of Italy, through Milan, Turin, Trieste, Genoa and Rome—at that time, the paperback edition of the cookbook was the number-one bestselling non-fiction work in Italy. Afterwards, Rebecca and I went to Sicily for a few days to recover from the bustle and the constant book-signing sessions.

But even at our holiday hideout, requests for more readings and cooking demonstrations kept coming in. The rights to *Polish-Jewish Cuisine in 69 Recipes* had now been sold to Iceland as well.

Rebecca and I strolled through the garden of our hotel, sat in the shade on the edge of the pool, had breakfast and dinner on our balcony, and occasionally I went into the bathroom and imagined I was going mad. Rebecca bought a barrette that made her look a few years younger.

Occasionally I referred to our days at Motel Silver Lake, days that became increasingly mythical. Our happiness was a figment, but strangely enough it felt quite tangible and close-by, as though it were only seconds away. That was our happiness on Sicily: a bullet that had missed us by a hair's breadth.

*

I don't remember whose idea it was to go to the opera. They were doing *Wozzeck*. On the outside, the opera house in Palermo had looked so beautiful that Rebecca said, "I bet inside it's even more beautiful."

The doorman at the hotel arranged tickets for us. And asked whether I'd sign a copy of *Polish-Jewish Cuisine in 69 Recipes* for his wife.

We prepared for the opera as though we were going to a big party. Late in the afternoon we took a bath together.

"We're famous," Rebecca said.

"Yes," I said, "that's right."

Then we lay on the bed, the heat coming in through the drawn curtains. Rebecca pointed to a dress hanging over the back of a chair. "Shall I put that on?"

"No," I said, "please don't."

I laid my hands on her body, which I knew almost as well as my own. I kissed her, she kissed me, we talked between kisses, I don't remember what about, I pulled gently on her hair, but I didn't get an erection.

"That can happen," she said. "We fuck six times a day."

"Not to me," I said. "It's never happened to me before."

"Come on," she said. "We have to go to the opera, let's get dressed."

We got dressed. A silent movie was playing in my head. Rebecca and I in the Museum of Natural History, a statuette by a psoriasis patient on the table between us. Evelyn and I in the limo with low-flying helicopters above, me in the all-night deli, waiting for customers, waiting for life.

"Shall I wear my barrette?"

"Do," I said. "And use the red lipstick, it looks good on you."

We walked to the opera house; it was a long walk, but that was all right on such a lovely evening. We had plenty of time.

"What are you thinking about?" Rebecca said. "Not about the erection, I hope?"

"A little bit," I said.

"Come on," she said, "get normal. We fuck six times a day."

"Tell me the truth," I said. "How many men have you made impotent?"

*

We had fantastic seats on the front balcony. We talked about the other people in the audience, because no one could understand us, and Rebecca flipped through the program in search of a summary of the opera.

Ten minutes before show time, I couldn't stand it anymore. "Wait here," I said. "I'll be right back."

I went to the foyer and asked a theater attendant the way to the men's room. He pointed to the right. I found a clean booth and locked myself in. I unzipped my trousers, pulled out my organ and began jerking off. I heard footsteps and men pissing. The men carried on a conversation while they pissed. And I stood there yanking my thing. My body shivered like I was running a fever, a strange fever, tumescent fever. Footsteps moved away, time passed, I jerked off, but nothing happened. I leaned my head against the wall, I panted, but even panting didn't help. I thought about naked women in seductive poses, women I had known, women I hadn't known, except in pictures.

In the distance there was the sound of applause, but it was not for me. The conductor bowed, the lights went down. And I jerked off, but nothing happened. My weenie remained as little and soft as a wee innocent babe.

I heard music. So this was *Wozzeck*. I'd never seen the opera before. Or heard it.

I thought about pornography, about whores, about Rebecca, about the fairytale princess and about Evelyn who made cappuccinos, and the music grew louder. Nothing happened. In the distance I heard footsteps, a theater attendant I thought, and above it all the music.

There was blood on my hands. The skin was torn. I wiped the blood off on the tiles.

My life had come to a halt, here was where it all stopped, in the opera house at Palermo, here my in memoriam could begin.

I kept on jerking. Maybe blood helps. Blood often seems to help. The music was even louder. It was starting to hurt. My life was a seaside village I wanted to run away from, because I knew every paving stone by heart. My weenie was getting smaller and bloodier, everything had been jerked raw. A skinned body part hanging between my legs. I buttoned my trousers. I was shaking like a Parkinson's patient in the terminal phase. I left the men's room. I stopped and leaned against a marble pillar. Then I saw Rebecca, looking for me. She was so beautiful. And lonely. Just like me, and better yet, the blood on my hands made me truly masculine. Truly masculine at last; it had taken a while, I'd had to go to the opera house in Palermo to get it, but there it was.

"Where were you?"

"Jerking off."

"What?"

"I was jerking off, so I'd get an erection."

"Idiot." She tried to hit me, but I sidestepped it. I usually see it coming, the rabbit punch, the bullet of happiness, I see it coming and I dodge out of the way.

"Let's go back to the hotel."

"What's wrong," she said. "Aren't you feeling well? Are you sick?"

"Yes," I said, "I'm sick."

"But what about the opera?"

"Forget it, it's a lousy rendition."

"Don't get all worked up about an erection, we make love all the time."

But an erection was all I was, my whole life was one big bloody erection, I'd finally become what I should always have been. After my first book appeared, I'd received a letter from a reader saying: "He who lives by the dick will die by the dick."

We walked back to the hotel in silence, we stepped right along. What a lovely evening it was, enough to bring tears to your eyes.

*

Back at the room, Rebecca said, "Still, it's a pity about the opera."

We went out onto the balcony together.

"There," I said, "that's the harbor."

"Yes," Rebecca said.

"And there," I said, "that's the city."

"That's right," Rebecca said.

And suddenly it occurred to me that I had never unpacked that statuette from the psoriasis patient, that it had gone to the storage closet unpacked, and suddenly that made me roar with laughter.

"What's so funny?" Rebecca asked.

"Everything," I said, and I showed her the blood on my right hand and I held her tight, and we laughed about my blood and my erections and the opera, although by that point we had both left long ago.

"Do you still want to be Mata Hari?" I asked.

She shook her head. "I'm yours now," she said.

"That's stupid," I said.

The next day I got erections again as though they'd never gone away. According to Rebecca, I jumped onto the bed like the champion of the world.

"Sweet little Rebecca,

"A few days ago you asked me whether I felt the world was at my feet. I haven't felt that for ages. Despite my Austrian medal, the proceeds from Cooking after Auschwitz *and the meetings with numerous top-ranking dignitaries.*

"You do feel that way, apparently, which is fine; certain strains of euphoria are truly too costly for words. Or, rather, too costly to require words. Euphoria like that can do without words.

"You asked me a while back whether I still took you along because I felt guilty. I told you then that I did not feel guilty. Which is true. I do not feel guilty. At least not about us. And you, why do you still go with me? Or don't you need a reason for everything, is habituation reason enough?

"Rebecca, you said my kisses are becoming parched. Shall we cut through all the lies now, shall we try?

"I am not the man you'll marry, I'm not the father of your children, I'm not lying at your feet. I am the parched kisser, I have a weakness for you, a major weakness, and when I wrote that I needed to approve the men you'd flirt with later on, when I'm no longer around, I was flirting with you, but I'm not the one.

"Never quite finding each other creates a bond as well.

"Dear Rebecca, I'm not claiming that I loved you; perhaps that was the only thing that really bound us together, that we were bad at loving others. That we thought we loved each other and enjoyed the illusion, for a while, at the poolside, while in fact the world was spinning around us and we barely saw each other.

"Wanting to be desired by an even more desirable prince who comes your way, that's probably what's behind all the sorrow, the fretting, the blubbering, what's behind that desire to live greatly and compellingly. The unending and eternal longing for the prince on the white charger.

"I am not the prince on the white charger, I am the rat on the hobbyhorse. The Theater of False Hope is closing its doors.

"I'm going to miss you, and because I'm going to miss you I'll hate you, but time does heal.

"Hopefully a great new love will make its appearance soon, has perhaps already appeared, and hopefully that person will bring a kind of happiness to your head. Finer and better and greater happiness.

"That I choose not to witness your forthcoming happiness is not something for which I can accept the blame.

"Little kisses,

"Robert"

"What are you writing?" she asked.

"A letter," I said.

That evening we ate at a restaurant in Palermo that had been recommended to us by the hotel doorman, the same one who'd asked me to autograph the book.

Between the main course and dessert I read aloud from a book, I don't remember which one. It was a translation from Norwegian or Swedish, I vaguely remember that, there were some lovely passages in it, and it occurred to me that one should really do that more often, read out loud to another person between the main course and dessert.

When dessert was finished, I handed her the letter. It had been in my back pocket, and it was a little wrinkled and warm.

"Read it out loud," she said.

"No," I said, "I want you to read it."

She read and I played with sugar cubes, built a little house of sugar cubes, and ordered two coffees.

Then she finished reading. What followed was a scene, but nothing traumatic. A voice was raised, a glass of water landed in a lap, there were a few curses, the impotent rituals of sorrow. The god of missing was fed two more living sacrifices.

I was tempted to lay a hand on her leg under the table, to say a few words that would make everything all right, and then let the hormones do the rest. But my mind was made up. The way a writer rules over his creations like a stubborn and wrathful god, so I ruled over our romance. Not susceptible to reason, or pleading, or to references to all the pleasure that lay behind us and was now being thrown away. Susceptible only to the voice, the seductive and all-conquering voice that said, "Go away, disappear before it's too late, disappear before you can't go back, disappear before they touch the sore spot." No call so sweet as the call to flight.

"You're throwing it all away," Rebecca said.

"So much has been thrown away already," I said.

*

So I disappeared from Rebecca's life. I flew back to New York. Between the many letters from fans and would-be authors of cookbooks, I found a letter from Evelyn. Evelyn had gone back to Puerto Rico and become a live-in maid to a rich and friendly family. She and her children were doing well. She'd seen my picture in the paper.

I tucked the letter away in the same drawer in which there had once been a drawing of a dachshund. The drawing I had one day torn to pieces to banish dachshunds from my life.

Hate is the sea into which all the missing flows mingled down.

*

In New York I dreamed about dachshunds, cookbooks and the Jellied Carp Foundation. Rebecca left messages on my answering machine, but I didn't call back.

She said, "I fuck a new man every day, Robert, men who can really get erections."

Even my jealousy had no urgency. Besides, the game she was playing was too much lacking in subtlety to convince me that I would find something in her life that I hadn't yet seen or known.

Thirty-four letters I wrote, to publishers, newspapers, magazines, the organizers of cooking fairs and the ideal home exhibition, all saying the same thing: "We are very sorry to inform you that Robert G. Mehlman died in his sleep three days ago." That cheered me up. An angry publisher called: "People don't understand jokes like this!" Frederik van der Kamp left a message: "When you write the sequel to your cookbook, you'll come back to us, won't you, Robert?"

I ordered a limousine and a chauffeur to drive me to Canada—finding one took me a few hours in itself, several limousine services refused to drive from New York to Canada—and I wrote a letter to the fairytale princess.

"Dear Princess Fairytale,

"Now that I have a house in the Bahamas, an apartment on Malta, an equity portfolio the value of which exceeds our collective dreams several times over, now that it can no longer be denied that I have made my international breakthrough, with a cookbook, but enough of that, now it seems to me to be the right time to go away."

That's how I wanted it to start, and that's how I started the letter.

"I've left The Empty Vessel. I wanted to tell you that too. Why, I don't know. I don't know why I started anything with The Empty Vessel, and I don't know why I left her either. Is one supposed to know things like that?

"To make a long story short, I was impotent. At the opera house. But that was taken care of. Just so you know.

"But this leaving The Empty Vessel solves nothing. It wasn't The Empty Vessel that stood between us, you always realized that.

"I don't know what's got into me, and you, who had the opportunity to study me for years, and did, apparently don't really know either. So why tire ourselves with that question now?

"I have pilfered your time, it's true, I should have left you earlier, but apparently some farewells take a long time. Now that I

have left The Empty Vessel, I can make what I hope will be the definitive attempt to relieve ourselves of each other's presence.

"I have so much to say, it would fill a book, but there's no time for that. Life is nonsense, holy nonsense, but even holy nonsense remains nonsense. A rather paltry discovery after all these years. Maybe that's what we share, that we both find life nonsense, but apparently sharing nonsense is not enough.

"Seeing as you have access to my bank account and have been included in my will from the very start, it's not money that has come between us—that's the last I plan to say about that, because I know how odious the subject is to you.

"At the drugstore today I was offered a new gel that prevents shaving rash. For free. The girl behind the counter pointed at my Adam's apple and said: 'Doesn't that bother you?' I accepted the new shaving gel in all humility, so perhaps now I'll finally become better looking.

"I am heading north. The two of us have gone south together so often, I know the south by now. But not to write: the world has ruled that the cookbook is my magnum opus, they've even been so gracious as to forget completely about my bargain-basement books, and I in turn have decided to accept the world's ruling. It does, after all, have its advantages; I no longer have to explain my books to people on whom all attempts at explanation are wasted. Cookbooks speak for themselves.

"Let's not lose track of each other completely, although I don't know how that is supposed to work in actual practice. Postcards, perhaps? Telegrams?

"Is there anything practical I've forgotten? Of everything outside the realm of the practical, I can best be silent.

"Kiss,

"Your Robert"

I had to cancel the limousine that day, because my wife came home from work early and wouldn't let me go.

"Why the snow?" she asked. "Isn't that a bit far away this time of year?"

"Life itself is far away, if you look at it from the point of view of death."

"All right, so don't look at it from the point of view of death."

She opened her bag and took out a few medical dossiers she had to run through at home.

"Are you really bothered so much by having made your breakthrough with a cookbook?"

"It's not the cookbook," I said. "And it's not the breakthrough either."

"Maybe you should try medication," the fairytale princess said. "For a while."

"No," I said, "if I'm chemically imbalanced, then that imbalance only works in my favor. I see everything very clearly. I have distanced myself from people, and I have good reasons for that."

"You've distanced yourself from your own life," the fairytale princess said.

"I know," I said, "I'm the beast and you're the zoo, but it's good for beasts to change zoos every once in a while."

"You finally left The Empty Vessel, so why be in such a hurry to go to the snow? You've got all the money you could ever need, so why the snow?"

"I have to get out of here," I said. "Before it's too late. You're suffocating me."

"You're suffocating yourself, you idiot." She started weeping.

"Hasn't the tragedy ended yet?" I asked.

"You don't know anything about people," the fairytale princess said. "You need me to help you understand them, or else you have to give them the third degree and milk them dry before you can do it, but under your own steam you're incapable of understanding them—in fact, that's what makes you a bad writer. All your words, all your formulations, that so-called brilliant style of yours, can't hide the fact that you know nothing about emotions, that you don't want to know anything about emotions."

"The tragedy has ended," I said. "The lies are finished now."

"What do you mean, finished?" she said. "They've only just begun, haven't they? And why does The Empty Vessel still call you three times a day?"

"Why don't you ask her yourself?"

"You left her, didn't you?"

"She's still allowed to call me, I can't be held responsible for everyone who calls me. And besides, my phone calls are none of your business. This is still my house, you know."

"I don't want that woman entering my house, not even through the answering machine," shouted the fairytale princess.

"She wants to saw her head off, her own head is driving her crazy."

"So let her saw her head off!" the fairytale princess yelled. "That would be the best for all concerned. Make sure she starts sawing today. It's because of her that I still don't have a child."

"Listen. First I thought that when my father died I could finally start living. My father died, but the living didn't start. Then I thought: when my mother dies, I can start living. But my mother isn't dying. Now I think: when you die, I can finally start living. But you don't want to die, you want to have a child. I can't spend my whole life waiting around for people to die, can I? I've waited long enough."

The fairytale princess took a few steps back.

"You're crazier than people realize, Robert," she said. "You'll truly stop at nothing."

"No, of course I'll stop at nothing. What is there to stop at anymore?"

"I don't care, but I want a child."

"So make a child!" I screamed. "But not with me."

"Who am I supposed to make a child with? For most of my fertile life you've zoomed around me, like a bee around honey, and chased away all the men who wanted anything from me."

"I never chased anyone away, and I never zoomed around you. I don't owe you anything, because I never promised you a thing."

"You sucked the best out of me."

"The best out of you, don't make me laugh: poison is what I sucked out of you. If you remain without child then it's your own fault, and my mother says that all you have to do is look at you to see that you're as sterile as hell."

That's when she picked up a shoe and shattered the glass door of our bookcase.

I live in lies, but it's a comfortable villa. Complete with jacuzzi.

"When are you finally going to start whipping your life into shape?" said the fairytale princess, picking up the shards.

"That's not my job," I said. "What I whip into shape are sentences, chapters, stories."

*

It took me a few more days to convince the fairytale princess that I really needed to go to the snow. She, in turn, convinced me that I owed her a child.

She said, "You don't have to assume any responsibility for it, but at least give me the sperm."

"What do you need my sperm for?" I shouted. "Every man has sperm, why does it have to be mine? I don't want to give you my sperm, I don't want to reproduce. I want to be left alone!"

"I'll leave you alone," she said. "Is it too much to ask?"

The biological clock was ticking away, and that ticking drowned out the sound of all other clocks. It took another twenty-four hours for her to convince me that a single-parent family and happiness were no more mutually exclusive than a two-parent family and happiness: she also convinced me that I truly owed her sperm, if only to make up for some of the time I'd pilfered from her. What's more, she said, "I really want a child with curls." That cinched it. I owed her a child with curls. A child as a going-away present, why not? After all, a child is a hopeful ending.

*

We went to bed with each other twice.

The first time, passionlessly.

The second time, even more passionlessly. But tenderly. So tenderly, with such incredible tenderness, that I felt like jumping out the window.

"So," I said when it was over, "the kid's been made, now I can leave."

The limousine pulled up to the door. Canada was my destination. I had a bag with me, a couple of books, some old clothes. The fairytale princess had to go to work. She couldn't stick around to wave goodbye. I promised to call soon to hear whether the sperm had done its work; if not, I'd come back.

We drove north. The driver asked, "Why north?"

I told him I wanted to see the snow.

He said, "So why don't you take a plane?"

I told him I wanted to see everything along the way.

The trip was long. We slept in motels, but not in the same room. The driver didn't want to eat with me, either. He said he preferred to eat alone in the car. I respected that.

The sky grew grayer, the landscape starker.

Funny, I thought, this is what pain is like. Doubtless merely a tiny advance on all the pain to follow. And this was expensive pain too. A hundred and twenty dollars an hour, not including gas. The pain to follow would almost surely be cheap pain. Not the kind of pain you could write about. Pain you could write about wasn't real pain. Real pain was still to come.

I called Rebecca from a motel, but when I heard her answering machine I hung up.

And in the meantime, silent movies. Picking blackberries with Evelyn, the fairytale princess in the all-night deli, Mrs. Fischer in her kitchen, Rebecca lighting a cigarette and putting her ugly hands on the table to show me, and me, jerking off desperately in the men's room of the Palermo opera house, and again the fairytale princess crying over what I had made of my life, and throughout all of this, hotel rooms, with dachshunds on the wallpaper.

"How much further north do you want to go?" the chauffeur asked.

"Further," I said. "I want to see the snow."

This loneliness was made by me, stage-directed by me. I was everything. Audience, actor, set designer, playwright, lighting, prompter, fireman, cameraman, makeup girl, ticket-seller. This loneliness was my work of art; a pity no one could see it, it was so beautiful.

My delusions had been ethnically purified of the human race. I was the only one left in my own delusion. I had gone AWOL from my own firing squad.

I called the fairytale princess and asked whether my sperm had worked.

"Patience is a virtue," she said. "Where are you?"

"Somewhere in Canada," I said.

"What are you doing there?"

"Planning to go sledding," I said.

Indians went to the snow to die, I went there to go sledding.

Operation Survival had been a major success, soon there would be no need for me to even miss myself. The person I could have been. The bullet of happiness that had missed me by a hair, because I'd ducked just in time.

Some people had had the chance to die early on in life, but they'd ducked in time and spent the rest of their lives regretting that.

Thank God, there were no more extenuating circumstances. Just plain circumstances. That would also serve as my answer when people asked me "why?" Who, what, where and how were all questions that ultimately resulted in shame, and in all the things that gave reason for shame, and there were plenty of those.

To the question "why" there was only one possible answer: "Just plain circumstances, with no extenuation."

Here you didn't have to exist for anyone's sake, you were relieved at last of that impossible task. Here you existed only for The Museum of Loneliness. I was the museum guard, I punched the tickets and I gave the guided tours.

*

In a complete breach of custom, the chauffeur actually had breakfast with me. For two weeks he'd breakfasted alone, but apparently he felt the time was ripe for rapprochement.

Earlier that morning the fairytale princess had said, "We shouldn't be overhasty, but it looks like the sperm's done its work."

"I drove someone to Florida once," the chauffeur said, taking a bite of his pancake. "I also drove someone to Detroit, but I've never been as far as this."

"Neither have I," I said.

"What they say about you," he asked, and stopped chewing, "is it true? That you're a famous cookbook writer?"

"Everything is true," I said. "Only my rates have gone up."

3

DOES THE FUN START HERE?

The child they made, that's me: Harpo Saul Mehlman. I am the *Wiedergutmachung* for something that could never be *wiedergutgemacht*.

My father braved it out in the snow for three days. Then he came back, and it took him another twelve years before he was able to complete Operation Leave The Fairytale Princess.

*

This is the letter he wrote me on the day he left for good:

> *"Dear Harpo, weird little son of mine,*
>   *"My relationship with your mother, also known as Princess Fairytale, has survived a great deal. Too much to enumerate here, but I'll try anyway. Tumours benign and less benign, literary flops and bestsellers, penury and seven-digit wealth, hotel rooms dirty*

and clean, extramarital affairs and platonic loves, neuroses, scores of suicides, a child, a wedding in Florida, my mother, shaving rash, gray hairs, gums that no longer function, mild alcoholism, burials and cremations, stench, fame and obscurity, and for the rest all those of my incompetencies, shortcomings and defects not mentioned above.

"When a relationship has survived all this, why decide to finally split up anyway? That's a good question, little Harpo. And at this moment I can give you only one answer. You can't leave everything up to Death; sometimes, as a person, you have to help out a little.

"I think it's a good idea for you to go back to Amsterdam with the fairytale princess. I'm going to stay in New York for a while: maybe I'll go traveling, I don't know why I'm not finished traveling yet. There's no way you know everything. Maybe I'll finally finish The Empty Vessel and Other Pearls, *maybe I won't, maybe some things have to remain unfinished.*

"I think, but this is a secret between the two of us, that it's very good for the fairytale princess to leave her psychiatric patients behind.

"Too bad I didn't talk to you more when you were four, and five, and six, and seven, but I was too busy working on my magnum opus. I've come to know my magnum opus better than I know you. But believe me, I'll make it all up to you.

"Little Harpo, when you come home from school and find this letter, I'll be out for a bit, but I'll come home around five-thirty. Your mother has a party after work today, so we'll have to go to dinner without her. Maybe we can see a movie. I've heard that there's a good movie on about a dwarf. How does that sound to you? Your tastes seems to drift every which way at the moment, so if you don't feel like a movie about a dwarf, just say so. It's not a kid's movie, by the way, it's a movie for adults, just so you know.

"Don't be afraid that you'll never see me again: I'll come to Amsterdam regularly, and we can go on vacation together as always, maybe even with the fairytale princess. Although I think it would be

better for the time being if the fairytale princess and I didn't go on vacation together. Maybe in a few years' time. Our marriage has always been a trench, but lately the trench has become pretty narrow.

"If you like, we can buy sandwiches and have a picnic in Central Park. I know how much you like picnics, so I'd be willing to grin and bear it for your sake. My having a son who loves picnics and camping indicates that there may actually be a God, or in any case a kind of natural justice. There's no way I can explain these peculiar predilections of yours other than as a punishment for all my unforgivable sins.

"So it's up to you to decide what we're going to do this evening. Although I hasten to point out that the 'skip dinner' option is not open.

"I have to go now. I have an appointment with a man who's interested in buying the apartment on Malta.

"Please remember that the cleaning lady was in today and that the poor woman worked like a horse—fortunately I was able to cheer her up, or at least I did my best to cheer her up. I bought her a new vacuum cleaner and had it wrapped festively.

"Keep the peace, take off your shoes when you come into the house, your mother appreciates that so much.

"I myself have never sacrificed much to keep the peace, and don't ask any major sacrifices either, only a little offer on your part, that you take off your shoes. If you can't make major sacrifices, then make little ones. That's how I've always done it, because no matter how difficult I found it at times, I believe that in the long run you must see making sacrifices as a practical matter.

"Could you do me a favor and wear something presentable this evening? I know that tormenting me is the joy of your existence, that seems to be something you inherited from me, says the fairytale princess, so I'll just assume that you'll dress in a way that will make me feel a wee bit miserable. I, in turn, will deliver a full report on that wee bit of misery, because otherwise your torment will bring you no pleasure and that would be missing the point.

"Don't leave the house, I'll be back at five-thirty. Make little sacrifices for the peace.
    "Four kisses,
    "Robert"

Now that I've reread all my father's letters to me, I don't know whether he truly wrote them for me or with an eye to publication. But that no longer causes me any pain. I have other memories, and I don't have to write them down in order to keep them alive. Maybe that's because I've seen up close that writing does more to destroy memories than to preserve them.

At first I wanted to write about my father, but I soon discovered that writing is not a religion to me, not some idol to which living burnt sacrifices must be offered, and also that what I wanted to say about my father had already been said by my father. And that you don't have to find words for everything. Even though my father thought that a thing only existed once it had been properly formulated.

People who heard of my plans asked me, "Are you planning to rehabilitate Robert G. Mehlman?"

But he wouldn't want to be rehabilitated, especially not by me.

*

When my father left the fairytale princess, he began wandering through Europe. He was still living off the revenues from *Polish-Jewish Cuisine in 69 Recipes*. He traveled from one hotel to the next. Spain, Greece, Switzerland, Portugal, Italy.

Sometimes he called. A few times he came to Amsterdam for a day or two. But by then my mother was living with a Russian, and the Russian and my father didn't get along.

"I'm working on my magnum opus," he said. "It's my proof that I do understand something about emotions, my way of getting back at life, God and the world."

"I can't listen to this anymore," said the fairytale princess.

He sent quite a few letters at first, but as time went by they became less frequent. The four-page letters shrank to two, and finally became picture postcards containing nothing but platitudes. "The hotel is good, but my private secretary has lit out on me."

Sometimes he hinted at coming back to the fairytale princess. But she didn't think that was a good idea. And besides, by then it was already too late.

*

Ten days after I'd found him at the Hotel Santa Caterina, I returned to Amsterdam. When we parted, he said, "I'm practically finished with my magnum opus. After that I'm going to write a book about you, Harpo. A real book, not some epistolary thing. I think you've got a trilogy in you."

"Please, leave me out of it, Papa," I said. "You really don't have to write about me. In fact, I'd rather you didn't."

He went with me to the airport at Naples, and took his bag of unopened mail with him. He talked a great deal about his magnum opus and said the only thing he wasn't satisfied with was the ending, but it was only a matter of days, maybe only hours, it could come to him any moment now.

He said, "Do you ever have the feeling that you suddenly know how something has to end?"

I said I didn't, and he asked, "Do you have a girlfriend? Have you got a picture of her?"

At the airport we drank coffee and bolted down a croissant.

"I'm a natural for the royal family," he said. "I've got it in me to lead people. What this day and age needs is an enlightened despot."

I looked at the coffee dripping from his croissant onto the floor.

He walked me to the gate, until we got to the sign that said: PASSENGERS ONLY.

"You can't go any further than this," I said. I knew my father and I didn't want him to try sneaking along anyway.

"You're right," he said. "I have to get back to the hotel, I've got to put things in order. After that I'm going to Sabaudia. The beach there is a lot prettier. If you find a girlfriend, send me a picture, okay?"

Then he tried to lift me off the ground, but I was a lot bigger and stronger than him.

*

He actually did move to Sabaudia, to a hotel with a prettier beach.

One warm evening, a little less than three weeks after I'd said goodbye to him at Naples airport, he walked onto the beach at Sabaudia wearing his swimming trunks and a straw hat. He was carrying a carving knife that he'd stolen from the hotel kitchen. He threatened the other bathers and cursed wildly. The other bathers called the *carabinieri*. The first two *carabinieri* to arrive tried to persuade my father to drop the knife and go along quietly. But he cursed at them in bad Italian, and came at them, waving the carving knife.

In the end they shot him six times. Two bullets shattered his leg, one went through his right arm, the rest ended up in his stomach. He was taken by helicopter to a hospital in Rome.

*

"Something's happened to your father," my mother said that evening after I came home late from a party. "He's in a hospital in Rome." Even the Russian was upset.

The next morning we were on a plane, my mother and I.

Two days later, Robert G. Mehlman awoke from his comatose slumber. He didn't even seem surprised to see us. The first thing he asked was, "Where are my things?"

"They're being taken care of," I said.

"My manuscript," he said. "Bring it to me."

"In your condition, you shouldn't be worrying about your manuscript," said the fairytale princess.

"I'll decide for myself what I worry about," my father said hoarsely. "It's not up to you to tell me what to worry about, I want my manuscript."

"Papa," I said, "don't scream at Mama like that. She came all the way from Amsterdam to Rome for you. She loves you."

"I'll scream at anyone I like," my father said, "until they bring me my manuscript."

Two nurses came into the room and shooed us out into the corridor. Excitement could be fatal to Robert G. Mehlman.

My mother decided to return to Amsterdam rather soon; the arguments had gotten out of hand. I told her it was important that I stay with my father; after all, he had to have someone with him. It was a good way to wheedle some money out of her.

I took up residence in a cheap boarding house in Rome. Every afternoon I went to the hospital.

The events at Sabaudia had actually led to open debate in the Italian parliament. And on TV I saw the *carabinieri* who had shot my father. They were both quite young. One of them said something to the effect of, "Now my life is ruined too."

The papers wondered out loud why the *carabinieri* hadn't tranquillized the crazy man with a hypodermic needle, why they hadn't thrown a net over him. In an editorial, one paper wrote: "Instead of shooting at the Mafia, they shoot crazy people."

My father would have been proud of himself.

Only one minor evening paper noted, in the very last paragraph, that the crazy man in question was the former cookbook author Robert G. Mehlman. I think he would have regarded even that ignominy as his own creation.

*

The doctors say there's almost no way my father can ever lead a normal life. They're even afraid it may come to an amputation, but I have a hard time following them. His head was the only thing he was able to move.

"Is this where the fun starts?" he asked me one afternoon.

"What?" I asked.

"In that story we're working on."

"This is no story, Papa," I said. "This is real. You went to the beach and threatened people with a knife."

"Yeah, good one, right?" he said.

The doctors said I should talk to him a lot, even when he was asleep.

There were days when he said nothing at all, and others when all he did was ask, "Where's my manuscript?" Another time he actually said, "You have to write your own obituary, Harpo. If you leave it to some third-rate journalist, you'll end up tucked away at the bottom of page ten."

*

The hotel in Sabaudia sent me his things. I went through his steamer trunks and his bag full of mail. Some of the letters and bills were more than three years old. There were also letters that had been returned to sender. Proposals of marriage to people who no longer existed.

Nowhere did I see anything that even remotely resembled a manuscript. Until, at the bottom of one of the steamer trunks, amid socks and underpants, I hit upon a package wrapped in a garbage bag and bound together with rubber bands. The package consisted of a large quantity of paper, notebooks, beer coasters with addresses written on them, a piece of cardboard and money in various currencies. I kept the money and the piece of cardboard. The rest I brought to my father in the hospital.

"Just send it all to David," my father said when he saw the garbage bag. "He'll fix the typos. Tell him we're in a hurry."

Six weeks after I'd sent the package to David, it came back. With the patience of a saint, he had arranged everything in the right order and attached a memo to it: "I think it would be wise to wait with publication until all those involved have passed away. Good luck, David."

*

Weeks went by. My father's condition remained unchanged. The fairytale princess said I should stay in Rome, if the doctors thought that was good for my father. I told her that was exactly what the doctors thought.

After four weeks I asked, "Why did everything have to be ruined, why ruin it all over and over again?"

He tried to turn his head and look at me.

"I'm bored," he said. "Does the fun start here, or what?"

For a while he said nothing. Then he asked, "When's my book coming out? My magnum opus? When's it coming out, and are they doing anything about publicity? Or is that still too much to ask?"

*

I've visited the people he told me about, the ones he wrote about, the ones who served as models for the characters in his work. Perhaps in the hope of finding out more about him, perhaps to find out that there are things you shouldn't want to know.

Josef Capano is in a sanatorium in Liege. The American authorities threw him out of the country. And there wasn't a sanatorium in Antwerp that would have him.

I sat at his bedside for three hours, and he spent three-quarters of that time hacking. He kept forgetting my name, and complained about how they'd forbidden him to smoke, and how he was going to smoke anyway. A few times he mumbled, "We were made men." But it was unclear whether he was referring to himself, or to my father, or to someone completely different. A nurse finally came along and put an end to the interrogation.

"Your father still owes me money!" he called out as I was heading for the door.

*

How it could be possible, no one knows, but Mrs. Fischer is alive too. I went to visit her. She still lives in her house, with five nurses. She talks to herself and laughs out loud, maybe she's in contact with her Indian guide.

Evelyn is still living in Puerto Rico, working as a live-in maid. When I finally got her phone number, I had to call three times before she had time to talk. It was a bad connection. At first she couldn't believe that my father had a son.

She remembered different things, things my father hadn't told me, and things he hadn't written about either. A few hours out rowing, a visit to the movies, the blackberries in her memory were wild strawberries.

She asked, "Do you look like your father?" And, "How could you not love a guy like that? But I made cappuccinos, I came from Puerto Rico, I was another class of people."

Perhaps her fantasy had slowly overgrown reality, perhaps she remembered things that had never existed. If happiness isn't an expectation, then it should at least be a memory.

I decided there was no sense in traveling to Puerto Rico.

"Call me again sometime," she said.

Her children were doing well.

*

I did look up Rebecca.

I called, and she invited me over for tea. She lived close to the Vondelpark.

"Oh, you've changed," she said. "You've gotten so big!"

I laughed, half embarrassedly, half clumsily. What do you say to your father's lover, the one you knew as Aunt Rebecca and, when she wasn't around, also as The Empty Vessel?

She had children, two girls. We sat on pillows on the floor, her younger daughter played next to us. "I was young," she said, "and a little crazy, but I have no regrets, it was a wonderful time."

She showed me pictures. I flipped through them quickly. The pictures weren't meant for my eyes. Maybe you shouldn't want to know everything about your father. In any case, I didn't want to see naked pictures of my father.

"Yeah," Rebecca said, "I even went with him to Japan," and she lifted her daughter onto her lap.

I didn't know what to say, so all I said was, "That was before I was born."

I took a good look at her hands, maybe to see whether they were really ugly. They were old hands. Her hands had grown old faster than her face.

"He broke up with me on Sicily," Rebecca said, "but after that he wrote me even more letters. So I just went and saw him again."

"Why did you actually leave him?" I asked while I built a tower of blocks with her daughter.

"After twelve years," Rebecca said, "he still couldn't choose. It got a bit too much for me. I met my husband, and I didn't have to wait for him. I remember calling your father and telling him, 'No one will wait for you as long as I have, Robert. No one.'"

"And what did he say?"

The tower was almost finished.

"That everyone was waiting for him: publishers, newspapers, his wife, his family. That you'd be better off waiting for the messiah."

Rebecca's daughter was trying to climb onto my lap.

"And then?"

"Then I said that it had taken him twelve years not to choose, and that enough was enough. That I'd met someone who could choose, and that I was going on vacation with him. And he said, 'How am I supposed to choose? I'm working on my magnum opus, don't demand so much of me.' I said, 'Robert, have I demanded too much of you? The fact is, I've demanded very little of you, but even that was too much.' After that I received at least forty letters from Robert, and about ten telegrams, but I didn't open them. I knew that if I opened them it would start all over again. If I opened them it would never stop, and you can't go on like that all your life, can you?"

"No," I said, "you can't."

I thought about Mata Hari. There was a silence, then I said, "You have a very nice daughter."

At seven her husband came in with the other little girl.

Rebecca said, "This is Harpo Mehlman. Robert's son, you remember?"

"Yes," her husband said, "I remember."

He asked me to stay for dinner, but I said that was impossible; unfortunately, I had to leave that same evening for Rome.

"And what are you planning to do?" asked Rebecca.

"I want to be a photographer," I said. "None of that artsy business. I'd like to work with fashion models."

Rebecca wanted to give me a few of my father's letters to take with me.

"Keep them," I said, "they're yours."

She walked me to the door. "Why are you going to Rome?" she asked.

I wondered whether I should tell her. I hadn't said anything to Evelyn, why should I? What good would that have done anyone? But in Rebecca's case, it seemed different.

"My father," I said, "went onto the beach at Sabaudia one evening with a carving knife. First he threatened a few bathers, then the *carabinieri* came and he threatened them too. He cursed at them. They had no choice. They had to shoot him."

There I stood, across from my father's mistress, the woman I'd known as Aunt Rebecca. There was nothing more to say. She had married and borne children, I had gone back to Amsterdam with my mother, my father had run out onto the beach at Sabaudia with a carving knife. Apparently that's what's left of lives once you've summarized them.

I had promised myself to ask Rebecca a lot more questions, but when I was finally with her it suddenly seemed senseless. Not because I already knew or sensed everything, but because it wouldn't help.

In her bookcase, I'd seen a copy of *Polish-Jewish Cuisine in 69 Recipes*.

*

As soon as I arrived in Rome, I went to the hospital. The nurses greeted me like a long-lost friend.

"Where were you?" my father asked.

"I had to go back to Amsterdam for a bit," I said. "I had to see Mama."

One of the nurses approached me in the hall. "Your father is impossible," she said. "He keeps shouting at us that we should be getting the publicity rolling."

It had taken him twenty years to disappear from my mother's life, and he'd been trying to disappear from his own for almost that long. In the end he'd needed the help of two *carabinieri* to complete the operation.

It seems as though that image of my father, one I never saw myself—on the beach at Sabaudia in his swimming trunks, waving a stolen carving knife—has pushed aside all other images and memories. As though a part of him had always been pacing the beach at Sabaudia, waving a carving knife.

I didn't tell him where I'd been. All I said was, "Everyone says get better quickly: the fairytale princess, The Empty Vessel, Mrs. Fischer, Evelyn, Josef Capano. They all wish you a speedy recovery."

"What do I need their wishes for?" Robert G. Mehlman shouted. "Let them come here and tell me in person, if I really mean anything to them. And Josef Capano still owes me a linen suit. I paid him to buy me a linen suit, he left with the money, and I never saw any linen suit."

A nurse came in to give my father a shot.

"Has David sent word, or is he too busy with his dog again?"

The shot started working, and I went to my boarding house to call the fairytale princess.

"That woman has started calling me again," my mother said. "That Empty Vessel wants to know what hospital your father is in. She must have found my address. Can't she leave me alone, even now? How did she get my number?"

"I have no idea, Mama," I said.

The fairytale princess swore. "Does she have to pursue me even on his deathbed? Doesn't that woman have any sense of propriety?"

*

I cannot and will not live in my father's reality, because that reality is uninhabitable.

The tiny space where our two realities intersect is a hospital room in Rome. And I'm not even so sure about that. Do our realities actually intersect there? Who does my father see when he looks at me, and who do I see when I look at him?

I'll have to accept that my father is a stranger to me, and always will be a stranger to me. Even now that I've pored over his things, precisely now that I've pored over his things, he's stranger to me than ever before.

There is no longer anywhere I can meet him: all that's left of us, of his letters to me, our walks, our dinners with the fairytale princess, even of how we bought clothes for The Empty Vessel, is an irreducible sorrow for which no correct formulation can be found. A thing that evades the power of words and therefore, according to my father, shouldn't be able to exist at all.

*

In front of me is a piece of cardboard.

"To Mr. R. Mehlman. Please call 212-573-9653. I have a package with me from the Netherlands that should be handed to you personally."

The handwriting is graceful. The telephone number no longer exists. It's nighttime in Rome, and the lady who runs my boarding house thinks I'll never leave, that I'll continue to sit in my room every night with a piece of cardboard in my hands.

This is the moment when I should tell you about The Empty Vessel, everything I know, everything I've seen, everything I can remember. The way the police reopen a closed case, that's how I should tell you about The Empty Vessel, but I don't want to be a footnote to my father's life. I want to work with fashion models, maybe even begin my own agency. Harpo Mehlman, for all your fashion models. Something along those lines.

*

The doctors say my father still hasn't reconciled himself to his situation, and that it would be good if I would start drawing his attention to what can't be altered.

"Papa," I say, "you threatened people with a carving knife on the beach at Sabaudia, and they shot you. And now you're lying in a hospital in Rome and can no longer use a large part of your body."

He twists his head to the left, so he can look at me.

"Don't you go believing that," he says. "Those are rumors your mother is spreading around."

Green Tea
short story
(published by the author; out of print)

Voices from Hell
Short stories
(published by the author; destroyed by the author)

Costly Meat
Play
(published by the author; out of print)

268th in the World
novel
(out of print)

A Garden Facing East
novel
Part 1 of the Sidney Brochstein cycle
(out of print)

Of Ribbons and Ravishment
short stories
Part 2 of the Sidney Brochstein cycle
(out of print)

It Takes a Sharp Eye . . .
pamphlet
(out of print)

A Dead Negro
poems
Part 3 of the Sidney Brochstein cycle
(out of print)

I Just Love Men with Women's Voices
short stories and critical essays
(removed from circulation)

Not Much of a Walker
columns
(out of print)

All My Readers Fit in One Cab
poems
(out of print)

Polish-Jewish Cuisine in 69 Recipes
literary cookbook
(34th edition)

Letters to Harpo
letters
(out of print)

The Empty Vessel and Other Pearls
novel
(manuscript; unpublished)